The Whisperer Returns

The Children of Light – Book Three

Vicki Wootton

Stargate Publishing

The Whisperer Returns – Revised Edition

This is work of fiction; all the characters, names, and places are strictly the creations of the author's imagination and are not intended to represent any person or place on the planet earth, although some of the names may exist there.

ISBN - Print book 978-0-9950102-8-4

THANK YOU

I owe special thanks to Teri Saya, Pauline Van Havere, Laurie Campbell, Aubrey Baptist, Patricia Dygula and Lisa Pepin for having the patience to read and re-read this manuscript. Many thanks for helping to correct errors and offering helpful suggestions for improvement. The responsibility for any overlooked errors is strictly mine. I also want to express my gratitude to Carlos for his help and encouragement throughout the lengthy process of writing and editing, and for washing the dishes so that I could go on working.

Other Books by this Author
NOVELS

The Whisperer – The Children of Light Book 1
The Whisperer's Journey – The Children of Light Book 2
Where Have All the Young Girls Gone?
At War with Terror
Forbidden World
Reluctant Warriors
Fatal Harvest

NON-FICTION

Names of the World

1 – Crossing the Desert

Felindra and her companions—Farah the communicator, Sastin the healer, Tirzah Lin the Master Wizard, and the two defenders, Barengush and Vertan—were becoming accustomed to sleeping in the daytime and traveling by night. Shortly before sunset, they were up and eating their evening meal—two small desert rodents, baked while they slept, and some dates from the last oasis; not much for five people, but they had to make do with whatever they could scavenge from the desert.

Three days had passed since they had escaped from Basrind and slavery, and they still performed scans to detect anyone following them, but that didn't mean they were completely free. Now the Basrindian military was after them with charges of desertion and treason, although to them, such charges were unjustified. They had been brought to Basrind against their will and sold as slaves, although the two defenders had been taken on by the Basrindian military to train recruits after Pangast and Nedra had invaded Basrind six days earlier. The two Albasinians had left their posts as soon as the opportunity arose and joined their companions at the plantation of Dom Ash where they were being held as slaves.

Now, they were traveling west across the Basrindian desert to the border of the neighboring land of Nedra, where they hoped to seek asylum. Nedra was one of the nations that had invaded Basrind but was a minor player; Pangast was the instigator of the invasion.

Vertan glanced back as he slung his pack on his shoulder. The setting sun had turned the sky a portentous shade of rust. "That sky looks a bit threatening," he said. "Do you think we're in for a storm?"

Tirzah Lin, the Master Wizard, studied the sky for a moment before replying. "I fear we may be." He blew out his breath.

"You don't sound happy about it," Lady Farah said. "I thought we needed some rain."

"We do indeed, but it will not be that sort of storm. I fear a *samoon* is building up ahead of us. We must find some shelter before it arrives. We could not survive out here in the open desert. I suggest we continue this way and keep our eyes open for a place to shelter. Some high rocks would be best. And cover your faces," he added.

"What about a wadi?" Barengush asked.

"The blowing sand fills in low-lying places and we could be buried."

Their energy was beginning to flag by the time they found a suitable place to shelter. The ominous sounds of the approaching storm were rising from a whistling rumble to a deeper moaning that created an almost musical undertone.

"What's that?" Barengush said, pointing to a shadowy form approaching from the west.

"It looks like a camel," Vertan replied. "And it doesn't look very steady on its feet,"

"There's someone on its back," Farah added. "He's hurt."

"Get them in here," Tirzah Lin urged, taking charge. "Lady Felindra, will you bring the camel into the shelter?"

They'd found a large rock formation, and a couple of power blasts from Barengush had created a shallow cave in one of the bigger rocks.

Felindra was the best candidate where animals were involved. She tightened the cloth over her face and staggered against the blowing dust towards the camel. As soon as she touched it, she felt the pain in its haunch and found the arrow that caused it. Soothing it as best she could, she persuaded it to go in between the rocks to the more sheltered space. A groan from above alerted her to the rider, a young boy from the nomad tribe they were following.

Tirzah Lin rushed over to the camel and looked at the boy, who was still conscious. After a brief conversation, he turned to the others. "He was sent to warn us of some dangerous people coming this way. When he came near the strangers, he coaxed his camel to speed past, but they shot arrows at him as he went by. One hit him in the shoulder and another got the camel before they were out of range." He kept his hand on the boy's uninjured shoulder and turned to Vertan and Barengush. "Could you gently help him down and sit him on a mat in the shelter?"

Sastin was already sorting through his healing supplies when they sat the boy down next to him. He looked up at Tirzah Lin. "Would you translate for me, please, Lin?"

"His name is Kemal," Tirzah said. The boy looked at him questioningly when he heard his name and Tirzah patted his knee to reassure him. "This man is a healer. He's going to help you. First he will examine you and then ask a few questions."

"Before I start, I'll give him something to ease the pain," Sastin said.

The noise of the storm was now a constant rumbling roar with intermittent whistles and moans. A fine dust was filtering through the narrow gaps, but the rocks sheltered them from the full force of the driven sand. Above them the sky was covered by a roiling blanket of orange-tinted black cloud.

The removal of the arrow from Kemal's shoulder was complicated by the fact that it hadn't gone completely through, and the head was buried in the flesh of his shoulder. "He's lucky it hasn't damaged anything vital and has only pierced the muscle. I'm going to get the arrow out," Sastin, said, "but it will be a bit tricky. I'll have to push the head out first. It will be very painful. Can you help control the pain"? Tirzah talked to Kemal and then answered the question. "I told him what you will do. I'm going to put him to sleep so he won't feel anything."

By the time the arrow was removed, and the wound covered with a clean cotton bandage, the sandstorm seemed to be right on top of them, the sound deafening.

"What a touching sight!" a loud voice proclaimed. "All my little friends together.

Startled, everyone turned to see who had spoken. "Oh no," Barengush groaned. "Not again."

2 – Old Enemy Reappears

The noise of the storm and the unexpected appearance of her old enemy were so overwhelming that Felindra couldn't take it all in. Her heart started to pound, and she froze with her hand on the neck of the injured camel. She had been trying to sooth it until someone could come and remove the arrow from its haunch. The poor creature was very uncomfortable and unable to sit down.

She felt a hand on her shoulder and recoiled. "It's only me, little sister," Tirzah Lin said. He withdrew his hand and patted her shoulder. "Don't be afraid. I'll protect you."

"I'm worried about the camel," she murmured. "She is suffering a lot of pain from the arrow in her thigh."

"I'll see what I can do," Tirzah said. "I think you should move into the shelter with your friends. Leave this to me."

As she moved away from Tirzah Lin and the camel, she became aware of a lot of movement and mumbling.

"You're completely surrounded, so don't try anything," Tumma, the grand wizard of dark magic, shouted. Get their weapons and tie them up!"

"What are you doing here?" Barengush asked contemptuously. "I had hoped never to see your smirking face again."

"Now, now, my old friend. Don't be so hostile. I'm here with a contract to bring you back to Kirkur. You won't get away this time. They're going to have your head on a pole, traitor." Tumma ended with a murky laugh.

Everyone was silent for a moment, trying to come to terms with this and, at the same time, trying to think of a way to get out of the dilemma. Two soldiers from the Basrindian army came farther into the sheltered clearing and started relieving the escapees of their belongings, covered by two of Tumma's wizards. They knew trying to resist would be useless.

"Why do you have to take everyone?" Farah asked. Farah was a powerful telepath, older than most of the other members of their group and had the courage to assert herself.

"Because the contract includes everyone, deserters and escaped slaves." Tumma sounded smug as he said this.

"But we were set free by Dom Ash after the invasion!" Felindra protested.

"So why did you run off?" Tumma retorted.

"We want to go home."

"Enough of this! It looks as if the storm is dying down. We must go before it gets light. Is everybody ready?"

Don't resist; you'll only get hurt. Go with them, Tirzah Lin sent. I'll work out a way to free you. I don't think he's noticed me, so I'm going to hide until you're all gone.

What about the boy and the camel? Felindra was always concerned about animals.

I'll take care of them.

"Are you communicating?" Tumma snarled. "Do I have to block you? I will anyway, as a precaution." He watched the prisoners. "Use a long rope and tie them in a line. I don't want anyone wandering off. Now, get moving!"

"I was sure there was another one," one of the wizards said. "But I can't see any sign of him."

"Did you see what he looked like?"

He must have used a camouflage spell, Felindra thought.

"Just a shadow through the dust, but I got the impression he's tall and thin."

"What about the boy and the camel?" the wizard asked.

6

"Leave them. They're both wounded and would only slow us down."

The noise of the storm had subsided to a dull whistle, and the driven sand had been replaced by fine dust. Felindra was thankful for the cotton scarf covering her face, although some of the finer dust managed to seep through. She looked up at the sky and saw a few stars among the tattered remnants of the dust cloud. This made her think of Varan. *I'm beginning to wonder if I'll ever see you again, my love.* She thought despairingly.

Dawn came upon them sooner than they expected in a hazy orange glow. Tumma ordered his men to be on the lookout for a shelter where they could rest. The sun was up completely before they came upon a cluster of trees and rocks on a hillside. Even with the sun above the horizon, the air was still hazy with dust.

"We'll stop here and rest for a while." Tumma said. "Men, split up into pairs, a soldier and a wizard, and take turns standing watch." He dumped his backpack on the ground and sat down in the shade of a bush. He opened the pack, took out a water skin, and gulped down a few mouthfuls.

"What about us?" Farah asked. "You took all our water."

"Give them one water skin," Tumma ordered. "They'll have to share it."

"What are we supposed to do if we have a call of nature?" Vertan asked.

Felindra could see Tumma building up to a rage. "Why do you people always give me so much trouble?" he growled, his face turning red. "Untie the two women from the line and tie them together." He scowled at them. "Does that satisfy you? How about you, princess? Is that good enough for your royal highness?" He smirked at Felindra.

Felindra wouldn't deign to respond. She'd had enough of that the last time she'd been his prisoner. Just because she was sworn to the son of a duke, he had insisted on calling her 'princess'.

After the men had relieved themselves, Farah and Felindra took their turn, having to push their way into some bushes to get away from the two men guarding them.

"I wonder what Lin is doing," Farah whispered, so the guards wouldn't hear. "I'm glad he got away."

"He said he would find a way to help us, but I don't know what he's planning." Felindra replied.

"He's an incredible man, isn't he? He's sure to come up with something totally unexpected."

"Do you think we'll get away?" Felindra said. She stood up and straightened her clothes.

"I hope so. I couldn't face whatever they have in store for us otherwise." Farah ran her fingers through her hair. "What I'd like more than anything right now is a cool bath with lots of soap."

"Me too," Felindra replied. "We'd better go back before he has a tantrum."

Tirzah Lin

Tirzah worked for a long time to get the arrow out of the camel's hip, eventually resorting to putting her to sleep after maneuvering her onto her opposite side. As with the boy's arrow, this one hadn't gone all the way through, which in this case was fortunate because it had come to rest against the hipbone. If it had gone further, it could have pierced vital organs and caused a painful lingering death.

Once he had cut down to the arrowhead and pulled out the entire arrow, Tirzah stitched up the wound. He applied plenty of Aloe gel and bandaged it with one of Kemal's head cloths.

Now he had to think of a way to rescue the Albasinians. Since the storm had died down and the sun had risen, they would probably be sleeping somewhere east of his present location. He wondered if they'd stopped at the oasis they'd left the previous night. It would be a good place to rest with plenty of water and fruit. He was beginning to feel drowsy himself, but before he could rest, he had to check on Kemal and talk to him if possible.

The boy was awake when Tirzah approached him, still lying where he had left him. "Are you well enough to travel?" he asked.

When Kemal struggled to sit up with only one hand for support, Tirzah helped him, moving him so that he was leaning back against a rock. "My arm hurts," he said, "but I can manage. What about Basma? She was hurt too."

"She's fine," Tirzah replied. "I took the arrow out and repaired some of the damage. She will be able to walk now, but her hip will be painful. She'll be fine so long as you take it easy. I think you should return to your tribe and tell them what has happened. They will be worried about you if you do not return."

"Why can't I stay with you?"

"I have to go and help my friends escape from those evil men. Besides, think how your mother will suffer if you do not turn up soon."

Once the boy was gone, Tirzah packed up his supplies and started trekking across the desert. There were no footprints to follow, so he had to rely on his senses to find them. He sent out mental feelers to locate them.

***

The Albasinians and their captors, apart from the ones on watch, slept fitfully until they were aroused by Tumma shortly before sunset.

"You're going to search for water and something to eat. The guards will go with you. I'm going hunting. Do you understand?"

"How about giving us some of our water?" Felindra croaked. Her mouth and throat were parched, and she couldn't summon any saliva to moisten them. The flying sand and dust had left her lips cracked and skin chafed, despite the head cloth she used to cover her face.

They'd had two full water skins each when they'd left the oasis, and the two defenders had each carried an extra one, but Tumma and his men had taken them with the rest of their belongings.

"You're going to look for water," Tumma replied. "You'll have to wait until you find some."

"Do you know what heat stroke is?" Sastin, the healer asked. Felindra was surprised to hear him challenge Tumma. He was usually a more retiring man.

"What are you babbling about?" Tumma responded.

"It's extremely painful. A person can die of it very quickly when it starts to boil the brain," Sastin replied. "We need water if we are to survive in this heat."

Tumma obviously wasn't aware of this by the fearful look that momentarily crossed his face.

"We have, or had, enough in our water bags to sustain us for another day," Vertan added. "I'm not sure the Basrindians will pay you much for our dead bodies."

"You are such weaklings," Tumma snarled. He turned to his men. "Get your cups out and give them one measure each." He turned away to pick up his pack and then turned back. "Then get going. It'll be dark soon and you won't be able to see anything with these clouds.

Once they had left the rock shelter and were away from Tumma, Farah said, "The oasis shouldn't be far from here. I wonder if we can reach it."

"I don't know," Felindra replied. "It's hard to tell where we are after wandering around in a dust storm." She looked over at the three men who were still tied together. "Can anybody tell how far we are from the oasis?"

Vertan scratched his head and Barengush shrugged.

"I couldn't even tell which direction it is," Vertan replied.

"All I know is, it should be east of here, but whether it is northeast or southeast, I couldn't say. The sun is setting behind us, so go the other way."

"What oasis?" one of the wizards interjected.

"The one we rested at two days past," Felindra replied.

"And now you don't know where it is," one of the wizards said. "Lot of good that will do us."

"Maybe you could find it with your magic," Barengush replied contemptuously.

"Let's keep moving, it'll be dark in a few degrees," One of the soldiers said.

***

You're on the right track, Farah received.

Lin! I'm surprised to hear from you; Tumma had blocked us. Where are you? What should we do?

He's too far away from you for the spell to hold. I've led him in another direction by putting the idea in his mind that there are some animals for him to kill that way. All he'll find is some snakes and scorpions.

That's a bit harsh, isn't it? Farah replied.

I suppose it is. I'm sure he'll be able to sense danger, but how he acts on it is up to him. I wanted to put as much distance between him and his cohorts as possible. If you veer to your right now and keep going in that direction, you'll reach the oasis before sunrise.

I doubt they will listen to me, Farah replied.

Just tell them you can sense it. The others will back up your ability.

When will you catch up with us?

Before dawn. Let me know if you have any problems.

"I sense plenty of water over that way," Farah said, pointing towards the right. She winked at Vertan and he nodded.

"She's good at sensing things like that," Vertan said to the soldier nearest to him, probably the senior member of the team judging by the corporal's emblem on his shoulder. "I think we should go where she said."

The man looked at him suspiciously. "How do we know it's not a trick?"

"Do you have a better idea?" Vertan asked. "It's time for us to have some more water," he added, using his conviction ability to make sure he was obeyed.

The corporal called a rest and made sure the men distributed water to the prisoners. Although it was now completely dark, they kept moving, even though everyone was exhausted and hungry. The defenders, Vertan and

Barengush, ended up supporting Felindra and Farah, walking arm-in-arm with them when they began to weaken.

"So, I assume Tirzah Lin is not far away," Vertan said to Farah, who was holding onto his arm.

"He said he would catch up with us near the oasis."

It's not far now. Turn slightly to your left, Farah received from Tirzah Lin.

"Did you hear that?" she asked Vertan.

"I did. I'm so glad we have him with us. I don't think we would have survived without him."

3 – Sunrise at the Oasis

The sandstorm of the previous night had changed the desert in some ways. In many places, hollows had been filled in with loose sand, making them hazardous to cross due to their tendency to slide underfoot. Rocks, on the other hand had been cleared of debris and looked smoother and cleaner. Although a lot of the vegetation had been destroyed and blown away, much had survived, albeit stripped of their foliage and fruit, and left flat on the ground.

"You'd better tell them to turn," Farah said after a while.

They continued through the night until a faint pinkish light on the horizon ahead announced the imminence of dawn. A few degrees later, they crested a massive sandbank and saw the oasis highlighted against the rising sun.

"Finally," Felindra said, letting go of Barengush's arm. *I've never been so relieved to see anything since Ashala appeared just in time to save me from the demon Ogryn.* She started to walk down the sandbank but ended up on her back sliding to the bottom. The rest of the group followed her with varying levels of decorum. They staggered across the level plain into the oasis, automatically making for the pools, only to find them empty apart from a sandy slurry in the muddy basins.

Barengush

"What happened to the water?" Felindra cried.

"It must have been blown away in the storm," Barengush said.

"The sand filled the hole," the Basrindian corporal said.

"What we do?" Barengush asked in his broken Basrindian.

"Dig!" The corporal illustrated with gestures. "There's water under the sand."

Barengush turned to his colleagues. "He says we have to dig for water."

"With our bare hands?" Farah asked.

Barengush and Vertan had another conversation with the two Basrindian soldiers. They responded by pulling out two shovels attached to their packs and giving them to the two defenders. "Dig!" was the order.

"We can't possibly work without drinking some water and resting for a while," Vertan protested. "Give us our water bags!" he added. He used his gift again to make sure they obeyed him.

The Albasinians got their water bags and looked around for a shady place to rest.

14

Much of the foliage of the oasis was damaged and most of the fruit had been torn from the date palms, although a few clusters had come to rest on the leeward side of obstacles like rocks and tree trunks. Sastin staggered over to the nearest bunch and brought it over to their resting place among the palm tops that now lay on the ground. They tried to ignore their captors who seemed to be undecided about what to do now that their leader was missing.

"We could probably take them quite easily if we tried," Barengush murmured to Vertan.

"We could," Vertan replied. "But not before we have some rest."

Felindra

Felindra woke with a start. Something wet had landed on her face. She sat up and looked around. The sky was clouded over again, but this time, it was rainfall.

"We're in for a storm," Tirzah said, patting her on the shoulder.

"Brother Tirzah! I'm so happy to see you." She stood up to give him a hug. "Did you just arrive?"

"I've been here for a while, but I thought I'd let you sleep a little longer. As I said, there's a storm coming, so we should prepare for it. Higher ground would be better, but that sand dune wouldn't be stable; the water would wash it away in no time."

Already the raindrops were falling with more force. "Couldn't we stay here?" she asked.

"It's probably the only solution," Tirzah replied. "We could secure ourselves among the date palms. The most serious hazard would be flooding, but it may not be that bad."

Seeing that everyone else was awake, Tirzah greeted them all and advised them to take shelter among the date palms. Even though the palms had been damaged, their trunks were still held firmly in the ground and would provide something to hold onto.

"What about them?" Barengush asked.

"I'll talk to them," Tirzah said and walked over to where their captors were huddling in another clump of foliage. They stood up when he approached and came to meet him. After some talking and waving of hands, the two soldiers and wizards picked up their packs and went over to another cluster of palms. Each one took a ground sheet from his pack to hold over his head, but when Tirzah spoke to them again, they handed two of them to him.

The storm was fierce and violent, with loud rumbling thunder, but it soon passed, leaving the air cooler and fresher. They found water in the two larger pools but needed to wait until the silt settled to the bottom before using it.

There was still some daylight left, but the Albasinians were eager to move on. "What are we going to do about them?" Vertan nodded towards the two Basrindian soldiers and their wizard companions.

"I'll take care of them," Tirzah Lin said. "Fill your water skins and gather as many dates as you can find while I talk to them again."

Seeing the activity of the Albasinians, their captors got up and joined them. "It's time to move on," the corporal said. The other three nodded agreement. "Get them ready to march, tie them together like before!"

The Albasinians had long since removed the ropes with which they had been bound together and stowed them away. "Where are the ropes?" the other soldier asked.

"You won't be needing them, will you?" Tirzah Lin said. "Come over here; I have to talk to you." In the mildest voice, he directed them to one of the groups of date palms. Felindra watched as they came along obediently, wondering what Brother Tirzah was up to. "Sit down," Tirzah said.

The next time she looked, their four captors were lying on the ground. "Bring the ropes," Tirzah ordered. When Vertan and Barengush reached him, he said, "Tie them up. They'll sleep for most of the night and by the time they wake, we'll be far away." He turned to Farah and Sastin. "Would you search their packs and retrieve what they took from you. Take their weapons too."

"Can't we leave them something to protect themselves and for hunting?" Felindra said.

"You are too tender-hearted, young lady," Tirzah replied. "Don't you realize what they had in store for you? Very well, leave them two knives."

"And they'll need some water when they wake up."

Tirzah Lin sighed and shook his head. "Go ahead."

4 – Crossing the Border

Felindra

When they left the oasis, Brother Tirzah led them towards the north. "We'll make it look as if we're heading for Pangast. Once we leave a good track, we'll turn west again towards Nedra."

"I wonder what happened to Tumma," Felindra said.

"I cannot sense his life force," Farah said. "Can you, Lin?

"It's very weak," Tirzah Lin replied.

"Will he pass?" Felindra asked.

"It is likely," Tirzah replied.

"That's so sad. I don't suppose we could help, could we?"

"Why would you care about him after what he did to you, and me? He's only getting what he deserves."

It's just.... I don't like to think of anyone dying out there in the desert, alone and probably very frightened. He had a mother once and people who loved him."

"So why did he turn to evil?" Barengush said.

"We'll never know. Something awful may have happened to him. Like you, he may have been abused by his father."

"Don't fret, little sister," Tirzah Lin said, patting her on the shoulder. "There is nothing we can do. He will pass on to the fields of the Great Spirit and suffer no more."

Oh light, please help Tumma. Felindra felt the warm, peaceful current flow through her, the sign her prayer had been received.

***

The only sign of a border between Basrind and Nedra was a line of stone pillars set in the ground about a span apart and shoulder-high to a man. Some of them were leaning sideways, others were broken off at varying levels and all were adorned with thorny weeds and vines.

"Not much of a border," Vertan commented. "Anyone could cross it at will."

"Like us," Barengush added.

"It's only meant to be a marker," Tirzah Lin said. "It's there as much for administrative purposes as anything. It lets travelers know when they've entered or left the country. If you could see through all that foliage, the names of the border states are carved into the stone. If a military force crossed the markers, it would be treated as an act of war."

"Like the current situation," Farah said.

"Precisely," Tirzah replied.

The six travelers pushed through a gap between two pillars, trying to avoid being caught up in the prickly vines. They walked on across the arid landscape until they came to a road of hard-packed sand.

"This must lead to a settlement," Tirzah said. "Let's follow it and see what we can learn from the people."

"Won't they be suspicious of us?" Vertan asked. "They might think we are spies."

Tirzah Lin shook his head. "I will speak to them and explain our situation."

"Do you think many escaped slaves come this way?" Sastin asked.

"Since the Pangastians freed the slaves, it seems inevitable that some have passed here."

Not far from the border, they saw a cluster of small dwellings that appeared to be made of sand. Further scrutiny revealed that they were built with sun-dried bricks. It must have been an oasis because there was plenty of greenery around the village, including date palms and some fields of grain, as well as several fruit-bearing trees, which they discovered later were olives, figs, and apricots.

As they approached, several men appeared on the road, carrying broad-bladed knives not unlike the bolos used by the farmers on the islands of Motu Ataahua, but these looked as if they doubled as weapons.

"Hold your hands up facing them," Tirzah Lin instructed them.

"Are they hostile?" Barengush asked.

"I doubt it. They are always prepared to protect their families and homes, but they don't usually attack without a reason.

The three men stopped about five steps in front of them and their leader said something that only Tirzah understood. Tirzah stepped forward and responded, occasionally gesturing towards his five companions.

The three Nedrans came closer and inspected the Albasinians, nodding their heads and muttering to one another as they passed each one, then the leader shouted. "Hah!" and beckoned them to follow.

The men were brown-skinned, like the Albasinians, but they were taller and more rugged looking. They wore long robes of natural cotton and matching head cloths with colored bands.

They are impressed with us, Farah sent.

In these rags? Felindra replied. The clothes they had escaped in were now dirty and tattered after being worn for days and subjected to everything nature could give.

I think Tirzah must have told them we were important people in our homeland.

Tirzah came back to walk between the two women. "We make them nervous," he said. "They are probably afraid the Basrindians will seek reprisal against them for harboring escaped slaves. We won't stay long. It would be helpful if we could do something for them while we are here. Shall I see if there's anything they need help with?"

"Yes, go ahead," Felindra replied. "We'll keep our eyes open, too. Would it be wise to reveal our magical gifts?

"I think it would if the circumstances present themselves."

Rosy streaks were beginning to appear in the sky ahead; the sun would be setting soon. They could see the smoke rising from cooking fires ahead and smell the aroma of roasting meat.

"It smells too good to be true. I hope they offer us some," Vertan said.

"You will find they are a hospitable people. They would feel dishonored if they did not share their meal with us, or if we declined their offer," Tirzah said.

A crowd of children galloped up to meet them, looking at them with varying expressions. Some of the younger ones laughed and pointed, others just stared, their eyes round with wonder. Some of the older boys squinted suspiciously, and several girls giggled behind their head cloths. They skipped along beside the visitors, chattering excitedly with one another.

A woman shouted something and most of the bigger children ran back to the village. Moments later, the former slaves entered the village, which consisted of seven brick houses around three sides of a tamped-earth square with a large cooking fire in the center. An animal the size of a sheep or goat was roasting on a spit over the fire with a boy at one end turning it slowly. Several women were preparing food on a table outside the biggest house, the one in the middle.

The first thing the men did when they arrived was order some of the bigger girls to bring them bowls of water. They placed them on the ground in front of the visitors, smiling shyly and then covering their mouths with their head cloths. They said something, but no one understood but Tirzah Lin. "We should use the water to wash our faces, hands, and feet," he said. "It is their ritual ablution before a meal."

"Very practical," Sastin said. Something caught his eye. "You see the boy turning the spit? He looks as if he's injured his leg or foot. Lin, could you find out what happened? I might be able to help him."

After they'd finished their ablutions, the villagers invited them to share their meal, serving meat with a spicy mixture of vegetables and cooked grain on baked clay plates. For a beverage, they had the fermented goats' milk with which they were already familiar. Despite their gnawing hunger, Felindra and Farah ate slowly, savoring every mouthful, closing their eyes ecstatically over the mouthwatering flavors. This was their first real meal since before the Pangasti invasion of Basrind more than seven days gone. The invasion that had enabled them to escape.

Felindra looked up and Tirzah smiled at her. "Good, eh?"

"It's the best meal I can remember; it's been such a long time since I ate anything like this. Would you tell them and ask if there's anything we can do to repay them? Maybe I could look at their animals ... you know what I mean."

She noticed that Barengush and Vertan had already cleaned their plates, wiping the final drops of gravy with bread. The village women watched them, nodding with satisfaction at the travelers' response to their cooking.

The sun had set by the time they finished eating and the younger children had been taken indoors and put to bed. "Where are we going to sleep?" Vertan asked.

"I'll find out if they have somewhere for us to rest," Tirzah Lin replied. After speaking to the village elder, he came back and reported that they could sleep on the roofs of the houses.

A woman came forward and led Felindra and Farah to a staircase along the side of one of the houses and up onto the roof. The flat roof had a brick, knee-high barrier all around it, and several straw-filled pallets scattered around on the floor. As they looked around, the woman gave them each a wool blanket that she'd been carrying over her arm.

Not knowing the language, the only way they could thank the woman was with their palms together in front of their faces and a bow. "Thank you, and Light bless you," Farah said with a smile.

After the woman left them, Farah and Felindra took two pallets each and piled them, one atop the other, by the eastern barrier, and then they wrapped themselves in the blankets and lay down.

Farah yawned. "I'm exhausted," she said. "Good night."

5 – Leaving the Village

The next day was spent helping the villagers with a few problems. Barengush used his gift of controlling elements to blast away a rock from the middle of one of their grain fields; he also removed the stump of a tree that had been struck by lightning.

Sastin and Tirzah looked at the boy with the injury they'd noticed the previous evening. Apparently, he'd sprained his ankle when he'd stepped on a stone while running, twisting his foot sideways.

After examining him, Tirzah explained to the boy, who had around twelve years, how to take care of it. A woman was watching them from a distance, wringing her hands anxiously, so Tirzah beckoned her closer. After discovering she was the boy's mother, he told her what he'd told the boy, which was basically to keep the foot cool with cold water and rest with the foot raised higher than his heart. Other than that, all they could do was apply a supportive bandage.

Farah saw a woman watching her and felt a tendril of thought reach out to her. The woman obviously had some telepathic ability but seemed unsure what to do with it. When Tirzah had finished helping Sastin, she beckoned him.

"I think that woman is a telepath," she said. "Do you think we could help her? She may be afraid the villagers would find out and punish her as a witch."

"I'll talk to her," he replied. "Come with me. I don't want those men to get the wrong idea."

After a brief conversation, Tirzah turned to Farah. "Walk with us. Perhaps we can put her fears at rest."

"How should we approach this?" he asked when they had reached an orchard of olive trees.

"All we can really do is reassure her. Tell her we have four telepaths in our group and the gift is invaluable to us especially when someone dangerous is near."

Felindra had gone with two of the herders to visit their flocks of sheep and goats and check on a camel family of two parents and a young calf. Some of Felindra's most joyful moments were spent communicating with animals, so she was in her element walking among the herds and listening to their problems. She was happy to report that the herds were healthy, with no major problems, just a goat with a thorn in its foot, and a sheep with a stomach ache, but the herders were impressed when Tirzah translated her assessment. One of them said something to Tirzah and laughed.

"He asked if you would like to stay here and help them."

"I wish I could, but I have to return to my family in a land far from here."

***

The sun was setting. They'd eaten their last meal in the village and were preparing to leave when they heard galloping from the direction of Basrind.

"Quickly, we must hide," Tirzah Lin said. "Come on, into the barley field. We can lie down on the ground there and not be seen." After a few words with the village head man, he nodded. "Let's go."

25

They grabbed their bags and ran down the slope to the fields on the other side of the orchard and threw themselves on the ground among the dense stalks.

"I told the head man that if they are looking for us, to send them south along the road."

As they watched, kneeling among the stalks, four camels rode into view. Even in the twilight, they could see that they were Basrindian soldiers. After a terse discussion with much arm-waving and shouting, the soldiers lowered their camels and dismounted.

"They're going to search the village," Vertan said.

The villagers watched the soldiers as they entered homes and workshops. Mothers hushed their children, men paced angrily with clenched fists. Entering another country in a time of war was tantamount to invasion, but there was nothing they could do although the Albasinians could sense how much they wanted to fight.

They heard the crash of breaking dishes and the louder sound of something heavy being knocked over, then the Basrindians gave up the search and questioned the villagers once more, this time with threats, but the people stood steadfast, shaking their heads, and pointing to the southwest. Finally, the Basrindians mounted their camels and rode on along the road.

"The headman told them we passed by around midday and asked for some refreshment and then continued south," Tirzah related.

6 – The Road to Kum

After leaving the village, Felindra and her team, now led by Tirzah Lin, who was a long-time resident of the area, took the trail north towards the border with Pangast. One of the reasons for the Pangasti invasion had been to release slaves, many of whom had been taken in border raids, but they made it their purpose to release all slaves, no matter where they originated. Many of Dom Ash's slaves had chosen to stay because Dom Ash was a good master who cared about their well-being and didn't abuse them.

They were now heading for Kum, Pangast's major port city, where Tirzah Lin hoped to be reunited with his sister, Rasamé, another slave who had been released by the Pangasti. Dom Ash's father had granted Tirzah his freedom after he'd saved the life of his son, Ash. Lin and Ash had become friends and grown to manhood together. Tirzah Lin had been allowed to go wherever he pleased, but if he stepped too far out of line, he knew his sister, who had a different master, would be punished.

Tirzah Lin came from another country far from Basrind, a place he called 'the home of his heart', and longed to return to, but he hadn't been able to leave Basrind while they held Rasamé hostage.

The people in the village had given them bags of fruit and nuts, in addition to a pile of freshly-made flatbread, wrapped in cloth, and two clay pots of goat cheese, to sustain them for a day or two. All they needed now was to find a spring or stream for water. The moon was almost full and there were no clouds to veil the stars, so they kept up a steady pace along the sandy trail.

"They are good people," Felindra said to Tirzah.

"Most people are," he replied with a sigh. "It's greed for wealth and dominance over others that causes most problems."

"It's like the nomads we met at the oasis, working hard for their livelihood, only to be robbed of everything they'd struggled for." She thought for a moment. "You know what amazes me? They're so generous; even when they have so little, they are willing to share what they have with strangers."

"That's the root of brotherliness, knowing what it feels like to be hurt and in need, and applying that to their relationships with others. I think you call that empathy in your country, don't you?"

Felindra nodded. "That's right. I wonder if we'll see the nomads again. I'd like to know that the boy and his camel are safe."

"We may cross their path again. We are going in the right direction."

Farah came up beside them, "Mind if I join you?"

"You are welcome any time, Lady Farah." Tirzah said. "What do you think? Are we safe?"

"I can't sense anything threatening," Farah replied. "What about you?"

"All calm and peaceful."

"There's quite a lot of animal activity," Felindra added. "But nothing hostile."

"Barengush and Vertan have gone hunting," Farah said. "Men and their craving for meat."

"Barengush has improved a lot since I first met him," Felindra said. "When we escaped from the dungeons in

ValkonenMaa, he was horrified when I bought *vegetables* for us to eat."

Felindra look up at the stars and thought of her betrothed far away in Albasiny. They'd pledged to think of each other every time they looked at the stars but thinking about Varan these times brought more pain than joy. After the effort he and his father had made so that they could marry—she a commoner and he the son of a duke—they were so far apart. This reminded her of her father and his reluctance to accept a knighthood until he realized it was for her, and she smiled. *Dear dadi, I wonder where you are now.*

"Thinking about home?" Farah asked.

"Yes, I was. It must be daytime in Albasiny. Can you contact anyone? I want Varan to know I'm safe and on my way home.

"We could do that now," Farah replied. "Do you want me to send a message to the palace?"

"That would be nice," Felindra replied. "Maybe we should call my father as well. Could you to try to contact Ashavan?"

Farah didn't close her eyes while she was sending because she needed to see where she was walking. After a few moments concentration, she turned to Felindra. "The sender at the palace asks if you want her to send for him so you can talk to each other."

Felindra thought for a moment. She had always been a bit shy about her romance with Varan. Oh, what did it matter? Everyone knew about it anyway. "All right," she said.

"Let's stop and rest for a while," Tirzah said. "I don't want you tripping over something on the path."

"He's here," Farah said. "He wants to know if you are well, and when you are coming home?"

Felindra felt awkward having an intimate conversation through two intermediaries. "Tell him I am quite well, and we will be coming home as soon as we can find a ship going in the right direction. Ask him what is happening in DarSolas and how is the duke."

They'd found some boulders to sit on while the conversation continued. Felindra found it so unsatisfactory, she wanted to bring it to a hasty conclusion. All they could talk about was trivialities. After they'd exchanged assurances of love for each other, Felindra said goodbye. After it was over, she let out a long breath. "Thank you, Farah."

"Shall I try to get Ashavan now? I wouldn't be surprised if they're back in Albasiny by now."

By the time Farah had finished communicating with Ashavan, the sun had almost reached the eastern horizon and the sky had taken on a pinkish-yellow tint.

"Let's look for a place to sleep," Tirzah suggested. "That way, we'll have time to have a meal before the temperature becomes unbearable."

As if they'd heard Tirzah's words, Barengush and Vertan chose that moment to return from their hunt. Vertan had a long-legged rabbit and a lizard, while Barengush carried two rabbits over his shoulder.

Felindra flinched when she saw them, but she tried to keep her feelings to herself. She hated seeing animals being hurt, but she realized it was the unavoidable law of nature that some creatures were predators and others were prey. Even her beloved wolf, Ashala, had had to kill to sustain her life.

"It looks as if we're going to have a feast," Sastin said.

Tirzah nodded. "Well done, you two. Let's find a place to start a fire."

While they were searching for a sheltered place to sleep, Felindra asked Farah about her communication with Ashavan.

"They are still at sea," Farah replied. "They were delayed on the way back to Albasiny." She smiled at Felindra. "You'll be happy to know they've captured Gremulkin."

"Thank the light! That's wonderful news. How did they manage that?"

"One of his wizards turned him in, after some negotiation. The wizard wanted to trade his life for Gremulkin's. They all knew what was at stake if they stuck with him, so it wasn't too difficult to turn them."

"What will happen to them now?"

"He will be turned over to the queen and tried for treason, among other things. The wizards that were with him will also go on trial, for lesser charges."

"What's the penalty for treason?" Felindra asked.

"Public decapitation," Sastin, who was walking with them, said.

"I suppose that's just, given all the suffering he caused in the Dark Brotherhood conflict." Felindra said. She had personal reasons for despising Gremulkin. He had destroyed Varan's family, leaving only him, his father, and an uncle alive. He was also responsible for the destruction of the duke's castle and the theft of the Trethawynd treasury, as well as Felindra's kidnapping and incarceration in the dungeons of the Valkonen monastery when she only had thirteen years. Everyone she knew and loved—some of whom no longer lived—had been affected in some way by Gremulkin and the Dark Brotherhood.

***

Felindra woke suddenly sensing something was wrong. The sun was still shining, and even in the shade, the light was dazzling. Feeling someone standing close to her, she peered through half-closed eyes and saw a pair of feet in dusty leather sandals. Raising her focus higher, she traced her way up past dirty white britches to a pair of hands holding a large, curved knife, and then up to see a bearded chin and pair of dark eyes looking down at her.

As she opened her mouth to raise the alarm, the man pointed the knife at her and put his fingers across his lips.

Felindra stared at him, but refrained from making a sound, instead, she sent to everyone, *there's an armed man standing over me.*

The result of this communication was chaotic. People shouting, weapons clashing, the scream of an injured man. When the man close to her turned his attention to the melee, Felindra sat up quickly, grasped his ankles and upended him in the sand. In his surprise, he'd dropped his knife, so she stood up and grabbed it before putting her foot on his chest and holding it over his face.

She could now see what was happening with her friends but taking her eyes off him was a mistake. He pulled her feet out from under her and sent her floundering on the ground. As she fell, she lost her grip on the knife, which he grabbed and pressed to her neck, grinning at her and shaking his head.

He said something she didn't understand. "What you want?" she asked, using the few words she had picked up in Basrind.

The attacker replied with another flow of words, the only one of which she understood was "you".

"Who are they?" she called loudly. "What do they want?"

"They're bandits," Barengush replied.

"Everyone, stay calm and wait a moment." Tirzah said.

"Shall I try to blast them?" There was a thump. Barengush let out a groan and said no more."

"Something like that would hurt all of us," Tirzah Lin said. Another thump silenced him as well.

If only I could see what's going on, Felindra thought.

It's hard to say, Farah replied. I don't think they want to rob us. It's obvious we have nothing to steal. I fear it may be something more sinister.

What do you think it could be?

They look suspiciously like Basrindians. Slavers maybe?

I think that's a possibility, Tirzah Lin interjected. Don't try to resist; you'd only get hurt.

Wouldn't you know someone would take advantage of the situation, all those escaped slaves wandering around the desert with no protection? Farah sent.

We'll overcome them, Tirzah replied, but for now, go along with them. I'll try to find out what's on their minds. Help me, Farah.

The men who had attacked them tied their hands behind their backs with rope and then joined them all together with a longer rope threaded through their elbows. As on previous occasions, all their belongings and weapons had been confiscated. There were four men in the group, one of which acted as their leader. He yelled some orders, the essence of which was 'get moving'.

It was fortunate that the attack had occurred just before sunset, so they weren't bothered by sunlight. Nevertheless, it was still very hot, and their water supply was getting low.

Let's summarize what's on their minds, Tirzah Lin sent. Then we will decide what to do. I noticed one of them is feeling ill and is getting weaker. I think he will collapse soon if he doesn't get treatment.

I think the most significant fact is that they are all deserters from the army. Farah added.

How can they take us into Basrind and sell us as slaves if they deserted? Vertan asked.

"No doubt they have contacts outside of Basrind who will pay them for capturing us. Tirzah Lin replied. Now, here's what I suggest, and we must do this quickly, before we reach the border: I will put them to sleep, just as I did before. It will be easier this time because they don't have any magic to use against us.

They had barely covered a hundred paces before Tirzah went into action, leaving four sleeping Basrindians lying on the ground.

Once everyone was freed, Tirzah said, "let's put them in a shady place. They're going to sleep for a long time."

"We ought to leave them some water as well," Felindra said. "We don't want to kill them."

"I'd like to examine the one who is sick," Sastin said. "It won't take long, and I might discover something useful."

He knelt beside the fallen man and checked his signs without touching him. If it was contagious, he didn't want to transmit it. The man's heart was beating rapidly, although it sounded weak, and his breathing was becoming labored. Although his skin was hot, he wasn't producing much sweat, in fact, it looked quite dry. Then he noticed the rash around the man's ankles.

"What do you make of this?" he asked Tirzah. "It's like nothing I've seen before."

Tirzah knelt beside him and looked the man over, nodding his head as he did so. He stood up when he was finished and spoke to Sastin in a faint voice. "It looks bad. He may not survive."

"What is it?" Sastin asked anxiously.

"They call it desert fever," Tirzah replied. "The symptoms are the result of a parasite invasion. It is spread by an ant that lives in the desert. See the rashes on his legs? That's where he was bitten."

"You mean any one of us could catch this? Sastin stood up and moved away from the sick man.

"It's possible. Anyone who is in good health should be able to fight it off. This fellow is obviously on the verge of starvation."

"Poor man," Sastin said, "What a way to die. Is there a cure, or treatment?"

"There's an herbal remedy that will flush the parasite from the body but finding it might be a problem. Otherwise, you just have to make the victim comfortable and make sure he drinks lots of water and nutrient-rich broth."

"Are we ready? Barengush asked.

"I'll lead," Tirzah said. "We could reach the Pangasti boarder before dawn if we hurry. We can eat as we walk, if we still have any food left."

"They took it all, but I retrieved most of it." Vertan replied.

"I hope you didn't take anything from the sick man," Tirzah said.

Vertan shook his head. "I couldn't bear to touch him or even get close; I was afraid I'd catch something."

7 – Out of Danger

Tirzah Lin

Crossing into Pangast was like going into a new climate zone. The desert gradually became greener, trees started to dot the landscape, and grasses grew in the soil instead of cacti and other desert plants. The sun had risen by this time, enabling them to see their surroundings. After a while, farms appeared, although the crops they were cultivating looked wilted and droopy.

"Here you see one of the reasons Pangast invaded Basrind, in addition to freeing slaves," Tirzah told his companions. "Pangast has suffered from drought here for several years."

"I suppose that's the reason they took all the food from the plantation," Farah said.

"But don't they have wells like those in Basrind?" Felindra asked.

"In order to dig wells, you need an underground reservoir to supply them. Unfortunately for the Pangasti, they aren't as blessed with underground water as the Basrindians," Tirzah replied. "As we move farther north where the land becomes hillier, you'll see more streams and rivers, but even they are running low. The problem is lack of rainfall."

"I wonder if we can help them with that," Barengush said. "If Gremulkin's wizards can summon up storms, surely we can bring some rain."

He refrained from calling them Dark Wizards; he didn't like to remind anyone that he had once been one himself, until she came on the scene and convinced him of the advantages of following the Light.

"That's a good suggestion," Tirzah replied. "But I don't think we should try anything like that without consulting the authorities."

"I agree," Barengush said. "But if we do something to help them, they might help us get home."

They'd been traveling northeast since crossing the border, but when they came to a road going directly east, they turned onto it. The first thing they saw was a military checkpoint manned by four Pangasti soldiers. One of the soldiers stepped into the road and signaled for them to stop. It was fortunate that the military had made their inspection point beside a grove of trees because the questioning took a while and the sun was already a few degrees above the horizon.

"Is there somewhere we could get some water?" Tirzah asked. He'd done most of the talking with the soldiers because of the language barrier.

The soldier who appeared to be in charge pointed to a barrel in the shade of their shelter and answered the question. "He said we can fill our water skins from the barrel." He told his companions. "They have plenty because it's refilled every day."

They walked on, keeping to the shade of any trees they encountered. The road began to climb after they'd walked for several degrees and everyone's energy was flagging.

Felindra

"Can we take a break?" Felindra asked. "For some reason, I'm feeling a bit weak." She bent to scratch her ankle. *This damned itching is going to drive me out of my mind.*

She noticed Sastin scratching his lower leg. *Why are we itching?* she wondered but didn't want to complain about it. She looked around at the others, but no one else seemed to be affected. *Oh, Light, please don't let it be those ants.*

Everyone else welcomed the idea, so they all sat down under a tree, and took several sips from their water skins.

"Is there any food left," Barengush asked.

Vertan, who had been carrying their food, pulled his bag towards him and drew out a cloth-wrapped bundle. He opened it on the grass and showed them the sparseness of their food supply. He looked at his companions and shrugged.

"How long will it take us to get to Kum?" Farah asked.

"If we can keep going until sunset and then sleep through the night, we could be there by sunset on the morrow," Tirzah replied. "That's providing nothing happens to hold us up."

"Are there any villages or towns in between?" Farah asked.

"There are several, according to those men at the checkpoint."

"It's too bad we don't have any coin to buy things," Barengush said.

"We'll come up with something," Tirzah said hopefully. "There's always something to trade, even if it's only the sweat of our brows."

"What does that mean?" Barengush asked.

"We might be able to trade our labor for food and other needs."

"Do you think it's safe to eat what we have?"

Tirzah smiled and nodded his head. "The Creator provides."

After eating the scanty meal, mostly dates and nuts with some leftover meat and bread from the previous day, they leaned back against the trunk of the tree.

Before closing her eyes Felindra saw Sastin scratching his foot and it set her scratching again. The rash seemed to be spreading. "Does anyone have some Aloe? I've got a terrible itch on my leg." If she didn't admit what she suspected, there might be a chance she was wrong.

Sastin

Tirzah's eyes snapped open. "Don't scratch it!" he snapped abruptly.

Sastin was alerted by the urgency of Tirzah's response and looked down at his feet. "I'll check in my supplies," he said, with a knowing look at Tirzah. After rummaging around in his pack, he drew out a thick spikey leaf wrapped in some clean cotton. "Only this. It's a bit dry, but there should be enough gel for both of us. Let me slice it.

As he was slicing the leaf Tirzah Lin moved over to sit between him and Felindra. "Let me see," Tirzah said to Felindra. He next turned to Sastin and examined his foot, then he sat back and nodded.

"What?" Sastin asked. "Is this the same...?" he ended with a cough.

"It looks like it."

"Like what?" Felindra asked coughing into the hand she'd just used to scratch her ankles.

Tirzah slapped her hand away from her mouth. "Don't! Don't touch anything with your hands."

"You're scaring me," Felindra said shakily. "What is going on?"

"One of those bounty hunters had a rash like yours and now he's dying or may have already passed on. It is something very dangerous and we need to be extra precautions if you are to survive." He turned aside to receive the sliced half of the aloe leaf. "Here, daub this on the rash. Make sure it is thoroughly covered. Clean your hands after you've finished.

"What else can we do?" Sastin asked.

"We need to find the herb that will destroy the parasites. There should be some around here; remedies often grow in the areas where the problem exists, although heliban is not a common plant. There may be a healer or medicine woman in the next village who has some."

"I sincerely hope so," Sastin said. He looked over at Felindra, whose skin had turned as pale as putty. He could see beads of sweat on her forehead, whether from the disease, or from fear, he couldn't tell. "Don't lose heart. We'll beat this," he said. "With the Light's help...."

"I know," she replied, "But I feel so awful." She leaned back against the tree trunk and closed her eyes.

"A few more precautions," Tirzah Lin continued. "Drink lots of water to wash out the toxins, and don't eat any more food; it would only feed them. I've heard that eucalyptus juice can also drive them out, so if you have any, add a little to your drinking water."

Tirzah Lin

Tirzah Lin leaned back against the tree and closed his eyes. He had done his best to mask his anxiety about the two Albasinians, trying to play down the seriousness of their conditions, but Sastin must have realized that himself. Felindra was another matter. She hadn't even been close to the sick Basrindian bounty-hunter. *I should check them all.* He stood up. Everyone appeared to be sleeping, so he went ahead and checked the ankles and feet of Vertan and Barengush, leaving Farah 'til last.

She opened her eyes when he got close to her. "You're worried, aren't you?" she said, shading her eyes to look up at him.

He nodded and reached out his hand to her. "Would you walk with me for a few moments?"

When they were out of hearing range of the others, Tirzah said. "You are right. I am very concerned. I need someone to talk it over with. I'm not sure how to handle this."

Farah looked at him compassionately, making him conscious of what an attractive woman she was. "What is your main concern right now?"

Tirzah thought for a moment. "Not being able to find the heliban medicine they need."

"You think they will cross over without it."

"It's not a certainty but given the state of their health after walking so far and not having enough food, not to mention the other mishaps they'd had to cope with ... all that reduces their chance of being able to combat the infestations."

"It's too bad Sastin is infected. He's really an excellent healer."

"He could probably heal himself if he had the strength and endurance. It's Sister Felindra I'm more concerned about."

"How long would it take someone to get here from Kum? That's where you expect your sister to be, isn't it?"

"I never thought of that," Tirzah said, looking a bit more optimistic. "She's also a healer like our mother. She might be able to find some in the city, or in one of the villages on the way. In answer to your question, if she left now, she could be here by sunrise walking, or she could be here by sunset this day if she had transportation. I will contact her and find out what she can do."

Farah waited with Tirzah while he was communicating with his sister. He gestured and nodded his head as the conversation progressed. He blew out his breath when he'd finished and beamed at her.

He took her arm. "We are both tired. Let's rest for a while before we move on". As they walked back to the shade tree arm in arm, Farah asked, "Aren't you going to tell me what she said?"

"She will meet us at the next village, but first she is going to check the herbalists in the city to find the heliban. She has a horse, so it won't take her too long."

Felindra

Felindra feels as if she is walking in thick mud; every step is an effort to pull her gigantic feet out of the mire and move them ahead a little, only to have to repeat everything again and again. Her head feels as if it is stuffed with fleece. She can't see anything through the thick fog that surrounds her. I can't go on, I'm too... her head begins to float away like a balloon, spinning through the fog.

She felt someone shaking her by the shoulder. "Felindra! Wake up," a gentle voice said.

When Felindra opened her eyes, everything seemed to shimmer, and Farah's image floated in the air. *Why do I feel so awful? I must really be sick.* "I feel dreadful," she said shakily. "I'm so hungry."

Tirzah's face appeared beside Farah's. "You can't eat anything, Felindra; all you can have is plain water. Can you sit up?" She shook her head weakly. "We'll help you up." He and Farah took an arm each and raised her up into sitting position. "Now, drink this." He put the cup to her lips and she managed to take a sip or two before her eyes closed and her head fell sideways. Tirzah shook her. "You must drink more than that, Felindra. Come on, try again."

Even though her head was buzzing and threatening to fly away again, she managed to choke down half the cup, although at least a quarter of it ran down her neck and soaked into her clothes.

"I have to attend to Brother Sastin now. I'll leave you with Farah for a while."

Farah sat down beside her and took her hand. "How are you feeling now?"

"Where am I? What's wrong with me?" Felindra's voice was weak and sounded as if it was coming through liquid, then her body convulsed, and she vomited a stream of water and pale mucus all over her clothes.

Fortunately, Farah had been given enough warning and rolled away to avoid being spattered. Felindra had fallen sideways onto the ground.

Tirzah Lin

Tirzah rushed over to them. "What happened?" he asked.

"She just vomited and collapsed."

"You'll have to get these clothes off her, they'll be contaminated. No! Don't touch them! Did you get any on you?"

"I don't think so. I got out of the way in time. Can you see any wet patches on me?" Tirzah examined her clothing, feeling uncomfortable, as if he was invading her privacy, and quickly looked away.

"No, you're fine." He wiped his brow with the back of his hand. This was quickly getting out of hand, and to make matters worse, the heat was stifling.

By now Barengush and Vertan were awake. "Is there anything we can do to help?" Vertan asked.

"We need medicinal herbs and some clean clothes. I wouldn't be surprised if all our clothing is contaminated. We should burn everything."

"How far is the next village?" Barengush asked. "Maybe we could go there and get some clothes for her and Sastin.

I don't know how far it is," Tirzah replied. "It could be around the next bend, or it could be a league away."

The clip-clopping of hoofs coming from the direction of the checkpoint alerted them to the approach of riders. After a while, a couple of camels appeared, led by a man and a woman.

"Maybe they can help," Vertan said.

Tirzah nodded and went to meet them, holding his palms forward. When he was close enough, he bowed to them. When they stopped, he went closer. "Greetings, friends."

The man replied, "Greetings to you, my friend. Is there a problem?"

"It is a trifle. Two of our company are sick and we need a few items to help their healing. I perceive you are traders and hoped you could help us."

"You seem to have fallen on dark times, brother," the man replied, looking up the road at the rest of the group. Tirzah Lin felt a touch of shame at their bedraggled appearance. It had been so long since they'd been able to bathe or wash their clothes, he had grown used to it. He bowed his head. "Forgive the way we look, brother. We have recently crossed the desert from Basrind, escaping from enslavement." A thought occurred to him; maybe the man suspected they couldn't pay for the goods. "We do have a few items we could trade," he added.

The man nodded. "What is it you seek, friend?"

"Some cotton garments for my sick friends, and healing herbs."

"We don't trade in herbs or medicines," the man replied, "but we have some clothing."

"Ah, that is good news. Would you excuse me while I talk to my companions? Come with me if you wish."

The trader looked at the woman and nodded.

She whistled, and the two camels started forward. Tirzah went ahead and spoke to Vertan and Barengush. "They have what we need; not the herb, but some clean clothes. Now we need something to trade for them."

Barengush and Vertan looked at each other. Vertan patted his backpack where he'd tied the sword he'd confiscated from the bounty hunters. "Do you think they would take a sword?"

The couple glanced at Felindra lying under the tree and took their camels to the opposite side of the road where they stood well away from Tirzah and Vertan. "Show them," Tirzah said.

Vertan untied the weapon and held it out hilt first. The man took it and turned it over, rubbed his thumb down the blade and turned to Tirzah "It's old and not in good condition," he said.

"It's a bargaining tactic, so don't worry." Tirzah said to the two defenders. "I'll ask him to show us what they will give us in exchange."

Farah joined them when the woman took down one of the packs from the camel's back and watched as she drew out some cotton garments that looked like long nightgowns, and some head cloths.

Eventually they settled on five gowns in various sizes and five headcloths for two swords.

"Where are you traveling to?" Tirzah asked the trader.

"We go to the next town, Urgua, for the market."

"How far is that?"

The trader looked up at the sky. "We could be there at sunset," he replied. "Is that where you are going?

"Yes. We are meeting someone from Kum there."

"It will be difficult with two sick people. Are they able to walk?"

"If they cannot, we will carry them."

"Wait. I may be able to help you." He went over to the other camel and brought down a package from the back of the camel's head. He undid it and produced several rolls of heavy material that looked like tent cloth. "Perhaps you can use these to carry them." He handed two of the rolls to Barengush and said to Tirzah, "We will be staying at the inn in the market square. You can leave them there when you have finished with them. Tell them to keep them for Amfor. They all know me there."

8 – Reunion

Farah

After Farah had washed Felindra and put on a fresh gown, Tirzah helped lift her onto one of the tent cloths. They settled her on the cloth and took away the contaminated clothing to be burnt. "She's nothing but skin and bone," he commented when they were out of earshot. "If she doesn't get some nourishment soon, I fear she'll fade away. I hope Rasamé has been able to find that herb."

"She's always been a tiny girl, but I've never seen her like this," Farah replied. "She was always so active. She had to be with a wolf for a companion."

"I'll check and see how they're managing with Sastin. "I'll send Vertan to help you carry her, and I'll help Barengush."

The tent cloths were long enough for the invalids to lie lengthwise on them and leave enough room to tie a knot at each end so that those carrying them could hold them over their shoulders.

The sun was on the verge of setting by the time they were ready to leave for the nearby town. Even though the two casualties weren't heavy, it was exhausting work for the four friends who were themselves weakened by malnutrition and all the walking they'd been doing in the past few days. With frequent stops to rest, it took them until almost midnight to reach the small town, much of which was dark by that hour. Through the gates, they could see a few lights dotted around the center of the community.

The town gates were open, but the guards on watch stopped them. They came closer to examine the bundles they were carrying wrapped in tent cloth. The two men recoiled when they saw the bodies inside. "Are they dead?" one of them asked. That was when Sastin opened his eyes, making them retreat even farther.

"My friends are sick," Tirzah Lin said. "We have come a long way and are very tired," he added. "We have to find somewhere to rest."

"Where are you from?" the spokesman asked.

"We have come across the desert from Basrind after your military freed the slaves." He turned to address Farah. "Let's put her down on the grass over there. My arms are going to sleep."

"My whole body's going to sleep," Farah replied. "I'll stay with her."

The guards watched as they lay the two invalids on the ground.

"So, you're freed slaves?" The spokesman asked when they returned to the gate.

"That is correct. As you can see, we are very short on resources and very tired. We have to find somewhere to rest."

"I'm sorry we can't allow you to enter the town with anyone who is that sick. It might be a plague and spread to the whole population. You can take them over there by those trees. There's a stream where you can get water. Do you have any food?"

"Only some berries we picked by the roadside," Tirzah said, a wave of shame washing over him.

"All right. Go over there and get settled. We have orders from the capital to do everything we can to assist former slave refugees, so I'm going to send into town to rustle up some food. How does that sound?"

"Like a blessing from Tovah," Tirzah said with a shallow bow. "There is one more thing. We planned to meet someone else here. She was going to bring medicine for my friends. She would probably be on horseback. Have you seen anyone like that?"

"It's hard to say. So many people came through today for tomorrow's market. Where was she coming from, and what does she look like?"

"She was probably traveling with a companion. She is my sister, so she looks like me, only she is much smaller." He placed the side of his hand by his chin.

The guard shook his head. "Can't say I've noticed anyone like that, but we only came on duty at sunset."

Tirzah nodded. "Would you permit me to go into the town and search for them? If my friends don't get the medicine soon, they will not survive the night."

"What do you think?" the guard asked his partner.

The other guard shook his head. "I don't think so. He may have it too, but it doesn't show yet."

I could force them to let me in, Tirzah thought. I'll go and examine them and see how they're doing and if it's bad, I will have to use persuasion.

He went over and knelt by Felindra. When he put his hand on her forehead to test her temperature, her eyelids flickered. "Where are you? Ashala, come to me." Her voice was faint, as if coming from great distance.

"Felindra! Can you hear me? It's Brother Lin."

49

She moved her head from side to side, touching her lips with the tip of her tongue. "Thirsty...."

He touched her shoulder. "I'll get you some water. Hold on."

Farah, who had been standing nearby, met him as he walked away from Felindra. "How is she?"

"I'm worried about her. She's very feverish. She needs more water. If we could get her to the stream, we could immerse her. That would cool her off a bit. Is there any water left in the skins?" Tirzah, who was exhausted himself, felt as if he was running around in circles, trying to do too many things at once.

"I have a few drops in mine. I'll ask the boys to go for more."

"We should move closer to the stream," Tirzah said. "Come on, help me lift her."

Tirzah Lin

Halfway to the trees by the stream, they heard hoofbeats coming towards them from the east. Tirzah Lin stopped and watched until they came into sight, his heart drumming with hope. The lead rider was on a splendid chestnut stallion .... surely it couldn't be.... *I must be seeing things."*

It looked as if the small woman riding the horse was having a hard time controlling it. It bucked and snorted when she tried to bring it to a halt. Finally, she laid her face on its neck, murmuring, and stroking it gently. This calmed the horse a little, and she took this opportunity to take her feet out of the stirrups and slide to the ground.

"Is that you, Rasamé?" Tirzah Lin called.

The young woman looked at him and waved.

"Someone, hold this horse!" she shouted. "Be careful; he's

wild." Barengush and one of the guards ran over and took hold of the reigns while the young woman ran across the ground and all but jumped on Tirzah, smothering him with kisses. "At last," she said. "We're free! We can go home! I'm so excited." She pulled back and looked at him. "You look exhausted, Lin. Where are the patients?"

"Now that I can get a word in, I am delighted to see you." He kissed her on the forehead. "We aren't allowed into the town because of the fever, so we are going to camp over there by the trees. There's a stream there, so you might as well take your horses too. After we get them settled, I'll turn the two infected ones over to you. Did you get the heliban?"

"Of course I did. It took a bit of hunting though. That's why we are late. Here." She handed him a small packet of leaves wrapped in paper. "You know how to prepare it?"

When they'd finished moving everything, a couple of women arrived at the gate carrying two boxes. They spoke to the guards, glanced over at the strangers, and laid the boxes on the ground by the guardhouse. Barengush and Vertan went over to pick them up when the guards beckoned them.

The town had been quite generous. The boxes contained bread, fruit, cheeses, and some roast chicken broken into pieces. In addition, there was a canister of hot tea and two small bottles of wine.

Rasamé's friend joined them holding by hand a little boy of about three who had been riding with her. The woman, who was introduced as Vita, was a few years older than Rasamé.

"Where do you want me to start?" Rasamé asked as soon as she'd drunk some water.

"Mama," the boy shouted when he heard her voice. He pulled away from Vita and ran to her and jumped into her arms.

Tirzah Lin looked at his sister, startled. "And who is this?" he asked the boy.

The boy buried his head in Rasamé's shoulder. A look passed between the two women. The friend nodded.

"This is my son, Zanda," Rasamé said with a fond smile.

"I didn't know you had a child," Tirzah said. He had mixed feelings about her becoming a mother, not knowing the circumstances of the situation.

"I didn't want you to worry about me," she replied, punching him in the arm. "I know how you worry, but don't. It was consensual."

"Was he another slave?"

"No, he was the son of a friend of the master. A free man, a high-born free man."

Tirzah mulled this over for a moment. "I see. He's a fine-looking boy."

"You'll love him as much as I do once you get to know him."

Rasamé beckoned her friend. "Could you watch him while I work, Vita?" she handed Zanda over to Vita. "He might be hungry; there's plenty of food by the looked of it."

"Lady Sarah can help you tend to the young woman—she's the worst affected—and then I'll help you with the man. He's our healer, by the way. Do you need help preparing the herb?"

Rasamé looked at the ground for a moment. "I've never had to use it before. All the herbalist said was steep it in very hot water and let it cool. Do you know how to prepare or administer it?"

"Let me see it. We may have to experiment with small doses at first, since neither of us has used it before. You go ahead and look after Lady Felindra. Farah is with her now."

Felindra

Felindra's ears felt as if they were filled with water and her head stuffed with cotton. *Why am I so wet?* she wondered. *I'm soaked to the skin.* She began to shiver uncontrollably. Opening narrow eye slits, she tried to look at the sky above her. The sun had set, but there was enough light to see the leafy branches of a tree. She turned her head sideways and saw she was lying on the ground. Voices coming from nearby were distorted, as if they were coming from inside a metal drum. *Where am I? How did I get here? Oh, Light, what's happening to me. I feel so sick.*

A hand touched her arm. "Felindra! It's Farah. Are you awake?"

Felindra opened her eyes and squinted at her friend. "Farah? I'm so cold," she murmured her voice shaking, and teeth rattling.

"I'll look for something to keep you warm," Farah replied. "We have a visitor; Lin's sister is here. Rasamé's a healer and she's going to make you feel better."

Felindra squinted at the shadowy figure next to Farah. "All right." She closed her eyes again. The effort of keeping them open was too much for her.

"I think we should start with cleaning her up. She's soaked through her gown. It's no wonder she's cold. I can

53

examine her while we do that. Do you have a clean gown for her?"

"Yes, they're in this bag. I'll get some water?"

As soon as the two women started to move her, Felindra vomited again. She'd already started to have diarrhea, so she was in quite a mess.

Tirzah Lin

While the two women cleaned Felindra and dressed her in a fresh gown, Tirzah had concocted a potion from the heliban plant. It came with dried leaves and berries, so he'd used both. After crushing them in a clay bowl with a smooth stone, he mixed them with water and heated the concoction over the fire, before straining it into a cup. He'd tasted it and found it very bitter, so he diluted it well with spring water.

He gave the cup to his sister who sniffed it and wrinkled her nose. "This may taste awful, Felindra, but it will make you feel much better. Lin will lift your head while I hold the cup. Are you ready?"

Without opening her eyes or moving her head, Felindra groaned in response.

"Here we go," Rasamé said. "It doesn't taste very nice, so try to swallow it quickly. We'll give you some water to wash it down."

After finishing with Felindra, they went to give Sastin his share of the medicine. He was sitting up when they reached him.

"Hello, Sastin. I'm Lin's sister. I'm a healer like you. How do you feel?"

"Quite awful, to be honest," he replied shakily. "I don't even have the energy to keep my head up."

"I've brought you some medicine called heliban." Rasamé said. "I know you're not going to like it, but it's going to get rid of those parasites. You'll soon be on your feet again." She had a cheerful, encouraging way of talking.

"I'm hungry too," Sastin said.

"I've talked it over with Rasamé, and she thinks it would be all right for you to eat some cheese, and maybe some chicken," Tirzah said. "How does that sound?"

"We could give you some milk, if we had some," Rasamé added.

"Anything sounds good to me. Now, let's get this awful medicine down."

When Tirzah and Rasamé returned, Vertan and Barengush were sitting by a small fire finishing their meal. "I hope you left something for us," Tirzah said.

"I think we can scrape up a few bites for you," Vertan replied. He got up and brought the two boxes closer, so they could see what was inside.

"I think we should save what is left of the chicken and cheese for Sastin and Felindra," Tirzah said. "Is needs to be cut up finely so that they can swallow it.

"I'll do that," Rasamé's friend offered and set about cutting them with a little knife she retrieved from her belt pouch.

"I'll help you take it to them," Vertan said. "They may need help eating. I'm Vertan, by the way."

"My name is Vita," she replied in a husky voice.

"Farah, Rasamé and Tirzah sat down on the grass and helped themselves to the food."

The little boy was sleeping on a small blanket away from the fire, but he woke up and murmured, "ma!" when he heard their voices. Tirzah watched the child crawl over and settle on Rasamé's lap.

9 – Kum

Felindra

The men had dug a latrine in the trees, away from the stream and it got a lot of use once Sastin and Felindra started purging the parasites. Felindra could walk with assistance the next morning, although she was still very weak. On the second day, after building up their strength with as much food as she could tolerate without vomiting, they were ready to travel. Sastin recovered faster than Felindra, although he was still too weak to walk a long distance.

"What are we going to do now?" Vertan asked as they ate their evening meal.

"We should go to Kum and find out if there is a ship that will take us to Albasiny," Felindra said.

Farah nodded agreement.

"There aren't many ships in the port," Rasamé said. "The war is keeping them away now that Basrind has its navy in action."

Felindra felt deflated. After all they'd been through, they still might not be able to get home. *Oh, Light help us, please help us.* She wiped a tear from the corner of her eye.

"Don't fret, Little Sister. There are other ports and shipping lanes," Tirzah Lin said, patting her hand. "You could leave from the north coast of the continent. There's one port northwest of Eleria, and it's a lot safer in that area."

"But it's such a long way," Felindra objected.

"Let's see what we find in Kum first," Farah said. "Don't give up hope, love. We'll get home, one way or another."

"How can we travel all that way on foot?" Felindra realized she was beginning to sound petulant. *I'm too weak to make any decisions. I should let them work it out.* She closed her eyes.

She was alerted by a horse whinnying, sounding very annoyed about something. *I'll have to find out.* She looked at Rasamé who was the closest to her. "Can you help me up? I have to go and see what's wrong with that horse."

Tirzah Lin winked at his sister and nodded.

"He's always bothering about something," Rasamé said, as she drew Felindra to her feet.

"Is this your horse?"

"It's the one I've been riding. I'm the only person he will allow near him."

As soon as Felindra saw the two horses tied to trees at the edge of the stream, she quickened her pace. "Lex! What are you doing here, you naughty boy?" she also sent him waves of reassurance. The big chestnut stallion stopped his stamping and snorting and pricked up his ears, turning to look in her direction, then he snorted again and gave a soft whinny that sounded almost pitiful.

"You know this horse?"

"Oh, yes. He was my master's favorite. He and I were the only people, apart from the stable master, he would allow to touch him. How did you get him?"

"Like you, I was the only person who could handle him. The Council in Kum was trying to provide transport for the released slaves who lived far away. They had all these horses they'd taken from Basrind and were giving them to the former slaves. Nobody wanted this one, until I came along."

Felindra approached Lex and stroked his forehead, then she rested her face on his neck. "You're a good boy, aren't you, Lex? Did those nasty people take you away from your home? I know what that's like." She said this aloud for Rasamé, while she sent soothing, reassuring feelings to the horse.

"He looks a bit disheveled," Felindra said. "I don't suppose he would allow anyone to groom him. I know how temperamental he can be.

Lex had calmed down now and had started cropping the grass at his feet.

"You certainly have a way with animals," Rasamé said. "You must have a special gift to be able to calm him like that."

"The Great Spirit honored me with this gift. In our society, we call it Whispering."

"I've never heard of anyone with such a gift. It must be very rare, and useful. Shall we go back now and find out what they have decided?"

When they returned to the rest of the group, Felindra sat down and leaned back against a tree. "What did you find?" Vertan asked with a knowing grin.

"Dom Ash's favorite horse, Lex. I've been so worried about him, afraid they might have abused him because he was hard to handle. It's such a relief to see him with good people."

Tirzah Lin smiled to himself. "We've decided to continue to Kum," he said. "Even if we don't find a ship for you, we may be able to get some horses or camels to ride."

"Or donkeys," Rasamé added. "But that big fellow would need something a bit heftier." She grinned at Barengush who, being of Nordic blood from the northern duchy of ValkonenMaa, was the tallest person in the group.

"A donkey cart would be useful," Felindra said. Secretly, she hoped it wouldn't be necessary for the Albasinians.

***

The following morning, Rasamé and Tirzah Lin went into the town to buy some supplies. Rasamé had come equipped with a small amount of coin, another gift of the Pangasti Council.

Tirzah Lin also wanted to find the textile trader and return the tent cloths, which had been thoroughly scrubbed and laid out in the sun for a day, but when he went to the inn, he was told that they had left already.

"Do you expect him to return?" Tirzah asked.

The innkeeper held up both hands, fingers splayed. "Ten days," he replied.

"Would you keep these for him?" Tirzah pointed to the two rolls of material.

When they returned to the campsite, everyone was ready to leave. Half the morning had gone already, and the air was becoming very muggy.

Everyone agreed that Felindra should ride Lex and Sastin would ride on Vita's horse.

59

"Marmi! Look at me! I got big horse!" Zanda shouted, pulling on Barengush's hand.

Barengush crouched so that the little boy could climb on his back.

"Hold on tight," Barengush said as he stood upright, grinning sheepishly at his friends.

It was a slow journey with frequent rest stops. Felindra was still weak from the infestation and her body continued to purge, much to her discomfort. Shortly after midday, they stopped for a meal and everyone slept for a while. After several more leagues, the sun had set, so they decided to make camp for the night. They were running low on water, despite filling every container they could muster from the stream outside the town they'd left.

Felindra slid down from her horse into Rasamé's arms. "How are you feeling?" the healer asked.

"Better than yesterday," Felindra murmured. "Thanks to you and your medicine. But I'm so tired. I could sleep for a season." She was drooping and if Rasamé hadn't been holding her, her legs would have given way.

"Let's get you settled," She had Felindra clean, fed, and lying down on a clean blanket within moments of their arrival. "I have something else I can give you to boost your energy, but I'll have to prepare it first."

The travelers used the two horses to find a source of water. They appeared to have a special knack for detecting such vital necessities and they soon found a narrow stream, burbling down from the foothills. The water was upstream of the horses.

***

The family farms and smallholdings scattered around the outskirts of Kum gave way to small businesses like blacksmiths and country inns closer to the city, although everywhere they looked there were signs of neglect, fields filled with weeds and ditches with trash.

"It looks so tired," Felindra commented. "It's as if no one has the energy to do anything." *Like me.* "I know they've been going through hard times, lately, but I hadn't realized how much it has affected them."

"With so many men away at war, and recent droughts, most people use all their energy trying to put food on the table. It's not an easy life for any of them." Rasamé explained.

The people they passed looked half-starved and moved lethargically as they walked on the roadside or labored in their plots of land. They showed little interest as the former slaves passed them by. By the appearance of the refugees, they knew they could not expect anything from them.

The city walls were in a state of disrepair with broken bricks and crumbling mortar. They joined the throng of people entering the city, passing a guard post where the guards gave them a desultory inspection and asked a few questions before allowing them to pass.

"Where are you taking us, Rasamé?" Tirzah asked.

"I think the best place to stop would be Council headquarters."

"What is this Council? Is it a government facility?"

"No, it's run by the congregation of one of the Tovar sects. They call it 'Tovar's Council" Rasamé replied. "Their members volunteer to help people in need, and at this moment, their main project is aiding former slaves."

"They sound like followers of the Light," Felindra interjected.

Tirzah smiled. "It's the One God, whatever name you put on Him, and that is how his true followers would behave. Brotherly love underlies all true faiths."

They turned left inside the gate and followed a road that ran along the inside of the wall. It was a narrow road that was mostly gravel, bordered by tired weeds. The road went gradually uphill, and eventually turned right onto a paved road lined with walled dwellings and gardens on the upper side, and a large walled complex on the right, dominated by the dome of a temple.

Vita and Rasamé went up to the gate and pulled a chain on the wall.

"Who is it?" a young voice responded instantly.

"We are Vita and Rasamé," Rasamé replied. "We've brought some friends with us. May we come in?"

"Rasamé! I thought you'd left. Wait while I go and ask Sister Kadia."

Rasamé turned and smiled at her friends. "I love these young people who volunteer to help out here. I think it's good for them to have this experience. It teaches them that not everyone's life is filled with parties and shopping." Rasamé knew first-hand about how the children of the wealthy spent their lives.

"Are the people who run this center all from wealthy families?"

"Many of them are, but anyone can volunteer."

The sound of a bolt being drawn preceded the gate opening. A very small woman with silver curls peeking out from a pale blue head veil stood beaming at them. "Welcome. Friends," she said, "You look tired. Come in, let us take care of you."

She pushed the gate open further and revealed a girl of about twelve shyly watching them.

"Why did you come back, Rasamé?" the girl asked.

"Now, Loanda, that's not very polite," the older woman said. "Why did you come back?" she asked Rasamé with a grin.

By now, they were all assembled in a shady courtyard.

"This is my brother, Tirzah Lin," Rasamé said by way of an answer. "And these are his friends who escaped with him. Two of them are recovering from an infection and are still weak. They are from Albasiny and they want to find a ship that can take them home." She turned to the Albasinians. "This is Sister Kadia. She's a member of the Council."

"Come inside," Sister Kadia said. "I can see your friends are tired. Let's see what we can do to help them."

They passed through an arched tunnel into a large inner courtyard where tables and chairs were set out. The sunlight was filtered into the courtyard through pierced brick walls, keeping it comfortably cool and light.

"Sit down here, and I'll have some refreshments brought out for you." She turned to Rasamé. "Would you like to take the two invalids to the health center where they can lie down and rest? They can eat and drink there."

Felindra was too exhausted to enter the discussion beyond saying thank you to Sister Kadia. Rasamé supported her as she staggered down a hallway to a large twilit room furnished with several raised cots, some stools, and a long table down the center. Two of the cots were occupied by patients who seemed to be sleeping, a man on one side of the room and a woman on the other. "Pick a cot on that side, Sastin," Rasamé said. "I'll get Felindra settled over here."

Felindra managed to consume a small amount of vegetable broth and drink a cup of water before she closed her eyes and fell into a deep sleep.

When she awoke, the room was even darker than when she'd fallen asleep. *It must be close to sunset.* She looked around the room and found she was the only one there. *I need to wash. Where did Rasamé say the facilities were?* She went outside into the hallway and looked around, then she remembered it was across the hall. After cleaning up, she went in the direction where she could hear people talking and found everyone in the large courtyard.

The whole building was light and airy with bare brick walls and floors tiled with polished stone. There was little ornamentation beyond wall lamps and a few potted plants.

She saw her friends sitting at a long table talking to other refugees. There were seven men and women here in the courtyard and three children who were sitting on the ground playing a game which consisted of rolling wooden balls into one another and screeching when one of them was hit.

"Here she is," Vertan said. "We were just talking about you. Come over here and sit down."

"What were you saying about me?" she asked with a wan smile.

"We were telling these people what an amazing person you are," Farah said, while Vertan winked.

"Oh, that's all right then." She sat down next to Farah.

"Are you feeling better?" Farah asked.

"A bit. I had a good sleep, but I'm hungry again. Is it all right for me to eat something?" she asked Rasamé.

"Yes. You must regain your strength now but try to eat some vegetables if you can. And before you start, I've got your medicine. Take it now and the food will wash away the horrible taste."

While she was eating her vegetable and egg soup, the discussion continued. "We are trying to decide what to do." She glanced at Felindra before continuing. "What do you think?"

"What have you thought of so far?"

"I contacted Ashavan to ask him if there were any Albasinian ships coming this way. I gave him a brief rundown of our situation, leaving out anything that might alarm them. He will communicate when he has the information." Farah told her. "Other than that, we were discussing what to do if we can't get transport from here."

"There aren't really many options, are there?" she replied. "It's either find a ship, or travel with Lin to a northern port. We can't stay here and be a burden on these good people. They have enough problems. We don't even have anything we can barter for food."

"Your comment about bartering gives me an idea," Tirzah said. "There are caravans travelling back and forth all the time. We have a pair of excellent defenders. Maybe we could hire on with a traders' caravan to offer protection against bandits. They often travel together in large groups for protection and might be amenable to hiring all of us for our assortment of abilities. If we make the right kind of arrangement, we could get transportation and food for the journey."

"That sounds like a great idea," Vertan said. "Talking of safety in numbers; we would also be protected with more people. How many more times are we going to be attacked because we are a small vulnerable group?"

"How would you go about arranging it?" Felindra asked.

"The three of us—Barengush, Vertan, and I—would have to go to the caravanserai outside the city and talk to some of the traders."

"Do you think they'd go for it?" Barengush asked.

"I don't see why not. We wouldn't be asking for gold. It would barely cost them anything."

"That's if we need to go that way," Vertan said. "We have to see what Ashavan finds out.

Felindra noticed Sastin looking at her. She was shocked by the change in him. He looked so frail and desiccated, a mere shadow of his former self. The infestation had taken a lot out of him. *I probably look the same to everyone else.* "How are you feeling, Sastin?"

Sastin sighed wearily. "Not as awful as I felt yesterday. I'm getting there, but I think it will take both of us a while to get back to normal."

That evening, they had a meeting with two members of the council, a man and a woman.

"What we need to decide," Tirzah Lin said, "is how we are going to get home. My sister and I are from Eleria, which is a fair distance from here, and I believe Sister Vita is from the neighboring nation of Karaganda. Our major problem is lack of funds.

"We do not wish to be a burden on anyone, but if the Albasinians are unable to acquire a passage home from Kum, we are thinking of bartering our services with a trade caravan in return for transportation and sustenance. But before we get into that, we'd like to know if there is anything we can do for you. My companions and I have many gifts we can call upon if there is a need for our magic abilities."

"Give us some examples of these magic gifts," the male councilor requested.

"We have two healers, although one of those is recovering from an infection. I also have a little healing power, although not as strong as my sister's. We have a telepath who can send and receive messages over long distances, and two members are Albasinian Defenders who have a variety of defensive abilities."

"We would welcome any advice you can give us," Tirzah finished.

"The way I understand it," the male councilor said. "You don't know how you will be travelling until you find out if your Albasinian friends can ship home from here. Is that correct?"

"Yes," Tirzah confirmed.

"I suggest we wait until you have that information and go from there. We'll also consider your offers of help with your gifts," the man said. "It's getting late and you must all be tired, so I suggest we retire and continue on the morrow."

10 – No Ships

Farah

The news from Albasiny came in the middle of the night, but Farah kept it to herself until everyone was up and gathered together in the temple refectory.

"I'm afraid Ashavan couldn't find any ships in this area or any that were planning to come here any time soon. It seems that, with winter approaching, they don't want to sail too far from home."

"But what about the northern port that Brother Lin recommends?" Barengush asked.

"I don't have an answer to that," Farah replied. "What do you think, Brother Lin?"

"We haven't exhausted all the possibilities here yet," Tirzah replied. "There might be other shipping in port that is going that way—even part way would help. We should visit the port authority first, before we think about the northern ports." He looked around the table at his companions. "Do you agree?"

The Albasinians all nodded. "That sounds like the best plan," Farah said. "What do you think, Felindra?"

Felindra was still pale and droopy, but her eyes were brighter this day. "That's fine," she said. "I just want to get home, any way possible."

"Did you tell them about Felindra and me?" Sastin asked Farah.

"Only that you had been ill and that you are recovering nicely," Farah replied. "I didn't want to alarm anyone when Ashavan updates them about our situation. As it stands, they are relieved that we have escaped and are safe."

***

Tirzah Lin, accompanied by Farah and the two defenders, went to the headquarters of the Port Authority to inquire about ships sailing east, while Felindra and Sastin rested on lounging chairs in the courtyard. They didn't return until it was time for the midday meal and waited until they were eating to report their findings.

"It doesn't look too hopeful," Vertan said. "There are several ships in port that are going east, but none of them was going far. We also looked over the ships and weren't impressed by their condition. They were small and a bit shabby-looking, not very well maintained.

"And we didn't like the look of some of the mariners. They looked more like bandits or pirates to me."

"Not very promising then," Sastin said.

"I don't think we'd be very comfortable, especially anyone who is sick," Farah added. "I had a very uncomfortable feeling about some of them. I wouldn't trust them. They might decide to sell us over again and we'd be back where we just started, probably in much worse conditions than those we just left.

I'm sure most of them were honest traders," Tirzah said, "but, as Sister Farah said, you would not be comfortable, and they wouldn't take you all the way to your homeland. You'd still have to find another ship to complete the journey."

"Not only that," Felindra said. "We don't have anything to pay for our passage."

"Well, I suppose we go to the alternate plan," Vertan said.

Everyone nodded.

Vita spoke up once there was a gap in the discussion. "I've decided to stay here," she announced.

Rasamé looked at her friend, startled. "Why? I thought you wanted to go home."

"I've changed my mind. I like it here, and there's no one for me in Karaganda. It's been more than thirteen cycles since I left. My parents have passed on and, from what I recall, it's a poor country. Life is very hard there, and I don't know what I would do. It would be like having

69

to start all over, and I'm too tired to make another change. I've been offered a post working for the council and I think I'll take it, for a while at least."

Tirzah Lin

After siesta, Tirzah Lin, again accompanied by Vertan and Barengush, went to the caravanserai. It was an enormous stretch of fenced land filled with wagons, camels, and traders, with an attached paddock for horses and donkeys, and even a couple of buffalo. Buildings lined the inside of the fence and there was a water tank sunk into the center of the field.

"What are all those buildings for?" Barengush asked.

"Various purposes," Tirzah replied. "Some are cafes—the people of this land love coffee—and food vendors, others are sleeping accommodations. The big building there is the administration and services headquarters. That's where we are going."

"What's coffee?" Vertan asked.

"It's made from roasted beans which are used to make a stimulating hot beverage."

"I'll have to try some if it's that popular," Vertan said. "There's something like that in Valkonen which was catching on when we left."

They entered the administration building through an archway. Inside was a spacious room with men standing at high desks on either side. Three other men were sitting at wide desks on the far wall facing the entrance. These men were dressed in richer garments than those who were standing.

Tirzah looked around, assessing the operation. "I think it would be best to talk to one of the clerks first and see what we need to do."

He led them over to an unoccupied desk and asked the clerk about hiring on as guards.

"You should talk to one of the administrators," the clerk said. "They handle that sort of thing." He gestured towards the three seated men at the end of the room.

"I'm glad we could get some decent clothes," Vertan said. "We wouldn't have made much of an impression in our old rags." Both he and Barengush were now wearing loose, off-white culottes that reached just above their ankles, and tunics with long, loose sleeves. They had also had their hair trimmed to ear-length; all these services provided by the Committee. Tirzah had traded his black robe for an off-white one which provided better protection from the sun.

All three of the administrators were busy haggling with merchants, so they had to stand in line and wait for attention. "Let's one of us stand in front of each desk," Tirzah said in Trade to his companions. "That way we'll get whoever is free first."

After several moments, the trader in front of the right-hand desk slapped some coins on the desk and turned away muttering angrily to himself.

Barengush stepped forward to the desk and the others joined him. Once Tirzah had explained their needs to him, the man rifled through a pile of papers and selected one. "Try this one," he said. "They're moving out in two days with about fifteen wagons. They were asking about guards, but I don't think they've found any yet." He wrote something on a piece of paper and handed it the Tirzah. "Oh, and you need to pay the finder's fee before you make the deal."

"How much?" Tirzah asked with a sigh of resignation.

"I'll give you a bargain price," the administrator said. "Two gold."

It's no wonder they can dress in silks and jewelry, Tirzah thought, they are fleecing everyone who comes here. "Where are you expecting escaped slaves to find that much gold?"

The administrator shrugged. "You must pay, it is the tradition, but in light of your situation, I will reduce the fee to five silver."

He'll probably charge the leader of the caravan too, Tirzah thought as he took a silver coin from his belt pouch and put it on the table.

When they got outside, Vertan asked him where he'd acquired the money to pay.

"The Council suspected we might have to pay something and provided a small purse for our expenses. Now we have to find this wagon master. The best place is probably the coffee shops." Tirzah said.

The cafes and eating houses were crowded with merchants and drovers, and the noise was horrendous, not only from men's shouts and the clatter of pots and pans, but the livestock outside were pitching in as well.

Once they found the wagon master, the person organizing the caravan, it took them more time to negotiate the terms. At first, he had balked at the idea of hiring magicians for the job but was soon persuaded by the skills that were available, a definite advantage for the merchants.

The journey from the eating house to the gate was an adventure in trying to avoid stepping in the dung left by the animals.

"I'm starving," Barengush complained. "A cup of goats' milk hardly substituted for solid food.

"We'll be back at the Council center soon. They said they'd leave something out for us," Tirzah replied.

When they arrived back at the center, Farah was waiting for them. "Felindra and Sastin went to bed," she informed them. "I thought I'd wait up and find out what happened. Were you successful?"

The three men sat down at the table and filled their plates with bread and cheese, adding a few dates for variety. There was also a carafe of clear liquid on the table and some clay cups. Barengush poured some and took a sip. "It tastes like coconut water," he said, finishing off the drink.

Tirzah took a sip of water and turned to Farah. "Sorry you had to wait; we're starving. To answer your question, I would say we were successful. The wagon master we dealt with—his name is Parghan—wanted Barengush and Vertan to demonstrate their skills, but I dissuaded them, say it would cause too much excitement, although Vertan added his powers of persuasion to the discussion,

"We were fortunate. There is a caravan of about fifteen wagons leaving in two days. We're to join them before sunset on the morrow so they can show us what to do."

"That's a lot of wagons for two defenders to protect," Farah said.

"The wagon master told us that every merchant has an armed guard to protect his own property, so in the event of an attack, I suppose we'd all work together." Vertan explained. "That must be why they want us there the evening before they leave: to introduce us."

"What about accommodation for us?"

"We'll have to work that out when we meet on the morrow. I did explain that we had two invalids, plus three women and a child who would need places to sleep. They have one communal cookout each sunrise, from which everyone saves something for his other meals during the day." He looked around at his companions. "Anything else?"

"Where is the caravan going?" Farah asked.

"From here, we will travel northwest to a city called Hil Goa. That's the capital of a country called Goa Sun."

"Is that close to our destination?"

"It's more than halfway," Tirzah replied. "We may have to walk the rest of the way, unless we can find some horses."

"Don't forget the stipend," Vertan said. "They are going to pay us, but not at the regular rate because we have passengers. It will probably be based on how useful we can be. I expect Felindra will spend most of her time talking to the animals, once she is well enough."

11 - Caravan

Felindra

They arrived at the caravanserai when the sun was a few degrees from the western horizon.

Earlier in the day, one of the Committee members took them to a large paddock filled with horses. This time Felindra went with them. They were to pick some more horses. Felindra and Sastin, still very weak, were to ride the horses they already had, so they needed two for Barengush and Vertan, and one each for Rasamé and Tirzah Lin. Felindra was to examine the horses available and find the most fit, and those with good temperaments. None of the animals in the paddock was in the best shape. Many of them were old, some had been maltreated, while others had old injuries. She chose two docile fillies for Farah and Rasamé, and a couple of sturdy, older stallions for the defenders.

Lex started to kick up a fuss as soon as he was led into the caravanserai paddock, so she had to take him to the tent that had been set up for them and tether him to a nearby tree. He didn't like that either and she had to spend several moments calming him.

The men, except Sastin, had gone with the wagon master to be introduced to the guards and arrange how they would work together.

The women decided to settle down for the night before they returned. The tent was set up outside the caravanserai and furnished with thin sleeping pallets and some flimsy blankets. Zanda had fallen asleep on the way to the caravanserai.

***

Just before dawn, amidst clouds of dust, men shouting, and animals braying and whinnying, the caravan began to assemble outside the caravanserai. By the time they were ready to leave, the sun was several degrees above the horizon. The two defenders were to split up, Barengush at the head of the column, and Vertan at the back.

By midday, Felindra was too tired to continue riding, so she hitched Lex to the rear of the wagon that had been allotted to them. "Could you help me climb up into the wagon?" she asked Rasamé.

One of the merchants, whose wagon was not quite full, had offered space for the invalids and the little boy to rest during the day, but they had to sleep in the tent at night.

For the first two days, they proceeded through semi-desert, but as the road slanted upwards, more trees appeared, and they began to see small farms and orchards. It looked as if the harvest was finished for this year. Some of the fields had already been ploughed, ready for next-year's planting.

Once, they passed fields of sturdy green plants that stood higher than a man. They grew close together in rows and had attractive palmate leaves, each frond tipped with thick buds. As they rode past, an unusual but pleasant herbal fragrance wafted over the caravan. In some of the fields, men and women were cutting the buds and storing them in cotton sacks.

"What are they?" Felindra asked Tirzah who was walking beside her.

"They call it Kush. It's a medicinal herb. You see how they're harvesting the tips?" Felindra nodded. "Those are the parts that contains the most powerful resin. The leaves are useful, too, but those buds are more valuable at the market."

"What sort of things is it used for?"

"It's useful for many things from nausea to pain and infections. It can also be used to treat some chronic ailments. By the way, it also induces a feeling of elation and euphoria."

"It sounds like a useful panacea," Felindra said, "Maybe we should get some. I'll talk to Sastin about it. He must have heard of it."

12 – Attacked

Felindra

The caravan had no trouble from bandits while travelling through the agricultural land because it was populated and well patrolled. Now that the caravan had ascended into hill country, it had to pass through forests, and the guards had to be more watchful.

Felindra noticed the guards who patrolled up and down the column constantly peered into the bush on both sides. She knew that if danger was imminent, her friends would sense it before the guards saw any signs, but they kept that to themselves, not wanting to either spook the guards, or make them rely on magic and become careless. Barengush rode ahead of the caravan to make sure nothing unexpected was coming up.

They had to be extra-watchful at night and the guards rotated guard duty from dusk to dawn. Barengush and Vertan took turns on watch throughout the nights.

"Are caravans often attacked?" Felindra asked Tirzah.

"Oh, yes, but they usually pick off smaller groups or individual traders, not big caravans like ours, however it pays to be vigilant. This road is close to the border with the neighboring country, Bindd, I'm not sure what the problem is with them—something political, no doubt—but they are an unruly lot, always fighting and attacking one another. I think it may be related to wizards."

"What sort of wizards?" Barengush asked.

"According to what I can gather from the traders and the guards, there seem to be two groups vying for dominance. As to their focus, I believe at least one of the groups is dark, or they may both be devoted to dark— destructive— magic. Whatever they are, they are causing much chaos in their country; that's why so many are turning to banditry. There is no peace or stability in which to make an honest living."

Felindra shuddered. "Let's hope we don't meet any of them. Do you think there are wizards in the bandit gangs?"

"It's hard to say," Tirzah replied. "Although some of the guards talk about strange happenings when travelers are attacked."

"I think I should join the night watch," Farah said. "I might be able to sense something. I've not had much to do so far on this journey."

"You could take turns with me if you like," Tirzah said. "I've been trying to stay awake and keep watch; another mind would be helpful. You don't even need to leave the tent."

It wasn't until they were almost out of the forest and entering the Great Plain that the attack came, just before sunrise. The first warning came from Lex, who had been tethered with the other horses a few steps from the tent.

Felindra groaned and crawled to the opening to see what was upsetting him and came face-to-face with a grinning stranger. She let out a little scream before a sweaty hand was clamped over her mouth while the other hand grabbed her arm and dragged her out of the tent. Outside the tent were several more men. The man who was holding Felindra talked to the others in what to Felindra was babble, and then dragged her away from the tent.

Felindra! Are you all right? Farah sounded afraid.

We're being attacked. One of them is dragging me away. What shall I do?

Can everyone hear this? Farah sent to the other telepaths.

I'm on it, Vertan sent. Don't be afraid, Felindra, we'll get you.

I'm here, Tirzah replied. Don't fight them, Felindra. I don't want you to get hurt.

As her captor dragged her into the bush, Felindra went limp, leaving all her weight on him. He removed his hand from over her mouth and used both his hands to pull her to her feet. He growled some instructions which she didn't understand, but she continued to sag and drag her feet. This time, he punched her in the stomach and yelled some more. The punch was just what she needed—another way of fighting back—because she immediately vomited all over his culottes and his feet. The bandit swore and punched her head, sending her flying dizzily into a tree where she lost consciousness.

Tirzah Lin

The whole camp was in utter chaos. Although it was hard to see much in the pre-dawn light, but he could hear all the noise, men screaming and cursing, horses and camels bellowing and shrieking, the clash of steel on steel, and the sudden shriek of someone wounded.

He sent his senses out to survey the area. Farah, Barengush and Vertan were doing the same. Although the attackers had the advantage of surprise, they were losing the struggle. There are few men fiercer than a merchant protecting his goods, and they all appeared to be armed with something. Although some of them had already fallen wounded.

Suddenly, he came upon something dark and threatening. *So, you think you are a great wizard, do you? I'll soon have you down to size, little wizard,* the threat came.

Altogether, he sent out to his companions. He could feel everyone joining him to create a forcefield against the dark wizard.

With a flash of anger, the other wizard vanished from their sense field.

Something's happened to Felindra, Farah sent. *I can't sense her.*

I think she's unconscious, Vertan replied. *I'll try to find her.*

Vertan

Vertan fought his way through the bandits into the forest where he could sense her weak life force. He found two of the bandits crouching by a tree, looking down at something on the ground. The area was filled with the sour odor of vomit. He stood silently for a moment, observing them. They were arguing quietly, but he couldn't tell what they were saying. One of them reached out his hand towards the tree.

"That's enough," Vertan said, using his power of persuasion. "You don't want to move. You want to stand away from the tree and look at me."

Although they didn't know what he was saying, the meaning got through to them. They rose slowly to their feet and turned to face him with fear in their eyes. One of them started to reach for the short sword hanging from his belt. "You don't want to touch your weapons, do you? You want to drop them on the ground."

Looking confused, both men removed their weapons. In addition to two short swords, they also had knives, and one had a bow hooked over his shoulder.

"Sit down," Vertan ordered angrily, glancing anxiously at the little body lying on the ground. "Don't move!" He kicked their weapons away from them towards the tree where he could examine Felindra and keep an eye on them at the same time.

As he was turning away towards Felindra, Tirzah Lin arrived. "That was very impressive," he said, nodding at the two prisoners. "I thought you might need some help with Felindra. It looks as if she's badly hurt."

Both men knelt on the ground. She was lying on her back with her head bent up against the tree trunk. "She's been sick," Tirzah Lin said. "I wonder what brought that on."

Tirzah Lin

Vertan leaned forward to move her.

"Don't touch her," Tirzah said sharply. "I need to find out what caused her to lose consciousness."

"Could it be her illness?"

"I don't think so, although she is still very weak."

Tirzah looked at the way Felindra was positioned. Her head was turned sideways, resting on her shoulder. He felt her neck and found a faint pulse, so she was alive.

"Vertan, I want to move her. Would you take her legs and pull her down while I hold her head steady?" As Vertan took hold of Felindra's ankles, he turned to the two prisoners. "Don't move!" he said, with a fierce scowl.

While Tirzah was holding her head, he found her hair sticky with blood. As Vertan pulled her away from the tree, he did his best to keep her head from changing position. If her neck *was* broken, there would be little hope for recovery, but he didn't want to risk causing any more damage.

"All right, let's lower her gently to the ground without jolting her. Good. Now I want to test something else." He looked around the ground and found a small twig. After breaking off a sliver, he lifted her hand and poked it under a fingernail. Felindra moaned, the hand twitched and drew back. "Very good. Now we need some blankets to carry her to the wagon. I'll go while you stay and watch over her."

While he was concentrating on Felindra, Tirzah had been oblivious to the battle that was going on with the raiders, but when he thought about moving Felindra, awareness came back in force. Would it be safe to try to reach a wagon? The screams and shouts continued along with the clash of weapons and the cries of desperate animals trying to get away from the turmoil. He cast around and contacted Farah. *How's it going?* he asked her.

It's terrible, she sent in reply. I'm desperately worried about Felindra. I saw her dragged away by the raider, but I can't contact her.

Vertan found her and rescued her from the two bandits. She was hurt, a bump on the head, but she's unconscious. I want to bring her to a wagon, but I don't know if it's safe. Where are you?

I'm hiding out under a wagon with Rasamé and the boy. The fighting seems to be tapering off. It's moved to the other side of the circle. I think our people have almost beaten them off.

Farah's last statement was punctuated by an explosion, followed by horrific screams, and then silence.

The moans of people in pain were almost drowned by shouts and cheering.

I think we've won, Farah continued. That noise was probably Barengush with one of his power blasts.

When Tirzah returned with the blankets, the first thing he saw was the gleaming coat of the horse that was standing over Felindra, pawing the ground with his hoof and nudging her body with his nose. Lex! He must have put up a terrific fight to free himself; his reins had dragged what looked like a whole sapling behind him.

"Now what are we going to do?" he said to Vertan. "I don't suppose your power will make him move?"

"I can try, but I don't think it works with animals. He's so difficult to handle, I'm afraid to touch him."

"Try, and if that doesn't work, I'll send for Rasamé."

Lex wouldn't budge, so Tirzah contacted his sister and asked her to come and get the horse.

Tirzah looked around the clearing. "What happened to the two bandits?"

"I just told them to go home, and they left."

"You have a good heart," Tirzah said.

"I didn't see anything to be gained from hurting them, and we certainly don't have the facilities to hold prisoners."

13 – Arrival in Hil Goa

Tirzah Lin

When they finally carried Felindra to a wagon, Sastin and Rasamé took over her treatment while Tirzah went to talk

83

with the leader of the caravan and find out how much damage they had sustained.

It turned out that their losses were minimal. One of the guards had been killed and another wounded. Several of the traders had been hurt trying to protect their merchandise, although none seriously, and a few bandits had escaped into the forest with things they had stolen.

"Do you need any help with healing?" Tirzah asked Parghan.

"We have a healer, but any help you can give would be appreciated."

It took until almost midday for the Caravan to start moving. There had been a lot of cleaning up to do, bodies to bury, wagons to repair and escaped animals to round up. The camels came back of their own accord, but the dray horses—some of which were injured—were more difficult to round up.

The main meal of the day was being prepared by the cooks while others took care of the cleanup, although there would be no fresh bread this day and they would have to make do with hard biscuits.

Barengush and Vertan joined the others around the cook fire as soon as they'd finished their work and freshened up in the river below the camp.

"I'm glad Felindra didn't have to see that," Barengush said as he wiped his wet hands on his culottes. "I hate having to kill animals." Because of the severity of their injuries, he'd been forced to put a camel and a horse out of their misery.

That reminded Vertan of Felindra's injury. "How is she?" he asked Tirzah.

"She's resting in the back of one of the wagons," Tirzah replied. "Rasamé is with her."

"Is she conscious?"

"Not fully, but she responds to stimuli and her life signs are getting stronger." Tirzah replied. "We did a deep probe inside her skull and there is very little bleeding; not enough to cause permanent brain damage."

Felindra

Her neck ached, and she could barely move it. People's voices created a persistent hum, advancing and receding like the waves on a beach. She could feel a warm hand on her forearm and wondered who it could be. *What happened? Where am I? Lex! I must find Lex.*

She moved her head slightly and moaned with the pain. Then she opened her eyes a crack, but the light hurt, so she closed them again.

"Felindra! Are you awake?" the voice was female, but the accent was strange.

"Mmm," she murmured in response. "Lex?"

"Can you open your eyes and look at me?" the voice said.

"No, light." She barely refrained from shaking her head.

The light faded in the space she was in. "Is that better? I covered the opening." She now recognized the voice as Rasamé's.

Is what better? Oh, my eyes. She slowly opened her eyes again and looked at Rasamé. "Where are we? Why is the floor bouncing?" Felindra's voice was weak and a little slurred.

"We're in the back of a wagon. Do you remember what happened?" Rasamé asked.

Felindra was about to shake her head again but stopped in time. "Lex!" she said. "What happened to Lex. He was calling me."

"Don't worry about him," Rasamé replied. "He's fine. He's a hero; killed one of the raiders. Would you like to see him?" Rasamé pulled back the curtain from the opening at the back of the wagon.

Felindra heard a snort and a soft whinny outside and opened her eyes wider. "Lex!"

The big chestnut stuck his head through the opening and nudged her shoulder with his muzzle. "Good boy," she said, sending him waves of affection, but she didn't have the energy to lift her hand and stroke him.

She began to recall snatches of the events after Lex had awakened her: Two men with black beards dragging her into the forest, then one punching her; after that everything was blank. Now all she felt was pain, pain in her head, pain in her neck. So much pain she was afraid to move.

"Why does my head hurt so much?" she asked.

"You hit your head against a tree trunk, and your neck got twisted when you collapsed. Are you thirsty? You need to drink something, and I can put a potion in the water for the pain."

***

The forest was behind them now and they were travelling on a high, grassy plain with a few scattered farms, but it was mostly home to herds of wild horses and clusters of circular tents. It was two days since the attack, and according to the wagon master, they should arrive in Hil Goa two days hence.

After a day resting in the wagon, Felindra had left her bed to spend a few hours riding on Lex. Her neck and head were still sore, and she had to wear a supportive band around the neck, but she was restless and wanted to see the wild horses that roamed the plain, realizing she might never see such a sight again. This was probably where Lex came from as there was a distinct resemblance, although the breed came in a variety of colors, varying from pure black and russet to silvery white.

The caravan halted at a horse market on the second day and the traders went among the horses in the big paddock with the horse masters, picking out the ones they wanted to buy. This was not an easy job as the horses were very high spirited, just as Lex had been when Felindra had first met him and did not hesitate to kick out when anyone came too close.

Tirzah Lin approached Felindra where she was sitting on the grass watching the animals. "How are you feeling today?" he asked.

"Much better, thank you. Most of the pain has gone, but I still don't have much energy."

"Do you feel up to a little work?"

"With the animals?" Felindra's eyes lit up as she tried to stand up.

"Yes. The merchants are having a slight problem examining the horses. I told them of your skill with animals and they asked if you would help them. They even offered to pay for your services. I told them you were not completely recovered, but it's up to you."

"There's nothing I would like more than to be among the animals. Help me up and I'll do it."

Tirzah held out his hand and pulled her up from the ground. "I'll go with you to translate and help you if it's too tiring."

Felindra enjoyed an exhilarating hour among the wild horses. Her very presence seemed to have a calming effect on them, although she enjoyed touching them and feeling their strength and vigor, she sensed their desire to leave the pen and run free. She soothed the ten horses, one by one, as they were led out of the paddock by the horse masters and tethered to the wagons.

"You should come and work for us, Little Sister. You would make much gold." The chief horse master said."

After Tirzah had translated, she smiled and thanked him. "I would happily take up your offer, if I didn't have a very important engagement waiting for me at home."

The caravan stopped just before crossing the frontier into Goa Sun, the nation of which Hil Goa was the capital. After a discussion with the wagon master, Tirzah Lin called his group together. "I have been asked to inform you that in Hil Goa it is traditional for women to be completely covered in public." He paused to allow the women to express their feelings with sighs, eye-rolling, and head-shaking, before he continued. "This bundle contains some items you may use." He dropped a cloth package on the tailgate of the wagon.

"What would happen if we didn't?" Rasamé asked.

"I don't know," Tirzah replied. "But the penalty is probably severe. Not only that, men might feel free to molest you."

Farah opened the bundle and revealed a pile of gauzy white cotton. She picked up a piece, a long robe which would only leave the hands uncovered. "This doesn't look too bad," she said. "At least it's light, so we won't get overheated."

There were also headcloths with crown bands to hold them in place. All they needed to do was put them on over their clothes, although Rasamé removed her clothing, keeping only her undergarments.

When they had finished dressing, the wagon master inspected them and nodded, then he noticed that Rasamé's bare feet and asked her to don some sandals. He said a few words to Tirzah and went back to his post at the head of the wagon.

"What did he say?" Rasamé asked.

Tirzah smiled. "Only that the whole caravan might be penalized for carrying 'indecent women'."

The caravan passed through the border post, but not as smoothly as they would have liked. The border guards wanted to know why the women were riding horses. Tirzah quickly invented a reason, telling the guards that the women were the guardians of the horses.

Felindra smiled when she heard this.

The scenery didn't change from the grassy plain until they were closer to the city and agricultural land covered the countryside. At one point, they saw farmers planting a crop that covered a massive expanse of land along a hillside.

"What are they planting this late in the year?" Farah asked Tirzah.

"That's a poppy plantation. If this were springtime, the whole hillside would be red with blossoms. It's a beautiful sight."

"Is this the source of Powder of the Poppy?" Sastin asked.

Tirzah nodded. "It's one of the sources. It grows in many places where the conditions are right. It's a blessing for healers, but there are those who abuse it, so the growth has to be controlled to a certain extent."

The city of Hil Goa was visible from several leagues away, mainly because of amount of industrial smoke it produced. Before reaching the city, they passed through small villages with inns, blacksmiths, and other services for travelers. People had set up little stalls along the edges of the road selling food, and drinks for travelers, and fodder for animals. Some even sold hand-made trinkets, clothing, and decorated clay pots. When they neared the city gates, their progress slowed, the noise became louder. and the air became foul with dust, smoke, and animal droppings.

"I should have followed your example," Farah said to Rasamé. Her clothing was soaked in sweat. "I'm boiling in these clothes."

"You could go into a wagon and change," Rasamé suggested.

As Farah approached the stalled wagon in which they rested, she saw the stallion Lex hitched to the tailgate. *Are you in there, Felindra?* she sent, hoping her friend wasn't sleeping.

Yes, Felindra replied, I was too tired to ride any more. Do you want to come in? There's plenty of room.

"I only want to get rid of some of these clothes." Farah asked, reverting to speech. "Will Lex allow me to pass?"

"He will if I tell him to," Felindra replied. "All right, it's safe now," she added after a moment.

Inside the wagon, Farah removed her tunic and culottes and donned the robe and head cloth. She blew out a breath. "That's better. Is there any water in here?"

Felindra raised her head from the pallet and pointed to some leather bags hanging from the rail that supported the wagon cover. "Most of those are full," she said. "Why don't you sit for a while and talk with me?"

Farah made herself as comfortable as possible on the board floor of the wagon. At least it wasn't moving, but she knew if it did start to move, she would be bounced up and down over the uneven road.

"How's Sastin doing?" Felindra asked. "I haven't seen him the last couple of days."

"He's making progress. He still needs plenty of rest, but he's been helping the healer care for the men who were injured by the bandits."

A sharp jolt announced that the wagons were moving again.

Farah got to her knees and crawled back to the tailgate. "I think I'll go back to my horse," she said. "My tail bone can't take all this bouncing. I don't know how you tolerate it."

"I have a secret solution," Felindra replied. She lifted the edge of the pallet to reveal the pallet-size leather sack underneath. "It's filled with water to absorb the shocks."

"Very clever. How did you get it?"

"The trader who owns this wagon brought it. They use them as shock-absorbers when they're riding in the wagons."

There was suddenly an increase in the noise outside, men shouting and animals protesting, but they kept moving. "What's happening?" Felindra asked.

Farah dropped to the ground, greeted by a snort and poke from Lex. She looked around the side of the wagon and saw they were moving into a shady tunnel. She opened the curtain over the tailgate. "It looks as if we're going into the gate."

"Thank the Light," Felindra said. "I thought this journey would never end. How long have we been on the road?"

"I'm not sure, but it must be at least fifteen days."

"Do you think I should be outside?"

"I think you are better off in here. If they think you're sick, they might not bother you too much. Cover your face if you hear anyone coming."

14 – Leaving the Caravan

After separating from the caravan and receiving their pay, Tirzah led to search for an inn where they could rest and plan their next step. They checked some of the inns in the center of the city but found them too expensive, so they descended a hilly avenue to the market district about halfway down.

"I don't think we should find a place too close to the market," Farah said. "It is much too noisy."

It was hard to make oneself heard above the shouting of vendors and customers, and the cries of animals.

"I agree," Tirzah Lin said. "Let's look around the neighboring streets. There's bound to be something to accommodate all the out-of-town merchants."

They strolled down the central avenue and paused at the first intersection to scan the crossing street.

"There are several big buildings this way," Vertan said, pointing to the right. "They could be inns."

As soon as they entered the street, the noise died down to a distant roar with the intervening buildings absorbing much of the din. The first building they looked at was an inn, but it had a sign posted on the door which Tirzah translated as 'No Room'.

"That's to be expected so close to the market on a market day. Don't lose hope. We'll find something."

They finally settled on one a few streets farther down the hill. It was more run-down that the ones higher up. Its sign was hanging by one chain, and the paint was flaking off the door, but when they entered, the aroma of food was too enticing to miss. It seemed fairly clean inside, although the floor needed sweeping, but that was understandable at this time of day, with such a crowd of patrons.

As they stood in the doorway and looked around to find the person in charge, the room fell silent and all eyes were trained on the strangers.

"Why are they all staring at us?" Vertan muttered. "Did we do something wrong?"

"I think we are about to find out," Barengush said, nodding to the burly, bald man coming towards them.

The man stood in front of them, preventing them from moving farther into the room. He said something that none of them, but Tirzah and his sister could understand, although his demeaner indicated that he was very agitated about something.

He and Tirzah had a short discussion as the landlord explained the problem with much gesticulating and shaking of his head.

Tirzah turned to the team and told them what had been said.

"Women are not allowed in here. When I asked about rooms, he said you must enter from the back and ascend the staircase to the women's quarters. Your food can be brought to you there. Once he ascertained that only one of the women had familial relationship with one of the men, he told me we must be separated."

"What are we going to do?" Sastin asked.

"We have two options," Tirzah replied. "We can leave and look for another place or stay here under those conditions. And since this is the law, we have nothing to gain from looking elsewhere. This place is probably the best we can find."

The others nodded reluctantly.

"All right," Tirzah said. "I'll tell him we accept his offer."

Felindra

To reach the rear entrance of the inn, the three women and the boy had to go back down the street and enter a cluttered alley smelling of refuse. They looked down the alley and saw a veiled woman waving to them and went to meet her, treading carefully through the rubble.

The back stairs of the inn were steep, narrow, and gloomy. At the top was a small landing with four doors opening from it. The woman opened three of the doors so that they could look inside. Two of the rooms were too small to accommodate all of them, so they selected the largest room, which had six pallets and some low tables on a plain wooden floor. The outer wall had two small windows that overlooked the alley.

"What a dismal place," Felindra said after the woman had left to get their food.

"Well, it's only for one night," Farah said. "Just as long as the mattresses aren't infested."

"I can fix that, if they are," Felindra reminded her. "And rats, if they appear."

By the time they'd finished eating, the sun had set. Felindra and Zanda, Rasamé's son, were exhausted and ready to sleep, so Rasamé put Zanda to bed and Felindra lay down on her pallet, covering herself with the blanket provided by the woman who served them.

"I'm not tired," Rasamé said. "What shall we do?"

"We could contact your brother and see what he recommends," Farah suggested. They tried, but Tirzah cut them off with a quick *no magic*! before they could send a single word.

The next morning after breaking their fast, they met the men outside and went to a nearby park to discuss their next move.

"It's safer to talk out here," Tirzah Lin said. "I'm having reservations about using our gifts in this city. There's a feeling of ... I don't know how to express it ... it's like a heavy cloud pressing down on us. Does anyone else feel anything?"

"With me it's a deep anxiety, as if something awful is going to happen," Farah said.

"I feel a bit jittery," Vertan added. "But that might just be because we're talking about it."

Once everyone had commented, Tirzah Lin said. "We should leave today and get as far away from here as possible. Just buy a few supplies, get the horses and go."

"What about the inn?" Felindra asked.

"I've paid them already. There's no need to go back." Tirzah stood up. "Come, let's look at the market, see what we need to buy for the journey."

At least half the stalls in the marketplace had been removed; vendors from outside town, who only came into the city once every five days, had left. With the fresh vegetables and livestock gone, they could still purchase fresh baked goods, dried meat and fish, and dairy products.

There were several clothing stalls, but when the vendors saw the women looking at men's clothing, they shooed them away. "What's the problem?" Farah asked. "All we wanted was some culottes and tunics for the journey."

"You'd better let us take care of it," Tirzah Lin said. "Go to the women's stalls and look at their merchandise."

"How much can we spend?" Felindra asked.

"Not too much; we have to save some for the journey. I'd say about five silver each."

Barengush and Vertan had gone to get the horses from the stable by the caravanserai, so they wouldn't have to carry their purchases all that way. While they waited, they bought fruit drinks and sat in the shade of a tree.

A group of men in red and blue uniforms entered the market square and looked around, finally fixing their eyes on Felindra and her companions, and started walking toward them. As they came closer, the friends saw they had crests on their red tunics, an eagle with a sword in its claws under a gold crown.

"They look like palace guards," Tirzah said. "Don't look frightened."

The five men stopped in front of them and bowed. They gave a long explanation for their business in a friendly manner, while Tirzah tried to refuse whatever they wanted. Finally, he turned to his friends. "They say the Shah wants us to go to the palace. He wants to meet the foreign visitors. I told him we don't have time; we're leaving, but they insist we can't refuse an invitation from the Grand Shah."

They had no choice but to pick up their purchases and go with the guards.

"I'll flash an image of us being led away to let the boys know what's happening," Farah said softly. "Done!" she added after a couple of heartbeats.

Sastin and Tirzah were the only men with the three women. "I know that women are not supposed to be alone in the company of unrelated men, we should be prepared to offer explanations of our relationships. I will say Rasamé is my sister, and how would you like to be my wife?" he asked Farah.

"I'd love to," Farah replied with a grin. "What about Felindra and Sastin"?

"I could say I'm her uncle," Sastin offered. "We're both a bit sickly looking right now, so that should be believable."

***

Felindra hoped they didn't have to go far because the walk would be all uphill, so she was surprised to see five horses and an open wagon waiting on the street behind the market. The wagon was not like those used by traders to carry goods; it was brightly painted with blue, orange, and yellow patterns, and was drawn by four richly appareled horses. The sides could drop down to allow passengers to climb up into the rows of leather padded seats. Tirzah and Sastin were directed to two seats at the front and the three women to the row behind them.

"How are you feeling?" Farah asked Felindra.

"I'm glad we don't have to walk. I feel tired, my head hurts, and I'm frightened."

Farah took her hand to comfort her. "They aren't hostile," she said. "In fact, they're treating us like royalty."

"So why do I have this feeling of dread in my stomach?"

"I have to admit; the air is a little heavy. We'll just have to find out why he sent for us and hope it's not anything bad." She squeezed Felindra's hand for emphasis.

The road on which they travelled was wide and smoothly paved. Large trees with feathery leaves lined the way, and an ornamental garden with flowers and similar trees ran down the center. Large buildings with rich ornamentation lined both sides of the avenue.

The palace came into view before they were even halfway up the hill. It looked at first glance like a collection of various-sized buff-colored boxes stacked upon one another with gaps in between, but it wasn't unattractive. Some of the sections had diamond-shaped window openings and there was delicate white tracery along the edges and around the windows. Other windows were tall thin rectangles with balconies opening off them. The corners of the largest sections had round towers on their roofs with red and blue pendants fluttering in the breeze.

From the distance, they saw what looked like bundles of rags hanging along the outer walls. The sight filled Felindra with dread. *Oh Light, please let it not be...*

She raised her eyes for a moment when they got a little closer, but she quickly averted them with a groan and they filled with tears. Her fears were confirmed. They were human bodies, men, women, and to her horror, children. It wasn't just the dead bodies that were so shocking, it was the horrific mutilations they bore. Some with missing body parts, eyes, ears, hands and feet, even scalps and, from the bloody mouths, it looked as if the tongues had been removed from some of them. There must have been more than twenty corpses in various stages of decomposition.

Beside her, Farah gasped and wrapped her arm around Felindra's shoulder. Rasamé, on her other side, took her hand and squeezed it

In front of them, Tirzah Lin leaned forward and asked the driver of the wagon something. It was obvious from the tone of his voice that whatever he had learned disturbed him.

"What ..." Farah cleared her throat. "What was their crime?"

Tirzah turned around towards them, his mouth pressed in a grim line. "Witchcraft," he blurted. "We must be very careful. Don't even think of sending, or even having negative thoughts. We are in grave danger here and must be very careful. Be conscious of every motion you make and don't make any move or gesture that might be construed as casting a spell."

It was impossible to hide their revulsion and Felindra knew they wouldn't be able to approve of the Shah's actions if they were asked. "That is the worst thing I have ever seen," Felindra whispered to Farah. "It's even more horrifying than the child's body we found on the way to DarSolas seven years ago."

Felindra's wolf, Ashala, had found a sack containing the body parts of a young boy, and a living werman in a clearing near the Monastery. Her Father had been summoned to the castle by the Duke of Trethawynd and, with another defender, they were on their way to the meeting when the discovery occurred.

Finally, their wagon passed through the palace gate, leaving the dreadful spectacle behind, but they couldn't forget what they had seen and knew they never would.

15 – Meeting the Shah

Felindra

The wagon drew up under a marble portico where they dismounted. One of their escorts told them to wait in the large hall they'd entered through the massive double doors. He then ran up a curved staircase and disappeared.

Felindra and her companions stood on the white marble floor looking around the hall without interest, too numbed by what they had seen outside. She was feeling very shaky and might have collapsed if Rasamé hadn't supported her. "You should sit down," Rasamé said, leading her to a marble bench. "Your skin is so pale. Are you afraid?" she asked.

Felindra nodded. "I feel ill. I wish we were away from this dreadful place." A few tears trickled down her face.

Farah joined them. "I wonder what he wants of us," she said.

"It's hard to say. Did anyone pick up anything from the guards who brought us here?" Rasamé asked.

"I was too afraid to scan them after Lin's warning," Farah said.

The other women nodded in agreement.

Sastin sat down next to Felindra. He looked as devastated as she felt. He touched her shoulder. "I know how you feel, but I don't dare try to heal you."

"I know," Felindra replied. "Don't worry, Sastin, we'll get through this. I know the Light is with us."

Further conversation was curtailed by the arrival of the guard and a tall thin man in a black robe trimmed with blue stars around the neckline, cuffs, and hem.

They walked towards the group that was now clustered around Felindra. And the five travelers stood up before the two men reached them.

The thin man dipped his chin in a perfunctory bow, lips pursed, and addressed them.

"This is the Grand Vizier. The Shah is waiting. He wants us to follow him," Tirzah translated tersely. His expression was not very happy, either. "Remember what I told you."

They formed a column and followed the vizier up the staircase with the guards behind them. The man turned around and scowled at them, uttering a few words, sounding irritated.

Tirzah replied, and the man turned away with a huff.

"He asks if we cannot walk faster. I told him that two of us are recovering from injuries." Tirzah translated.

Felindra was exhausted by the time they reached the top of the stairs and couldn't walk without Farah and Rasamé's help. Tirzah put his arm through Sastin's to support him.

The vizier led them to the right along a wide hallway and turned left into another hallway where he stopped in front of a pair of massive doors guarded by uniformed men armed with curved sabers. The doors were open, so they walked directly through into a long, lavishly decorated room where a large man rested on a padded marble armchair seated on a dais facing the door.

The man beckoned them to approach and the Vizier repeated the invitation.

"We have to go to the throne and bow to the Shah."

They followed the instructions, but their actions satisfied neither the vizier nor the scowling Shah.

"We have to get down on our knees touch the floor with our foreheads," Tirzah informed them.

I'm going to pass out, Felindra thought. *Oh Light, please help me.* A wave of warmth suffused her body as she carefully lowered herself to her knees and bent forward.

She had managed to get down without misfortune but rising from her knees was another matter. Her head was spinning now that she was kneeling upright, and it took all Sastin's energy to raise her up. After the effort, he was shaky too. Felindra knew that Tirzah couldn't come to their aid because she was an unrelated woman. She glanced at the Shah through her veil and saw that the Grand Vizier was now standing next to the throne, and both men were scowling.

The Shah said something to the vizier, nodding towards them, and the vizier repeated it to Tirzah. Tirzah bowed and gave a lengthy explanation. At that, the Shah bellowed something at some servants who were hovering nearby.

"He wants to know what is wrong with you. I told him," Tirzah explained.

Two chairs were provided for Sastin and Felindra, but the others were left to stand. "He only allows you to be seated in his presence because you are injured,"

Moments later pages arrived with trays containing beverages, some in gold flasks and the rest in silver-trimmed glass. The page with the gold flasks went to the Shah first and served him and the vizier. The glass and silver flasks contained water with a touch of lemon juice.

The Shah took a few sips and then turned to them and demanded … "Show me their faces," he said looking at Sastin. Tirzah translated, staring pointedly at the women.

"Shall I refuse?" he asked Tirzah, who nodded.

"My friend says she cannot do that. It is unseemly, and I agree."

The Shah's puffy cheeks flared scarlet and his eyebrows drew together over his bulging eyes. He attempted to stand up but was unable to raise his bulky body more than a hand's breadth before he flopped back into his seat and continued his tirade. By the time he'd finished ranting at Tirzah, he was out of breath and reaching out his cup blindly for someone to fill it.

Felindra and Rasamé looked at Tirzah curiously waiting for him to translate. Felindra was terrified; she wanted to find out why the Shah was so furious.

"He said he is the Shah, the supreme ruler and his word is law. You must do as he says."

The three women nervously raised their veils. Felindra felt no shame at revealing her face, but kept her eyes cast down, not wanting to look at the repulsive man. She could hear his wheezing breath, however and hear his voice making comments.

Felindra was suddenly startled when a hand grasped her arm. She looked up and saw one of the guards staring down at her. He pulled her to her feet. "What's happening?" she asked Tirzah.

"He has chosen you to be in his harem. He chose Rasamé, too."

She could tell Tirzah was furious but was trying to conceal how he felt. "I'm sorry I got you into this, Felindra. We should never have come to this place."

Before she could answer, the guard dragged her away by the arm, but she heard Tirzah say, "We'll get you out of this."

Another guard was pulling Rasamé away from the rest of her group. When Zanda started to cry, she shouted, "what about my son?"

"I'll look after him," Tirzah said. He went over to the boy and picked him up.

The Shah bellowed something at the guards, and the one leading her let go of her arm and pulled her veil down to cover her face. After that, he didn't touch her; he only prodded her gently in the back occasionally to keep her moving.

Once they were back in the hallway, having exited the room by a door behind the Shah's throne, Rasamé said something to her guard in another language, which he answered briefly.

"He says we are being taken to the harem to be 'prepared', whatever that means."

"Oh, Light, what are we going to do?"

"We'll have to see what happens and pray we can escape somehow."

The guard poked her in the back and gave them an order, which she assumed meant 'no talking'.

They turned a corner and approached a wide staircase up to a higher level. It was guarded by two men in blue robes with pink scarves around their necks. Although they were very obese, their bare arms and legs showed well-developed muscles. Both men were armed with spears that had heart-shaped blades and had small sickle-shaped swords attached to their waistbands.

The two palace guards greeted the staircase guards, although Felindra sensed contempt in their voices. After a short exchange, the staircase guards nodded Felindra and Rasamé towards the stairs, and the palace guards left.

"What did the guard say?"

"Just that these are the harem guards and we must do as they say."

Felindra could barely walk, so weak was she and filled with dread.

Seeing her condition, Rasamé put her arm through Felindra's to help her along. She turned her head to the harem guards and said, "She is very sick."

One of the guards grunted something to which Rasamé replied.

"He wants to carry you," she said to Felindra.

"I don't care anymore. Do as you think best."

"Don't give up hope, Felindra, Lin will think of something." She turned and nodded to the guard.

As he picked her up and rested her head on his shoulder, her veil came off and fell to the steps. The guard spoke to the other one and they both laughed.

"He said 'it's like carrying a baby'."

When they reached the top of the stairs, they found themselves in a lavishly decorated room with unusually dim lighting. Several women slouched listlessly on loungers and padded chairs. On closer observation,

Felindra saw that the furniture and decorations were tawdry and worn, but the most shocking realization was that most of the women were young girls.

An older woman approached them. After putting Felindra down, and explaining about her and Rasamé, the guards turned and descended the stairs.

The woman looked them up and down with a strange expression on her face, half pity and half determination. "Come!" she said in Trade.

Felindra was surprised that there was someone here who spoke a language she understood. "What is going to happen to us?" she asked the woman.

"You'll find out soon enough," the woman replied in a sympathetic tone. "You are sick?"

"Yes" Felindra said weakly. She staggered and grabbed onto Rasamé for support.

"You need healer," the woman said.

"My friend is a healer," Felindra replied. "Can she take care of me?"

The woman eyed Rasamé suspiciously. "What kind of healing?"

"Mostly herbal infusions and potions," Rasamé replied. "Sometimes I must also attend to the person's nutrition and activities as well, in order to hasten her recovery."

"No magic spells?"

"No magic," Rasamé affirmed, squeezing Felindra's arm.

Vertan and Barengush

"What was that?" Barengush exclaimed.

"All I got was a flash of the others being led away by some military-looking types."

"No message?"

"Nothing. They must be in serious trouble if they couldn't send a message. I think they were afraid to use their gifts."

"We have to find out what's happened to them and rescue them." Barengush asserted.

"We have to be careful," Vertan replied. "If it does have something to do with magic, we could be in big trouble. We need to get advice from someone who knows more about the situation here."

"And how are we going to do that? We can't even speak the language."

"We've both picked up some Trade language, and a bit of Basrindian. Let's go to the caravanserai and see if anyone we know is still there."

The stables where they'd left their horses were close to the caravanserai, so they took two of them and left the rest there for the time being. The two defenders set off down the narrow lane outside the city walls. When they arrived, it looked as if most of the wagons were still there and were loading new merchandise after having disposed of the load they'd brought here the previous day.

Barengush and Vertan dismounted and walked their mounts around the site until they found Parghan, the wagon master, who spoke Trade. He was busy giving orders to some drivers but left them as soon as he saw Vertan and Barengush. Most of the people in the caravan were welcoming towards the two Albasinians after their performance during the bandit attack.

After exchanging greetings, Parghan said, "You look worried, my friends. Has something gone wrong?"

"We are not certain, but we think the others in our group are in trouble." Vertan replied.

"We want to ask your advice," Barengush added.

The wagon master looked around and then said. "Come over here and sit down out of the way, then you can tell me about it."

"It's a bit vague," Vertan said. He leaned forward with his elbows on his knees. "We came to get the horses while the others stayed in the city buying supplies. We were just about ready to take the horses back when we received a strange message from one of them."

"You know we have some magic gifts?" Barengush said.

The wagon master nodded. "I assumed you had something like that after your performance during the attack. Go on. What was the message?"

"There were no words or explanation," Vertan said. "Just an image. It showed our people being herded into a wagon by some men in uniform. It felt as if the sender was afraid to use her gifts, didn't want to risk anyone knowing what she was doing.

"Aye, that does sound odd, and serious.

"What we want to know," Barengush said. "is if there is a ban on the use of magic."

Parghan rubbed his face with his palms and looked at them with a lugubrious expression. "I'm afraid to tell you, but I must. The Shah is fanatical about witchcraft, as he calls it. I wish I had known you were planning to go into the city; I would have warned you. Ah well, it's too late now."

"Brother Tirzah warned us not to use magic while we were there. He must have known something. The thing that puzzles me is how they found out about our gifts. We were too frightened to use them. The question is, were they taken because of using magic, or could it have been something else?"

"What other reason could there have been?" Barengush asked.

"That's what we need to find out. Did you get a chance to see what the abductors were wearing?"

"Yes, just a flash, but they had dark blue culottes and red tunics. The wagon they were putting our friends in was very fancy and ornamental. It was like an open carriage and had a liveried driver."

"Ah, that's interesting, but not good. Those are the uniforms worn by the Shah's guard, so it looks as if he has them." Parghan took a deep breath and gazed into the distance before continuing. "There are two main reasons why he might have had them brought in, one would be suspicion of witchcraft, and the other would be to add the women to his harem. The fact that he sent a royal carriage tends to make me believe it's the latter. Those young ladies of yours are very attractive, and he would think them exotic enough for his taste. Many a poor damsel had disappeared from the streets of Hil Goa and never been seen again."

Barengush and Vertan looked at each other in dismay. "What can we do?" Barengush asked. "We can't let them... Felindra is the betrothed of the Duke of Trethawynd. Something like this could start a war." He stopped when he realized he was rambling.

"What sort of person is he?" Vertan asked.

"He's a depraved monster, a predator of the worst kind. He has no mercy. His way of dealing with so-called witches is the most deranged thing I've ever heard of or seen." He shook his head. "Even children."

"Isn't there anything we can do?" Vertan asked desperately.

"I've been thinking," the wagon master said. "There is a possibility, if I can make the connection." Parghan stood up. "Come on, I'll take you to meet someone, if she's around."

He led them to a small tavern outside the city wall close to the caravanserai.

16 – Trickery

Felindra and Rasamé were taken by the woman who'd introduced herself as Minia, matron of the harem, to a bathhouse on the same floor. She ordered them to remove all their clothing and wash themselves thoroughly while she looked for some new clothes for them to wear.

Rasamé, who was more familiar with this type of bath, led her down the shallow steps into the tepid water, and gave her a jar of soap. "Would you like me to help you?" she asked.

Felindra was trembling, her teeth were chattering, and her skin was covered in goose bumps. She nodded to Rasamé.

"I'll do your back first, then you can sit down on the ledge." She took a rough cloth from a pile above the pool and dipped it into the soap, and then she scrubbed Felindra's back vigorously. When she finished, she scooped up water and rinsed off the suds. "All right, you can sit down now while I wash your front."

Despite the vigorous rub, Felindra was still trembling. "Why am I so cold? Do you feel cold?"

"No. It's just right for me. I think your fever is returning. In a way, that's a good thing, because he won't want to come near you if he thinks he will catch something." She reached over the rim of the pool and picked a large towel. "Here, you can get out now and wrap this around you. Sit on the bench over there."

"Are you two ready?" Minia asked, bustling in with a pile of garments.

"Almost," Rasamé replied, as she rubbed soap all over her body. "My friend is very sick, so I had to help her."

"She needs a healer," Minia said. She stopped and thought for a moment then shook her head. "We're in a tricky situation at the moment. Our healer was ... discontinued a few days past and they haven't replaced her yet. The Shah would not approve of a male healer touching his women."

"Not even my uncle?" Felindra said. "He is with us."

"I don't think he would permit him to enter the harem." Minia replied. "Come along, hurry up and get dressed, both of you. I've got other things to attend to." She laid two piles of clothing on the bench next to Felindra. When Felindra dropped the towel to don the chemise, the woman looked at her. "You're nothing but skin and bone. I don't know what he sees in you, but never mind, he likes little girls, and besides, you've got a pretty face."

She said it so matter-of-factly, but Felindra was almost paralyzed with horror and fear. Her trembling accelerated. She couldn't believe someone could be such an evil fiend, but then she remembered the bodies on the wall. She hastily put on the rest of the outfit, which was obviously

111

Vicki Wootton

designed to titillate a man, everything made of almost transparent material, even the chemise and under-wraps.

"Sister Minia," Rasamé said, "I can take care of her if I'm permitted. I have been looking after her ever since she got this disease."

"By the look of her," Minia replied, "you don't seem to be doing a very good job. How long has she been this way?"

"She contacted the infection in the desert near Kum. That was several weeks past, but she was wounded in a bandit attack on the caravan just before we crossed the border of Goa Sun and that has set her back somewhat. What she needs more than anything is rest."

"We'll see," the matron replied. "Come on, I'll show you where you can sleep. Bring the rest of your things; the extra clothes are for you to change. You must wash your clothes every day. By the way, did you say this disease is contagious?"

"I believe it is," Rasamé answered quickly. "Although I haven't been affected so far."

"How is it the rest of your group haven't caught it?"

"My uncle Sastin has. He is still sick," Felindra interjected.

"I believe it is spread by body fluids, blood, saliva, and so on." Rasamé put her arm around Felindra's back to support her. "Oh, there's one other way this disease may be passed on, that is by sexual contact. Although I'm not sure of this; I only heard of it by word of mouth."

Felindra decided she would allow Rasamé to lead the discussion from now on. She seemed to be handling it in Felindra's interest and she found Rasamé's manipulation of the facts interesting.

Minia reacted as if she'd been slapped in the face. She stared at the two women for a moment. "You're not just saying that to keep him away from her, are you?" she asked, narrowing her eyes suspiciously.

Rasamé squeezed Felindra's shoulder. "As I said, I don't know for sure if it is true. If he wants to take a chance..." she shrugged.

"Follow me," the matron ordered crossly. "I'm going to have to isolate both of you. I don't want the other girls to become sick."

Felindra noted that she called the harem residents 'girls', and she discovered this designation was close to the truth when she looked more closely at the residents of the harem. One thing they all had in common was their misery. There was none of the joy here that Dom Ashe's concubines often displayed. Some of these girls looked as young as eleven and twelve years, and none looked older than twenty. They all sat around the room looking listless and depressed, and some of the younger girls had tears running down their cheeks.

"They all seem so young," Rasamé commented, keeping her tone non-judgmental. "What happens to the older women?"

"He sells them in the slave market," Minia replied. "Unless work can be found for them in the palace."

"So they become slaves," Rasamé said.

"They already are," the woman said bitterly.

Aha, Felindra thought. She's not happy either.

"And if he's dissatisfied with a girl?" Felindra asked.

They stopped outside a curtained doorway. She pulled aside the curtain and waited for them to enter the room. She followed them inside, drew the curtain, and leaned against the wall. "You might as well know what you are up

113

against," she said with a sigh. "The Shah is unpredictable. There's no way of telling what he may do. We just must stay low and follow the rules. I'm here to make sure everyone stays in line, doesn't do anything stupid and arouse his anger. I may seem harsh at times, but my job is to protect you and prevent the girls from making mistakes that will earn them punishment. In answer to your question, Felindra, it depends on what kind of a mood he's in. I've known him to send girls to the dungeons to be chastised. They rarely survive that. As I said earlier, they may be sold as slaves. We've even had girls who have been charged with witchcraft and punished accordingly. You must be very careful in what you say and what you do; even the expression on your face can condemn you."

"So nobody is set free," Rasamé said.

Minia shook her head. "No, never." She sighed and turned to leave, then looked back. "I will try to convince him that you are both contagious and need a few days to heal." She pulled the curtain across the doorway after closing the door behind her.

Felindra looked around. The only furnishings were the pallets and some pegs on the wall for hanging their clothes. Compared to this, Dom Ash's concubines lived in luxury.

Rasamé's voice brought her back to the present. "He sounds like a truly evil monster," Rasamé said in a barely audible tone. "I don't know about you, but I feel trapped. I don't know how we're going to get out of this."

Rasamé sat down on the floor next to the pallet where Felindra lay and started to rummage through her medicine bag. "I'm surprised they haven't taken this. Ah, here it is. Now, if I could get some water and something to heat this in." She surveyed the room and then stood up. "I'll have to go and look around, see if I can find anything. She returned moments later with a metal cup of water and a lighted candle. "This will have to do," she muttered. She crumbled the leaves of the herb into the water and held it over the candle, moving so that her back rested against the wall. It would take a long time to bring it to boiling point.

Vertan and Barengush

The shades over the windows made the tavern gloomy inside after the brilliant sunshine outside, but as their eyes adjusted, they could see enough to realize that the room was almost deserted. A large bearded man stood by a high sideboard on the left-hand side, arranging some tankards and jars. He turned around when he heard the three men enter. "Parghan, my old friend! Welcome!" He wiped his hands on a cloth tucked in his belt and came forward to meet them. "As you can see, Brother, there's plenty of room for you and your guests. Pick a table and I'll bring you refreshment. The usual?"

"No, it's a bit early in the day for that. How about some iced lemon and mint?" he looked at Barengush and Vertan to see their reaction. They both nodded, and the landlord went into another room to get their beverages.

The two Albasinians looked around, noting the unlit fireplace in one corner and a staircase opposite the door. The ceiling was low with lanterns hanging at intervals from the beams. The room was furnished with ten tables of varying sizes. A man and a woman with her head covered sat at a table near the fireplace, glanced at them, and continued their subdued conversation.

The landlord returned with a large ceramic jug and three clay cups. "There you are. Anything else?"

"How about some of your famous crulinds?" Parghan said.

"Coming up!"

"What's a crulind?" Barengush asked.

"It's what he calls his secret mix, wrapped in dough and deep-fried. I know from the taste it contains cheese, tomatoes, onions, and various herbs and spices. You'll love it."

After taking a bite and savoring it, Barengush said, "this is the best thing I've tasted since ... I don't know ... maybe ever."

"Is your friend here?" Vertan asked.

"Let me check." He got up and went over to the sideboard where the landlord had resumed his work. After a brief conversation, he returned. "He said he'll send her a message. Come back at sunset; she should be here then. I told him something about the fate of your friends. It might influence her to help us. Don't worry; he's completely trustworthy."

Felindra

Felindra woke up, still feeling groggy, and looked around the tiny room. The walls were whitewashed bricks, and the only light came from a diamond-shaped window too high in the wall to see anything outside but a wedge of sky. She noticed a cup beside the pallet and sat up to examine it. It must be the medicine Rasamé was making for her when she fell asleep. She lifted the now tepid concoction and took a sip. It had the bitter taste she was used to, but no honey to make it more palatable. She drank it anyway, swallowing quickly. She lay back and gazed up at the tiled ceiling. *I wonder where Rasamé is.*

She wanted to think of anything but the hopelessness of her situation, but it kept coming back to her, accompanied by an icy hollow in her stomach. She rubbed her upper arms, trying to entice some warmth into her chilled flesh.

Oh, Light, what are we going to do? I'm so frightened. I'd rather give up my life than be touched by that monster. Please help me.

The warmth of His touch suffused her body, leaving her feeling much calmer. She knew he wouldn't desert her, but she appreciated the reassurance.

I wonder what Vertan and Barengush are doing. What have they done with Farah and the two men? Again, she felt the warmth.

The clatter of curtain rings against the rods alerted her to Rasamé's return.

"I see you're awake," her friend said. "Did you take your medicine?"

Felindra eased herself into sitting position with her back against the wall. "I did."

"How are you feeling?" Rasamé sat on her pallet across from Felindra and leaned back against the wall. "They don't believe in comfort, do they? It's a wonder we don't have to sleep on the bare floor."

"I feel a bit better, but I'm still weak. I've been thinking, Rasamé, about a way we might be able to keep him away from us a bit longer."

"Both of us?"

"Yes. It all depends on whether you have the right ingredients."

"Tell me about it," Rasamé said. "What would we need?"

"Do you have anything that can cause a rash? That's one of the signs of a disease, isn't it?"

Rasamé nodded. "Hmm, let me see." She opened her medicine bag in her lap and started looking through the paper-wrapped packages. She took one large package out and held it up. "This should work."

"What is it?" Felindra asked.

"In our culture, we call it 'witches curse'. It's a quite useful herb if it is boiled, but if you touch it without boiling, it causes a terrible rash, and fierce itching. It would do the trick, but could you endure it in your condition?"

"Do you have anything that would alleviate the itching without removing the rash?" Felindra asked.

"It's possible," Rasamé replied. "I'll have to think about it."

Just then, they heard scratching on the wall outside their little room. A timid little voice saying something that was incomprehensible to Felindra, followed by a rattling of dishes and something hard landing on the floor.

"It's our food. She's left the tray on the floor," Rasamé said, standing up to retrieve it.

The metal tray contained two bowls of something that looked like a cross between gruel and soup with some red and white chunks mixed in. There were also two small oranges and two mugs of white liquid. It might have tasted better if it had been hot, but it had obviously spent a lot of time between when it left the kitchen and its arrival at their room. The bowls' contents turned out to be a cooked grain mixed with some vegetables and chunks of fish. The drink was one of the fermented milk concoctions to which Felindra had become accustomed.

"It's nutritious enough," Rasamé commented when she'd finished. "I suppose they want to keep us healthy."

"Are we going to try the rash?" Felindra asked.

"I'm willing if you are. But before we do anything, I want to change the dressing on your head. If it's healed enough, we can leave it off from now on."

Barengush and Vertan

Having to wait had been very frustrating for the two defenders. Their anxiety levels increased as every degree passed. Vertan rubbed his hands together. *I should be doing something, but what can I do? It's this waiting, not knowing anything ... I hate having to depend on others.*

The time finally came around for them to return to the tavern. Parghan accompanied them to introduce them to the woman and translate if they had any problems understanding. This time the room was almost filled with men from all over the world, or so it seemed to Vertan. It was much more cheerful with the lamps lit, and much noisier. The room went silent when they entered, and every head turned to inspect them, but the patrons soon returned to their conversations and consumption of food and drink.

They followed Parghan straight to the high sideboard to speak to the landlord. He nodded and wiped his hands on a cloth. "Sit at the table near the stairs. I'll bring you something to drink. Finish the drink and then go up the stairs. She's waiting in the room at the end of the hall on the right."

Finally, Vertan thought as he drained his mug and stood up.

Parghan led the way and opened the door of the room. He stopped in surprise and bowed. "Your highness, I didn't expect to see you here, although I'm pleased and honored by your presence."

"Come in, Parghan, and bring your friends," a mellow voice said.

Vertan and Barengush followed Parghan into the room, dumfounded to find a member of royalty was there to meet them. They bowed in unison with their hands together and raised their eyes to look at him. He was sitting in a padded armchair by a large table covered with a richly patterned rug upon which stood a lighted lamp. He was a well-built man, around thirty-five years, with dark yellowish-brown hair, beard and trim mustache. His eyes were his most striking feature. They were a pale greenish grey color and radiated warmth.

Parghan bowed again. "May I present my friends, your highness? These two young men are from Albasiny. They are both what they call defenders in their country, something akin to guardians or soldiers, I believe. They were a tremendous help to us when our caravan was attacked by bandits. The tall one on the left is Barengush." Barengush saluted and bowed again. "And the other one is called Vertan." After Vertan finished repeating his bow, Parghan looked at them and continued, "It is my honor to present his highness, Shahbanu Kazim of Goa Sun. *Shahbanu* means prince or son of the Shah."

Barengush stared at him open-mouth. Could this be the son of the Shah who has taken our friends?

"Indeed," the prince said with wry smile. A look of deep sadness replaced the smile. "I know it is unseemly to derogate one's parent, but I have the misfortune to be his son. That is why I'm doing my work in secret."

Parghan signaled that he wanted to say something, and the prince nodded. "If you don't need me, I'm neglecting my work." Parghan said. "If you'll excuse me, your highness." He bowed to the prince who nodded.

"Until we meet again," Prince Kazim said. "Be careful; it's a dangerous world out there." Parghan smiled and left the room, carefully closing the door behind him.

"Sit down," the prince said to the two defenders, indicating the two chairs facing the table. As he pulled out the chair, Barengush noticed the woman sitting in the shade at the opposite end of the table.

She smiled when she caught his eye on her, and then nodded at the prince. An unspoken signal passed between them and then she spoke for the first time. "I'm Lemaya," she said. "Help yourselves to some water," she invited them.

"Now, let's hear your story, and then we will see what can be done about your friends." the prince said.

Felindra

When they awoke the next day, Felindra was feeling a little better, although the pain in her head was still bothering her and the rash on her chest and arms was very irritating. At least she had the energy to raise herself from the pallet. "I wish we could bathe," she said the Rasamé.

"Maybe we can," Rasamé replied. "Shall I go and find Minia? We also need to find out where to wash our clothes."

"I'll go with you," Felindra said.

When they left their room, a young woman coming towards them turned back the way she had come. Minia appeared in the hallway and flapped her hand at them to go back. As they backed into their room, they heard angry male shouts. When he continued the raging, Rasamé poked her head through the curtain to see what the commotion was about but withdrew it instantly.

"It's him," she whispered. "He wants to see us."

The voice roared again. "He said 'come out'. We'd better do what he says."

The cold hand of fear grasped Felindra's insides. She followed Rasamé out into the hallway, trying to control her trembling. The matron, who was cowering against the wall, beckoned them to come forward. The massive body of the Shah was being carried by two eunuchs like the ones she'd seen standing guard the day before. By their red faces and clenched jaws, she could see they were having difficulty keeping the base of the chair off the floor.

The shah turned on the two eunuchs. "Put me down, you imbeciles! You're making me sick with your clumsy fidgeting."

Although they tried to lower the chair to the floor carefully, they barely saved it from tipping over at one point, and it landed on the tiles with a thud. "Get out of my sight both of you! If I see you again, you'll end up in the dungeons."

"Come closer," the Shah shouted. "Why are you keeping me waiting?"

They crept a little closer, holding hands for mutual support, and stopped about two paces from him. "Take those rags off," he ordered. "I want to see you properly, see if you're worth all the trouble you're giving me."

"He wants us to undress," Rasamé whispered.

"No," Felindra uttered. "Light...!"

"We'd better do it. You don't know what he might do...," Rasamé began to slowly remove her clothes, starting with the head veil, Felindra got as far as removing the veil, but couldn't make herself continue.

From where they stood, they could see drool running from the corners of his mouth into his beard. His hand crept down into his lap and he began to massage himself. Just looking at him made her feel sick. She had never seen such a revolting person. Fear was building up to the point that her guts began to churn. She put her hands over her mouth and heaved, but nothing came up. Her head started to buzz and then her body slid to the floor. She could hear movement and commotion around her still, but it came from far way and through a fog. Unable to react, she just lay there and allowed it to pass over her. *Thank you, Light.*

17 – The Prince

Vertan and Barengush

After the two defenders had explained some of their experiences to date, the prince thought for a moment. "As I see it, your main problems are your magic gifts and the need to rescue your friends. I agree that you would be in great danger if you tried to enter the city. The Shah has spies everywhere, specially trained to detect magic, even from a distance, so we'll have to work around that.

"It all depends on where they are being kept. If they are in the dungeons, it will be much easier to get them out, but if the women have been sent to the harem, it will be a lot harder. It is virtually impossible for a man to get inside."

"Harem!" Vertan responded.

Prince Kazim nodded to Lemaya, and she continued explaining. "The Shah is a..." she looked at the prince, who nodded, "... is obsessed with young females. This has led him to commit the kidnapping and rape of hundreds of young girls and women. He created a harem in which to confine his ... victims."

"Is that like having concubines?" Barengush asked.

"Not exactly," Lemaya replied. "Usually, as far as I know, concubines are treated like wives because one motivation for having concubines is to produce sons for the master. The girls in the Shah's harem are slaves. He has no concern about their physical comfort or liberty; he just uses them and when he becomes tired of a girl, he discards her."

She looked at the prince, who smiled and nodded to her again. Vertan noticed that, when Kazim looked at her, his eyes glowed with tenderness and affection.

Lemaya took a deep breath. "In case you wonder how I know so much about this, I was one of his victims. Luckily for me, he just wanted to humiliate me and never ... suffice it to say I didn't lose my virtue." She blushed as she finished talking, lowering her head and focusing on the table.

"I'm sorry, my love. I hate to put you through this." He stood up and walked along the table to put his arm around her shoulder. She reached up and took his hand, looking up at him with tears in her eyes.

"One of the reasons I hate my father is what he did to my betrothed. We were in love, planning our marriage ceremony when she disappeared. I was fortunate to have a friend in the harem who told me she was there." He was silent for a moment. "Another reason is that he killed my mother."

Startled by this revelation, Barengush straightened up in his chair. His own father had killed his mother when he was a boy. "How... why did he...?" he stammered.

"Probably because she was a witch," the prince snarled. "At least that's the excuse he gave. She did have magic powers, which I inherited. I think he was angry because he'd already started his harem and she was trying to help the girls. He didn't want her interfering in his *private* life. His perversions."

"Did he know you both had gifts?" Vertan asked.

"He knew she did, but I'm not sure if he knew about me; if he did, he must have wanted to protect me, his only heir, although he never showed me any affection or kindness..."

The prince stopped talking and closed his eyes for a moment, as if listening. "That was the vizier. Something has happened at the palace. I have to get back there."

"Does it have anything to do with our friends?" Barengush asked.

"I don't know; it may, but it's the Shah ... I must go; it sounds urgent. Will you excuse me?" He squeezed Lemaya's hand and kissed her on the cheek. "Want to come with me?"

She stood up and took his hand. "Why don't we all go?" she suggested. "It should be safe now."

"Wait; let me check." He listened for a moment. "Yes, but I think you should lead them the secret way while I get my horse and go straight there."

Vicki Wootton

Felindra

Felindra woke up to darkness and cold. Even with her eyes open, she could see nothing but an occasional weak flicker of light. She could hear the ripple of water all around, and sometimes a grunt or a snuffle and a splash. She started searching around her and her hand touched another body. It stirred.

"You're awake! Good. I was afraid you'd never come around," Rasamé said.

Felindra sat up and moved closer to her friend. "Where are we? Why is it so dark and cold in here?"

"They call this place 'The Island'. It's in a massive cavern deep under the dungeons, and we are surrounded by water filled with crocodiles."

"I suppose there's no hope of it getting any warmer, or of our escaping."

"That's about it."

"Are they going to give us food?"

"I have no idea. Probably hope we'll die of starvation, freeze to death, or be eaten by crocodiles."

"What happened after I ... fell asleep?"

"Is that what you call it? It looked to me like fainting."

"I'm sorry, Rasamé, I was praying to the Light when it happened. I think it was His way of protecting me."

"You have some powerful friends," Rasamé said. "After you 'fell asleep', his grossness had a fit, bellowing and screeching at everyone until he ran out of breath. The essence of it was that we are useless to him, and so he ordered us to be taken to The Island, which is where we are now."

"How did we get down here?"

"One of the eunuch's carried you on his shoulder, again—I think they're beginning to like you. We descended hundreds of steps down and down forever, past three levels of stinking dungeons filled with the moans and shrieks of the prisoners, and finally arrived at this water-filled hole. They brought a little boat from somewhere, dumped us in it, and rowed us across to this platform in the middle. They had torches, of course, so they could see where they were going. And they introduced us to the keepers." She pointed to the water. "All around us. Can you hear them?"

"The crocodiles? Yes, I hear them. But I wonder why they don't jump up on this thing and attack us?"

"It's too high for them to get up on, I suppose. It looked almost a span above the water when we crossed."

"Do you want me to talk to them and see if I can influence them?" Felindra asked.

Rasamé shrugged. "Do you think you can? They're a lot different from horses and wolves." She'd heard of Felindra's long-time relationship with a female wolf back in Albasiny.

"I know, they are very primitive, I can at least try. There were crocodiles in a swamp in Trethawynd, but I never went near them."

Felindra reached out with her mind and tried to contact one of the creatures in the water. She found a mind, but it was very murky with no thoughts other than hunger and food.

After leaving that mind, she sent her sense out and scanned the rest of them—there were about fifteen of them. Some were sleeping, but those who were awake seemed to be preoccupied by nothing but food as they swam erratically around the platform. *They must be able*

127

to smell us. She took a deep breath and exhaled it. *Poor creatures.*

"Not much to work with there," she said to Rasamé. "They're all hungry. I wonder if they do feed them, and when."

Felindra? Are you all right?

"It's Farah," she said, grabbing Rasamé's hand. Farah! Aren't you taking a big risk contacting me?

Not anymore, Farah sent, her happiness obvious. You are going to be rescued, Barengush and Vertan are on their way, but they don't know where you are.

We're on 'The Island'. It's a cavern under the dungeons. The water around us is filled with hungry crocodiles

Oh, Light, that doesn't sound good. I'll have to talk to the crown prince and find out how to get you out. Is there anything they can bring for you?

Just some warm clothes and something to eat, Felindra sent. Farah, what is happening up there. Why are we suddenly allowed to use our gifts?

The Shah has passed on. The crown prince—who is as different from his father as fire is from water—is in charge now. He is also gifted.

How did the Shah die"?

Apparently, he succumbed in the harem during a fit of apoplexy.

Felindra had mixed feelings about the horrible man's demise and felt she may have contributed something to it.

Vertan and Barengush

"Follow me," Lemaya said as soon as the prince left. "Do you have any weapons?"

"Only these," Vertan replied, rolling back his sleeve to reveal the dagger strapped to his forearm. "Parghan gave us one each. But we have more. We left most of our defender equipment at the stables with our horses."

"Very well. I hope we won't need them, but it's better to be prepared."

Instead of going back downstairs to the tavern, she led them from the room to one on the opposite side of the hallway. Once inside the room, she slid the bolt inside the door and went over to the bed. "We'll have to move this out of the way," she said. "Would you mind giving me a hand?"

A trapdoor was revealed when the head of the bed was moved away from the wall.

She raised the trap door. "These steps are connected to a passage in the city wall." Once they were all through the trapdoor, she added, "a mechanism moves the bed back into place when the trapdoor closes."

Lemaya put her arm out in front of Barengush. "Wait!" As she concentrated on the message she was receiving, her eyes lit up and she smiled. It seemed as if a great burden had been lifted. She breathed out a strong breath. "The Shah has gone to rest with his ancestors," she said.

"Is that good news?" Barengush asked. "I mean, will things change?"

"With Kazim as Shah, everything will change. For one thing, there will be no more witch-hunts.

"Will it be safe for us to enter the city?" Vertan asked.

"I'm not sure about that. It might take a little time for everyone to get used to the new Shah and the new laws he will introduce, and the ones he will repeal. There are still many people in the city who hate magic users, and they might take the law into their own hands until stability is restored. Despite being such a monstrous person, Shah Firouz did have some powerful friends and supporters who, I'm sure will do everything in their power to obstruct Kazim." She took a lighted torch from the wall. "Let us continue," she said, starting to walk towards the right.

The tunnel they were in was wide, with brick walls and a clean stone floor. It was lit at ten-pace intervals by torches, the smoke from which irritated their throats, but it was preferable to walking in the dark. The curve prevented them from seeing more than twenty paces ahead, but they could hear the footsteps advancing behind them clearly enough. Eventually, the followers caught up with them and stopped. They were dressed in uniforms like those worn by the city guards.

One of them asked a question and, unperturbed, Lemaya answered, then she smiled. The two men bowed to her and continued down the tunnel.

"What did you say to them?" Barengush asked as they resumed their walk.

"Luckily for me, Kazim gave me today's password. I just told them we are on a mission for the prince."

They continued walking, meeting the occasional guard, but not being stopped by any of them. It seemed to Vertan as if they were walking all the way around the city. "Do you mind my asking where we are going?"

"To the palace," she replied. "There's an emergency entrance, or should I say exit? It's not far now, just around the next bend. Are you getting tired?"

"A little," Vertan admitted. "I would venture to guess it is many degrees past midnight."

They rounded the curve moments later. "Here we are," Lemaya said. She glanced down both directions of the tunnel, then added, "keep watch while I open it." While

Barengush and Vertan stood back-to-back behind her and watched the tunnel, she went to a niche in between two buttresses. A few heartbeats later, they heard a grinding sound, like stone grating against stone, and turned to see a narrow opening in the wall.

"Come," she whispered. "Hurry before it closes."

They darted through the opening and almost as the last heel passed the gap, the stone began to roll back into place.

"Is it set by a timer?" Barengush asked.

"Not really, unless you called it timed magic. You have to know the proper key or spell to open it, but it will always close after ten heartbeats. That's to prevent anyone nearby from following you."

"What happens if someone gets caught as it closes?" Vertan asked.

"Squish." she replied. "There's no way to block it open; it will crush everything in its way. Now, we must hurry. This way."

They had entered a dank room with stone-clad walls and no furniture, just stone stairs leading upwards. They climbed up several levels. Vertan began to fall behind after a while. Barengush could hear his panting breath and so, apparently, could Lemaya. "We're almost there," she said. "We are going to the royal apartments. That's where Kazim is."

They exited the stairway into another small room, but this one was a lot warmer and had plaster walls lined with storage shelves. She knocked on the door, using an arrangement of short and long raps. The door was opened instantly by a footman who bowed to her, said a few words of greeting, and gestured down the hallway.

Lemaya led them down a wide hall towards the sound of voices. The walls of the hallway were decorated with lifelike murals illustrating beasts and birds in their habitats. The artistic skill was impressive and must have been done many years past because paint was chipped and scratched in places, and parts of the surface were marred by stains.

"I hear Farah!" Barengush exclaimed. "Are our people all here?"

They had arrived at the door to a large salon and they could see the answer for themselves. Felindra and Rasamé weren't there.

Lemaya spoke to the footman at the door, and then she turned to the two defenders. "The prince had to leave. He was needed elsewhere. You realize how chaotic things are right now. He has so many matters to take care of, but luckily for him, he has the grand vizier to guide him and help him facilitate a smooth transition. I should be with him. You may make yourselves comfortable in here with your friends, but let me show you around, first."

They went into the room where they were immediately showered with hugs and kisses. Barengush saw Lemaya watching them with a smile, and he realized she was waiting.

"You said you wanted to show us around," he said to her. "But I don't want to keep you, I know you're getting tired. I will introduce you to my friends and they can show us where everything is." He turned to his friends. "This is Lady Lemaya, the betrothed of Prince Kazim. She's been helping with your rescue."

After receiving their thanks, Lemaya left them alone.

Felindra

Felindra and Rasamé lay together on the bare wooden platform, entwined in each other's arms for warmth. Neither their flimsy garments nor sharing their body heat could rid them of goose bumps or keep them from trembling. Felindra's feet seemed to suffer the most; she felt as if they were turning to stone.

"I wonder what's keeping them," She said.

"Maybe we should get up and move around, get our blood circulating," Rasamé suggested.

"I don't think I have the energy," Felindra said. "And I'm not sure my feet will support me; they've turned into blocks of ice." She sighed. Nevertheless, she stood up, with Rasamé's help, and they both started to walk around the platform. This started the crocodiles stirring and issuing grunts. "They're still hungry."

"Let's try to dance," Rasamé suggested when walking failed. Before they could decide whether to do so or not, they sensed an approaching light. "They're here!" Rasamé said joyfully.

"Light! Someone's coming. It must be Vertan and Barengush."

The light came closer and a tall thin man in a black robe appeared, carrying a lantern. Behind him, two other men came into view dragging a small boat. Felindra's heart sank when she realized they were not the two defenders. They looked more like guards. She gasped. "That looks like the Vizier," she said. "Oh Light, something must have gone wrong." She clung to Rasamé's arm for support.

The grand vizier! This can't be good, Rasamé sent.

Yes, it is I. Do not be afraid; we have come to set you free.

But you're the Grand....

Not what you expected, I know. I'll explain later. Now we must hurry. We've brought you warm robes and some water to drink.

The two guards pushed the boat into the water and climbed in, only to become surrounded by about a dozen hungry crocodiles. One of the guards picked up a lump of something from the bottom of the boat and threw it past their platform, sending the creatures snarling, snapping after it. The other guard threw another lump on the opposite side, making some of them break away and go after it. Once the crocodiles were distracted, they rowed hastily to the platform.

"Here, put these on quickly," one of the guards said. Being careful not to look directly at them, he pushed a package up over the edge of the platform. The two women quickly donned the garments and allowed the guards to help them climb down from the platform into the boat.

When they reached the other side, the vizier stood over them as they climbed out, Rasamé helping Felindra. "Good," he said. "Here's some water." He handed each of them a small metal cup.

He led them through a tunnel into a storeroom where the guards stowed the boat, and then he unlocked a door and ushered them through into another room. This room didn't appear to have a purpose, although the racks of instruments on the walls presented a grim clue as did the stains on the floor that looked like dried blood. Felindra began to shake and cling more tightly to Rasamé.

"Don't worry, we're not stopping here," the grand vizier said.

The guards opened another door, this time to a staircase. "Up we go," the vizier said, leading the way. The two guards followed behind.

"You may be wondering why I am rescuing you. You probably thought I was the lackey of the late Shah," The Vizier said. "That is what he believed as well, but I've always supported Prince Kazim. The prince has been forced to work undercover for many years to help the people his father abuses and, after the way he treated Kazim's mother and his intended bride, I felt I had to take a stand."

"Weren't you putting yourself in danger, being so close to him all the time?" Felindra asked.

"One thing the Shah didn't realize is that I have magic powers and could sense threats in time to avert them, most of the time. I must tell you that there have been times when only divine intervention could save me." He circled his thumb and forefinger and put them to his lips.

They started up the second flight, but Felindra was so exhausted, she stopped climbing and bent over, gasping for breath. She flopped down on the step, her head spinning.

"I can't...." she stopped to catch a breath.

The Vizier turned around, sensing everyone had stopped. "What's wrong with her?"

"She's very sick, your honor. She's too weak to climb the stairs," Rasame said.

"One of you must carry her," he said to the guards. They looked at each other, and then at the vizier, eyebrows raised and mouths gaping.

"Don't worry about it; I'll make it right."

"It is their custom," he explained. "They are not permitted to touch women not of their own family. They need your consent."

Felindra looked at the two guards. Both were young, dark-skinned and bearded. They looked harmless enough. "I permit you to carry me," she said, looking them in the eyes.

After the vizier explained what she'd said, the bigger of the two stooped down and hauled her up onto his shoulder, making sure she was completely covered by her robe before resuming the climb.

Do you feel comfortable? the vizier asked.

Yes, thank you.

But she wasn't really, the man was wearing a metal breastplate, the edge of which was digging into her stomach.

They continued to climb, flight after flight. Even the guards were becoming breathless by the time they finally arrived at another door, which the vizier unlocked with a key from his pocket. They entered a small storeroom containing cleaning supplies.

When they exited the storeroom, Prince Kazim and Tirzah Lin were approaching. The guard carrying Felindra gasped and quickly lowered her to her feet, then he fell face down on the floor and said something to the prince, pleading.

What's he doing? Felindra asked Tirzah.

He's afraid he will be punished for touching a woman.

The prince responded impatiently, and the man stood up and bowed to him profusely. The prince said a few more words, flapping his hand down the hall, and both guards walked away.

The prince told him 'an act of mercy is not a sin'. Tirzah explained.

"These poor people," Prince Kazim said in Trade. "It's a wonder they can function with so many taboos." He turned to Tirzah. "Would you like to introduce us?"

Tirzah, who was standing with his arm around Rasamé replied, "This is my sister Rasamé, and the other young lady is Felindra from Albasiny. She's a very talented woman, but unfortunately she has been quite ill lately." He turned to Felindra. "And this honorable man is Prince Kazim of Goa Sun, soon to be crowned Shah."

Prince Kazim dipped his head to the two women. "I'm delighted to meet you both, I know you both need rest and some warm clothing. We were just on our way to talk to your other friends; come with us. You will find everything you need there."

When they reached the salon, all Felindra's friends rushed to embrace them. Felindra wondered what the prince thought about all this male-female interaction. She turned and bowed to him. "I hope you can forgive our enthusiasm, your highness; it is our custom."

"There's nothing to forgive, my lady. You obviously care about one another. Now I suggest you and lady Rasamé go back through that door and make yourselves comfortable. I've ordered some food to be brought up as you must be very hungry."

After bathing and donning clean clothes, Felindra and Rasamé joined the others in the salon to share a meal. Felindra was so exhausted, she barely had the strength to raise a cup to her lips and she only nibbled at some of the food on her plate, all the time trying to stifle yawns.

"I think you need to rest," Prince Kazim said after looking at her drooping eyelids. "There's a bedroom back there you may use."

"I'll go with her," Rasamé said, standing up and going around the table to help Felindra stand.

18 – Attack at The Palace

Felindra

A ray of sunshine peeked through a gap in the window shutter. For a moment, Felindra was disoriented. She looked around the twilit room and saw Rasamé asleep in the bed next to her. Both beds were massive with enough space for three people to lie side-by-side. She stretched, and yawned, and then threw back the cover and sat up. *I must have slept right through the night,* she thought. The last thing she remembered was sitting at a table eating with all her friends. She knew that Rasamé had helped her to bed, but she didn't remember anything else, not even putting on the filmy white nightgown she was wearing. She slid down onto the luxurious carpet on the floor and went over to the window. After widening the gap in the shutter, she peeked through it, curious to see what was outside.

The balcony outside the window obstructed the view, so all she could see was the top of the palace wall far below and the rooftops of buildings beyond.

"You're up," a voice behind her observed. "How are you feeling this morning?"

She turned from the window to see Rasamé sitting on the edge of her bed. "Much better," she replied. "But I'm very hungry."

"Me too. Let's get dressed. There may be food in the salon."

A soft knock on the door startled them. Rasamé went to open it.

"It's only me," Farah said. "I wanted to see if you were awake. They've just brought food to break our fast." She came into the room and Felindra went to meet her. They embraced and then Farah held Felindra away from her so that she could see her better. "You look a bit better today, but you've lost a lot of weight." She turned to Rasamé. "How long before she will be ready to travel?"

"I'd say in about four or five days. That's if she obeys all the healers' orders and gets plenty of rest."

Farah let Felindra free and walked to the door. "Don't be long! We'll be waiting for you," she said as she closed the door behind her.

"I assume we don't need to wear veils," Felindra said as she finished dressing.

"You can never tell; it may be all right while we're with our friends, but we should put one around our necks, just in case."

"I want to hear everything that happened after they took me and Rasamé away," Felindra said after she sat down at the table to eat. She looked from Farah to Sastin and Tirzah Lin. "But first, I've a question for Lin. Can you tell us when we should use veils and when we don't need them?"

"Well, the tradition here is that women wear them in public and around unrelated men over the age of twelve." He shook his head. "I have a feeling that the future Shah may loosen those restrictions a little, but I'm afraid he may be up against some very conservative clerics."

"But how can a woman eat with a veil over her face?" Felindra asked.

"Men and women don't eat together in public, only in their homes. Even then, some men insist that the women eat separately."

"So that they can serve the men, I suppose." Felindra wrinkled her nose. "What about foreign women?"

"It's wiser to follow local customs out of courtesy if nothing else. Women may be molested by men if they are unveiled."

"How do you know all this?" Rasamé asked her brother.

"I've had a lot of time on my hands in the thirty odd years I've been in this part of the continent. I decided I would learn everything I could about the customs and traditions of neighboring cultures. It's always useful to know what you might be up against, so you don't get into trouble. Many people are upset if you don't observe their customs." He paused for a moment. "Now, I think Felindra wants us to share our experiences since we were separated."

Felindra nodded as she stuffed some bread dipped in fried cheese into her mouth. She was eating as if she wasn't sure when she would get her next meal. "What about you, Brother Lin?"

"The first thing they did after you left was separate us. Sastin and I were taken to a barred cell somewhere in the depths of the building."

"I think it was level one of the dungeons," Sastin added.

"We were told that there are three levels, each one worse than the one above. You were lucky," Barengush said.

"There's one even deeper down than those three levels," Rasamé added. "They call it 'The Island'. That's where we went. There was a torture chamber down there too."

"There are probably some of those on every level," Tirzah added. "We heard plenty of screams on level one." He turned to his sister. "What was it like down there?"

"It was like a nightmare. Cold and dark, and all the time the noise of crocodiles swimming around and grunting. All we had on were the flimsy rags they gave us in the harem, no food, nothing to drink. They probably thought we would try to get water from the pool if we got thirsty enough, but they never left anything to scoop it up with. I don't think we would have lasted many days. Felindra was unconscious when they took us down there."

"The shah came up to the harem. He wanted to see us. He didn't believe we really were sick. I was so frightened, I prayed to the Light for help, and then I fainted."

"I rubbed fire leaf on our skin, so we would get rashes," Rasamé said with a grin. "What happened to you, Sister Farah?"

"I was taken down to the kitchens and put to work cleaning dishes," Farah replied. "I became proficient cleaning up kitchens in the Basrindian slave center, so it wasn't a problem."

Barengush and Vertan related everything that had happened since they left their friends in the city. "And that's how we met Prince Kazim, and Lady Lemaya, who brought us to the palace," Barengush finished off.

"Did you know that she is Princess Lemaya?" Tirzah asked.

"Really? Is she a Goa Sun princess?" Farah asked.

"I believe she is the eldest daughter of one of the most powerful dukes in Goa Sun."

"How could the old Shah get away with treating her so badly?" Vertan asked.

"I assume he is of the old school," Tirzah replied. "Opposes witchcraft and probably supported his war against the use of magic."

"But his own daughter...." Vertan protested.

"Look what the Shah did," Barengush replied. "Killed his own wife."

Tirzah sighed. "Fanatics have no boundaries when it comes to a cause they are committed to."

"I hope things change," Felindra said. She stood up and walked over to the large window. The blinds had been folded back and the door to the balcony was open. "I'd like to see the view from up here," she said, stepping over the sill."

They were interrupted by a hullaballoo outside in the hallway: booted feet running, men shouting, a woman screaming. The door flew open and a palace guard came in. He looked around and picked out Barengush and Vertan. He yelled something at them, finger pointing fervently, but they didn't understand. The frustrated guard looked around for help and spotted Tirzah. "You say!"

"He says you are needed. Do you have weapons and armor?"

"We've got our swords, but no armor."

"All right get the swords and go with him. I'll come with you to translate."

With the door open, the noise was louder, but it began to fade as it passed to another section of the palace. While waiting for Barengush and Vertan to get their weapons, Tirzah asked the guard what was happening.

"The palace is under attack by fundamentalist witch-hunters. As far as I can make out, they fear that the prince will be lenient with witches."

Tirzah asked the guard a question and the guard left the room. He came back moments later with another guard.

"This man will guard the door. If those fanatics know you're here, they might come after you."

The two defenders were ready to leave and quickly disappeared into the hallway with the guard and Tirzah, closing the door behind them.

The guard who was protecting them locked the outside door and pulled a chair over to sit by it. He looked very uncomfortable, seeing the women without veils and kept his eyes everted as much as possible.

"We'd better put on some veils," Felindra said, moving towards their bedroom door. Properly veiled, they returned to the salon.

"What are we going to do?" Rasamé asked.

"Do you understand the language?" Felindra asked.

"No, well just a few words. Eleria is not too far from here and some of the words are similar. Lin tried to persuade me to learn more languages, but I was one of those stubborn girls. I thought he was wasting his time with all that studying but I see now it has paid off for him.

Tirzah Lin

The guard led them to the end of the hallway to a service door. While they were moving, Tirzah questioned the guard. "What exactly is happening?"

"All I know is that the palace is being attacked by witch-hunting radicals. His highness needs defensive help. I don't know why he needs your friends."

The sounds of battle faded slightly as they descended the stairs, but they could still hear crashes and shouts in the distance. They only descended one floor to a less luxurious level. "The Shah keeps an armory and guard room here for rapid deployment to the royal quarters in case of trouble. In here," he opened the door to a large storeroom where the walls were lined with weapons and a whole gallery of armor. "Pick what you need," he said to Barengush and Vertan. "You too, if you think it necessary," he added to Tirzah.

The two Albasinians donned chainmail shirts and hoods, and then glanced at the weapons. They picked out better swords than the Basrindian weapons they carried. While they were choosing, the guard sharpened his sword. All Tirzah wanted was a sharp stiletto.

"This way," the guard said, leading them back to the stairs.

Tirzah decided to try contacting the prince. *This is brother Tirzah, are you safe?*

We're barricaded in the Shah's council chamber, the prince replied, but it won't take them long to break in.

What do you need from us?

We understand that the Albasinians have powerful defensive magic. We need them to help them find the rebels and clear a passage to us.

Is the princess with you?

Yes, I'm here, brother Tirzah, Lemaya responded. Are your other friends safe?

They have a guard, and they can also use their powers. We're on our way, your highness.

When they reached the level above, the guard hesitated for a moment, as if listening.

"I just contacted the prince and he wants us to clear the way to the council chamber,"

The guard looked at him suspiciously. "That's where I was going."

The noise increased as they followed the hallway to an intersection. "This way," the guard said, indicating the right. "You go in front," he ordered the two defenders.

A woman screamed, then a door opened halfway along, and several men dressed in red came out dragging a woman and a girl of around fifteen.

"What do you say?" asked Vertan. "Can you make them let the women go?"

"I'll try but be prepared to back me up."

As they advanced, the rebels saw them and turned in the opposite direction. Vertan sent out a powerful conviction inducement, *you will put down your weapons and release the two women.* The men hesitated and looked back at the way they had come. Vertan repeated the command. *Do as I say, drop your weapons and let the women go.* The red-clad men looked at one another for a moment, puzzled, and then let go of the women and placed several weapons on the floor. *Stay where you are!* Vertan ordered. The women, who were already running towards them, stopped as well.

"What did you just do?" the guard asked.

"He was using a spell to disarm them without anyone being hurt," Tirzah explained. "We can continue now."

"What shall we do with the ladies?" the guard asked. "There might be more of them around."

"They can come with us," Tirzah said.

As they continued along the hallway, a large contingent of palace guards came rushing around the corner with several other men in military uniform.

"You can take them," the guard said pointing to the men in red. "They are disarmed."

Things became a bit chaotic after that, so Tirzah Lin decided to intervene on behalf of the frightened women and walk towards them slowly, holding out his empty hands. "My name is Tirzah Lin. I am a friend of the prince. Come with me," he said in their own language. "I will take you somewhere safe. The prince is waiting for us."

The woman looked at the girl, who shrugged her shoulders. "Very well. After what you just did, I believe I can trust you."

"Perhaps you could tell me which door leads to the council chamber."

The woman turned back towards the action at the end of the hall for a moment and watched the scuffle as the palace guards took custody of the five intruders. "It's the last door, down there."

It's safe to come out now, Tirzah sent to Prince Kazim.

The council chamber door opened, and the prince poked his head out.

"Uncle Kazim!" the girl ran towards him and threw her arms around him. He freed himself from her grasp and planted a kiss on her forehead. "Some horrible men came into our suite and tried to take us away. They were very mean and kept calling us witches. Where's Aunt Lemaya?"

"I'm here," Lemaya said as she joined the prince.

"Come in," the prince said. "Everyone, you too," he said to the highest-ranking guard and soldier, which appeared to be a sergeant and a captain, respectively.

Once inside, Prince Kazim told them to leave the door open. "I need a report from you so that we can plan our next move. Captain?"

"I believe many of the invaders are hiding throughout the palace," the captain said. "We've taken some of them and sent them to the dungeons, but my impression was that there were many more. What do you think, sergeant?"

"I'm wondering if they may be retreating or trying to. We need to be in contact with the other guards and soldiers on the lower levels."

"It looks as if we'll have to go floor by floor routing them out," the prince said. "We are fortunate to have with us today two Albasinian defenders. These men have many skills that we can take advantage of, especially in finding where they are." He extended his hand to Barengush and Vertan, "And also ...," he stopped talking and appeared to be listening.

They're outside the door trying to break in ... It was Farah.

"We must help them," Tirzah said. "Is it all right if I take one of our defenders?"

"Of course," Prince Kazim relied. "You can take some of the guards outside as well, Go now, hurry!"

Tirzah beckoned to Barengush. "Come with me." They both rushed out to the hallway, followed by the prince who ordered three of the palace guards to go with them.

"What's happened?" Barengush asked as they rushed down the hall.

"They're attacking our suite."

Barengush pushed ahead and disappeared around the corner. *I hope he's careful,* Tirzah thought, *we don't want to kill everyone.*

Rounding the corner, they saw the red uniforms of the witch hunters crowding the door to the salon, using a bronze statue as a battering ram. The three guards drew their swords and rushed forward, but before they could reach, them, Barengush let go of a power blast and destroyed the statue. He then drew his sword and faced the rebels, holding out his left hand as if casting a spell. They stood, frozen in place. By the time Tirzah reached them, the guards had taken them into custody and were hauling them off.

"That was spectacular," Tirzah said. "Not a drop of blood spilled."

"But do you think it will make any difference to them? It will probably make them more determined," Barengush said.

It's safe now, Tirzah sent to Farida. You can open the door to let us in if you can get it open. It's taken quite a battering.

Farah unlocked the door but couldn't open it. "Stand back, Farah!" Barengush called. He put his shoulder against the door and gave it two hard pushes. When it flew open, Farah was so pleased to be free, she rushed to Tirzah and hugged him, then pulled away, her face red.

"I'm sorry," she said.

It was my pleasure, he sent.

It took the rest of the day to clear all the witch-hunting rebels from the palace and into the dungeons. The task was made more difficult by having to sort out all the palace guards who had sided with them, because they

Felindra

"What are we going to do now?" Felindra asked at a late supper that evening.

"Now that Prince Kazim has invited us to his investiture as the new Shah, it would be discourteous for us to leave until that has taken place," Tirzah said.

"But don't they have to entomb the old Shah first?" Farah asked.

"Yes, there's that too. The internment will be tomorrow. It's their custom to have their dead entombed within three days."

"What about lying-in-state?" Vertan asked.

"Kazim has decided to forgo that because the old man was so unpopular with the people and he doesn't want to give them an excuse to demonstrate."

"I hope they've removed all the bodies from the walls," Felindra said.

"They have," Tirzah replied. "It's one of the first things he put in motion when he returned to the palace from his meeting with Vertan and Barengush. Another good piece of news is that he's going to set all the prisoners accused of witchery free and try to compensate the families persecuted in the witch-hunts, out of the royal treasury."

"That sounds like a step in the right direction," Farah said. "It's too bad he can't abolish witch-hunts altogether."

"He has a lot of things that need changing, but he needs the council's approval before he can change laws. The problem is that he's up against some very fanatical clerics. They appeal to lower classes and the less educated whom they stir up into mobs if they are displeased with anything the rulers put in motion. They don't have any official power; their power is in arousing the populace to revolt to get their way."

"You seem to know a lot about this," Farah said.

"Knowing the language helps," he replied. "It's amazing what you can find out from casual conversations."

"Do you think we should stay for a while?" Sastin said.

"I do," Tirzah replied.

"I hear there is going to be a royal wedding," Rasamé said. "Do you think we will stay for that, too?"

"It doesn't matter to me," Tirzah said "It's our Albasinian friends I'm concerned about. They've been away from home for more than a sun cycle, and I know one of them has an urgent reason to return home." He smiled at Felindra.

"I can't go back looking like this," Felindra interjected. "They'll think I've been in a famine, or a dungeon."

"You were actually below the dungeons, but we'll get you back into shape," Sastin said. "Resting here for a while could make all the difference."

"I suppose so," she said, then her face brightened up. "Do you think they'd let me work in the stables?"

"When you're strong enough," Rasamé said. "You'd better listen to your healers."

"Speaking of Albasiny, has anyone been in touch with them recently?" Felindra asked.

"Not in the last few days," Farah replied. "Do you want me to try now?"

19 – The Prince Makes Changes
Felindra

The following day, as they were breaking their fast, the Albasinians discussed their plans. "Ashavan told me that the queen is very concerned about our continued absence," Farah said.

"It's not as if we are late intentionally," Vertan protested. "I'd much rather be in Valkonen than what we've been through the last few moons."

"I know," Farah responded. "But, nevertheless, she is concerned. She's been thinking of sending a naval ship to bring us home." Farah turned to Tirzah, "What is the name of that port you told us about? If our queen did decide to send a ship, they'd need to know where to go."

"It's called Zimnyaya-gavan," he replied.

"Is it a big port?" Felindra asked.

"It's bigger than Kirkur. It's the major port on the north coast of Continent of Utrea."

"I'll let Ashavan know," Farah said.

Felindra finished her fruit bowl and exchanged it for some crisp bread and soft cheese. "What else did you find out?" she asked.

"Your parents are worried about you—both your and Vertan's mother—and have contacted the Monasteries several times. Lord Varan is also extremely anxious, the duke, too."

"What did you tell them?" Felindra asked.

"Ashavan says they are worrying about why we are taking so long. I said we have been traveling and it's a long journey. I played down the illnesses and injuries, just saying you and Sastin had caught a local disease, but you have recovered now and are resting."

"Good," Felindra said. "Can you send a message to Varan? Just tell him I have been unwell and am recuperating—say it was nothing serious—and tell him I'm thinking of him."

A knock at the door interrupted them. A palace guard entered and addressed Tirzah Lin. Tirzah made a response and the guard went outside. Then Tirzah told the others what had been said. "The prince wants to see us in the council chamber."

"All of us?" Felindra asked.

"That's what he said. I suspect he has some work for us."

The women went to their rooms to don veils before they set out for the meeting. When they arrived at the council chamber, several other people were there in addition to Prince Kazim and Princess Lemaya.

"Come in and sit down," the prince welcomed them. "Because you don't all know our language, we will talk in Trade language. First, let me introduce the others. This lady is Minia. She has been acting as the matron of my father's harem. The two ladies sitting next to Princess Lemaya are her sister, Lady Donya, and Donya's daughter, Azita, and the man on my left is Lord Omid. Lord Omid is the chairman of the Privy Council. And you all know the Grand Vizier." The Vizier, who was standing back and to the left of the prince, bowed his head to them.

The prince looked around the table. "We have many problems that need to be dealt with and we believe that you have certain abilities that might help us to find solutions."

No one answered, but they ducked their heads in respect and waited for him to continue.

"First the ladies. We have an important task for you if you are willing to do it. I'm sure you will agree that the harem is an abomination and must be closed. What I'd like you to do is go up there with Lady Minia and try to find a way to help those poor girls. We've already sent some decent clothing for them, but they must be relocated. We need to find out where they are from and if their families will accept them back. If not, positions must be found for them—we'll keep as many as we can as servants if they are willing to stay. All I want you to do is help them with any health problems they may have, see that they are fed, and find out where they are from and if they can go back. How does that sound?"

"Very good," Felindra said. "Is there a safe place they can go while they are waiting to be placed?"

"Yes. Knowing they probably don't want to stay in that place, we are cleaning out a vacant area in the Amber tower. It used to hold the old slave quarters and has all the facilities necessary—kitchen, bathing, heating and storage, but our carpenters are going to divide the open spaces into rooms so that they will have some privacy. Lady Minia will lead you. Are you ready to get started?"

The women stood up and bowed to the prince. "Not you, princess," He said to Azita. I need you to help me."

Azita's eyes lit up when she heard that. She looked at her mother, who smiled and nodded.

"We don't want her to see the scene of the old Shah's depravity," Lemaya said when they were out of the room.

"Besides that, she'll feel she is doing something important, working with the prince."

"Are any of the girls with child?" Lemaya asked Minia on the way up to the harem.

"No, thank the Great Spirit. He was ... how can I put this ...? not capable of...."

Probably because he was too fat, Rasamé thought. "Does that mean that some of the girls are still virgins?"

"Technically yes, they are, but that won't save them from abuse when people learn where they've been." Minia replied.

Felindra shuddered when they reach the staircase up to the harem and she thought about how close she'd come. The eunuchs were still there, although they were no longer armed.

"Blessed day, Jonah, blessed day, Bland," Minia greeted them. "Any problems?"

"Blessed day, mistress." Jonah shook his head. "Only some guards sniffing around, but we soon set them on their way. The eunuch who answered had a soft, gentle voice, which belied his muscular build.

When they were out of earshot, Felindra edged closer to Minia, and asked her, "They seem different from other men; why is that?"

"They are men who were castrated when they were little boys. It makes them ideal protectors of women. They can't molest them."

"Oh," Felindra said, A whole series of horrifying scenarios ran through her mind. "Where do the boys come from?"

"Many places, some are orphans, others kidnapped—usually from outlying areas—some are even sold to the slavers by their parents."

"That is so horrible. Those poor boys. Are they all slaves now?"

"I'm afraid so."

Minia pursed her lips and frowned as she stood looking around at the girls and the room in general. "You know, this is the first time I've seen this as the awful place it really is. It's so completely cheerless and drab, almost lifeless, despite all the decorations. I've been here so long, I've grown used to it, or made myself blind to the reality."

"You're right about it being dreary," Farah said. "It is depressing, and these girls seem to have no life in them."

"I'm going to talk to them," Minia said. She walked into the center of the room. "Girls, before I tell you the good news, is everybody here?" She looked around and saw three girls were missing. "Olen, would you and Berta go and find the rest of the girls?"

The other women of the team started looking around at the facilities, smiling and greeting the girls as they passed. "Look at these poor girls," Donya said. "Most of them are younger than Azita. What a horrible monster that man was." She wiped a tear from the corner of her eye. "I'm thankful Kazim kept her away."

When the other girls returned with the three that were missing, Minia asked them to listen while she told them the news and explained what was going to happen. "First, the old Shah has passed on and Prince Kazim will be the next Shah. He has ordered that you be set free and this place closed." Some of the girls sat up straighter, some whispered to their neighbors, and a few even smiled. It was as if they'd suddenly come to life.

"We have brought you new clothes. After you have changed, we are going to interview you—ask you some questions—so that we can find out where you may go when you are freed." She turned and pointed to some bundles on the floor by the back wall. "Those are the

155

clothes. "These ladies will help you unpack and sort them out. But before you go, is there anyone who needs a healer?"

The three girls who had been out of the room stood up. "This lady is Sister Rasamé. She is a healer, the one next to her is her helper." She pointed to Farah. "Go with them to the sick room and they will find out how best to help you,"

"Can we get some clothes first please, matron?" a tall scrawny girl asked.

The other members of the prince's team were already unpacking the garments and separating them into bundles of complete sets: undergarments, tunic, and veil.

"Go ahead," Minia said, picking out a dozen girls. She watched them move towards the clothing. "The rest of you wait until they are finished," she called to them. "If any of you needs to bathe, now is the time."

Rasamé

The only visible sign of illness was that the three sick girls seemed lethargic. Each girl was given a bundle before following Rasamé and Farah. "If it is permitted, I might be able to help by reading them," Farah said as they entered the side corridor. "This place is so gloomy, it would make anyone sick," she added.

"This is where they put me and Felindra when they brought us here." Rasamé pointed to one of the curtained alcoves. "And this is probably where he departed from this world," she added, pointing out some stains and deep scratches on the wall.

"Where are we going?" Rasamé asked the girls.

"There," The tall girl pointed to a wider opening with the curtains drawn back.

It wasn't much of a healing center. There were three raised cots and a high bench with some implements and half-filled jars without any notations to identify the contents.

"Where can I get some water?" Rasamé asked.

One of the smaller girls looked outside the curtains and pointed to a stone trough with a pipe over it. There were several buckets on the floor under the trough. "Do you want to help me?" she asked Farah. "These girls need to get washed before they put on clean clothes. Sit here and wait for us," she told the girls. "And don't touch the clean clothes."

They were like frightened children, she thought. I suppose that's what most of them are.

When they returned with the water, the three girls were sitting on the cots, a bundle of clothes, still wrapped, beside each one. "Now, time to get washed." They placed a bucket on the floor beside each one and looked around for cloths and soap. Luckily, there was a pile of cloths on the bench along with a jar of soap. "There. Now get those rags off and wash yourselves." Two of the girls did as she asked, but the third one, the smallest and probably the youngest, started to cry. She was the one who looked sickest of the three. Her cheeks were crimson, and her eyes inflamed and encrusted with pus, although the rest of her skin was very pale. She breathed through her mouth, making a wheezing sound in her throat.

"Let me help you, little sister," Rasamé offered. "I'm Rasamé. What's your name?"

"Bonda," she said nasally.

"Bonda, that's a pretty name."

"No, like this." She pursed her lips slightly and said the name again.

"Vonda?" the girl nodded and almost smiled.

She lay listlessly as Rasamé took off her clothes and dipped a clean rag in the water to wash her emaciated little body. She looked like a child of no more than ten years. "How many years do you have, Vonda? The girl held up the fingers of both hands and then two fingers. "Twelve? You only have twelve years?"

The little girl nodded, tears running down her face. Rasamé finished drying her and helped her don the undergarments. She took the bucket of water outside the door and came back. "I'm a healer," she said. "I am going to see if I can find out why you are feeling badly." The girl was now lying back on the cot with her eyes closed. "When did you first start to feel bad?"

No answer. She was asleep. *Poor child; let her sleep for a while*, she thought, picking up a thin blanket to cover her.

"How is she?" Farah asked.

"She has some sort of infection in her breathing passages. It won't hurt her to sleep for a while. I can give her medicine when she wakes up. How about the other two?"

"They're frightened," Farah replied. "They don't know what is going to happen to them and they don't feel well."

"Let's have a look." She went to the smaller girl first. She looked better in the clean clothing, but she was still lethargic. "Would you monitor her while I ask her some questions?" Rasamé sat on the edge of the cot beside the girl. "My name is Rasamé; I'm a healer" she started. "What is your name?"

"Pam," the girl said meekly.

"Tell me, Pam, do you have pain?" The girl nodded and squirmed. "Where does it hurt."

158

Pam pointed down towards her lap. "May I look at it?" The girl shrugged. "All right, lie down. I promise I won't hurt you." Rasamé was shocked by what she saw. The entire pelvic area was bruised and inflamed. "How did this happen?" She asked.

Pam shook her head. "I don't know."

"Did *he* do this?"

She nodded and started to cry.

"I'm sorry you've had to suffer like this, but you are going to be taken care of by some good people. Nobody will be allowed to hurt you again. Right now, I am going to put on some salve to help heal the damage." She used the application of salve to cover the deeper healing she was doing mentally to repair the damage. "There you are, does that feel better?"

Pam nodded, although she was still downcast.

"Rest for a while and when you feel like it, you can get up and walk around."

What do you think? She sent to Farah.

If that monster were not already dead, I'd kill him myself, Farah replied. Unable to perform the act himself, he poked her with implements.

Rasamé drew in a sharp breath through her teeth and shook her head.

The tall girl turned out to be a boy, recently castrated. His name was Radnim and he'd been a shepherd boy from the hill country outside the city. He'd been kidnapped while tending his flock by some men he described as bandits and brought to the palace. He had thirteen years when this happened a few months earlier. He didn't know why he had been put in the harem, although the former Shah had visited him a couple of times and fondled him, alongside one of the girls. He was now suffering from an

159

infection of the incision area. He was also deeply depressed and had thought of killing himself if he could find a way.

"There's nothing one can do to mend a broken soul," Rasamé said after they'd left the sick room. "That must be the ultimate crime. There should be a special place for such monsters."

"There is," Farah said. "Oblivion. They will never enter the halls of light."

They returned to the common room and found the other women interviewing the girls, making notes on each person in hopes of being able to place them somewhere they would be accepted and treated kindly.

"How many are left to interview?" Farah asked Princess Lemaya.

"All those on that side." She pointed to five girls sitting on chairs to her left. "We've done quite well, only five to go, but this is the most harrowing thing I've ever experienced. What these girls have suffered is soul-destroying. I doubt if any of them will ever be able to lead a normal life again."

A bell rang, and the girls stood up and started towards another room opening off the common room. They gasped and rushed forward when they saw what was spread on the tables, but the matron was there ahead of them to keep them in order.

"Be calm, girls. You will all get your share. As a gesture of his good will, Prince Kazim has ordered this meal for you from his own kitchens. Please sit down at the tables and help yourselves, but don't rush. There is enough for everyone." She beckoned the prince's team to join in the feast at a smaller table at the end of the room.

After the meal was over and the interviews were completed, they accompanied the girls to their new quarters in a different wing. It was two floors lower and across a courtyard. Rasamé noticed how the girls shaded their eyes as they left the building and it occurred to her for the first time that the reason for the harem being so drab was its lack of windows.

The prince had put Minia in charge of the girls' rehabilitation. She was an appropriate choice because she could empathize with their plight, having been a harem slave herself until her predecessor disappeared suddenly. She was one of the unfortunate women who had conceived a child. This was several years earlier, before the Shah's virility had declined. She never knew what became of her son; he was taken from her the moment he was born. She hadn't even been given the opportunity to hold him. "They probably killed him," she said. "*He* wouldn't have wanted any other claims against his throne."

When they returned to the council chamber, they reviewed their findings. Princess Lemaya took the chair and led the discussion.

"Out of the twenty-three girls and one boy in the harem, nine had less than fifteen years—one had only twelve years—eleven had less than nineteen years, and the rest had around twenty years." She flipped over another page filled with calculations. "This is where we come to the most shocking part—if anything could be more shocking than their ages—eleven of these girls were sold to the palace by members of their own families, usually an older male, father, brother, or uncle, although two were sold by their destitute mothers to provide for their other children. Two were claimed for default on debts and sold to the palace, three of the girls were the children of slaves, and the rest were kidnapped by bandits." She put the papers down and wiped her forehead. She looked at the faces of the women at the table, and Sastin, who had joined them. "This is a very harrowing experience. I don't know about you, but it makes me feel dirty."

"I understand what you mean," Farah said. "Even though I was not trying to listen to their minds, I couldn't avoid feeling their misery. Their most dominant sensation was intense shame."

"Yes, I can vouch for that," Minia said. "It grinds away at you, just below the surface of your mind. It takes away your self-respect and makes you hate yourself. It's something that will always haunt these girls for the rest of their lives. You feel like something not quite human, different from everybody else."

"You sound like an educated person," the princess said. "Would you like to tell us your story; please say no if you don't wish to."

"One of the things I've learned from life is that holding on to bad things, they fester and become worse. It's better to let them go. I lived in a small village about forty leagues from here, over near the border with Eleria. I taught the little children of the village. My father had taught me to read and calculate so that I could help with his business records. One day when I had thirteen years, a gang of outlaws attacked the village. They set fire to the wooden houses and killed some of the men who tried to resist. I tried to hide the children in a cave, but they found us because the little ones couldn't keep silent; they were too frightened. They bundled all of us, the children, some women and a few younger men, into one of the farm wagons, herded us like livestock. And I ended up here."

"What happened to your father?" Felindra asked.

"They killed him, and my mother who was hiding under the stairs." Minia sighed and started picking non-existent crumbs from the table.

"How do you plan to get them new homes?" Rasamé asked.

"I'm going to visit the Little Sisters of Alba on the morrow and see if they can give us any help," Lemaya replied. "I can take two of you with me if you'd like. It would be too much of a burden on them if I took more."

The friends looked at one another, trying to decide who should go. "I think Brother Tirzah should go," Felindra said.

"Thank you, Felindra. I'd be delighted. Who wants to come with us? How about Sister Farah?" Farah smiled at him and nodded.

"What does this organization do?" Rasamé asked.

"Mostly, they help the poor and distressed. Kazim and I have been talking about funding them so that they can expand their headquarters, and they may need more staff. I'm hoping that they can take some of our girls and help us place others in the community. We may be able to find work for some of them here in the palace." She looked around the table. "I can see you are getting tired, so, if there are no more questions or comments, shall we take a break?"

20 – Celebrations

Felindra

The ceremonial of the old Shah's internment was brief and sparsely attended. Very few noble families turned up for the event, although there were quite a few commoners who spent most of their time together scowling balefully at the prince and princess, and their foreign guests, or muttering comments to one another while eyeing them.

"What can you sense about those people?" Felindra murmured to Farah.

"One thing I'm sure of is that they don't like the prince and princess, or us, and they are rabidly against witchcraft. I wouldn't be surprised if they are the leaders of the anti-witch movement. I hope Prince Kazim is keeping a watch on them."

The High Priest led his attendants through the service, which comprised circling the catafalque with much genuflecting and chanting of ritual phrases. When that part was over, he removed the covers from the body and sprinkled it with fragrant oil, mumbling more words as he walked around it. Then he invited the congregation to come and bid him farewell, although not everyone; apparently women were spared that unpleasant task. Even some of the men, including Tirzah Lin and the Albasinians, declined the opportunity and stood shuffling uncomfortably. They'd done their duty and now wanted to be away.

Once the ceremonials were finished, eight men came in with poles to support the boards on which the body lay and carried it out to a high-walled courtyard behind the temple. A raised framework of wooden poles stood in the center of the courtyard above a pile of logs and kindling. The porters, with great difficulty, carried the old Shah's body up a stairway and placed it in the frame. After descending to the ground, they rolled the portable stairs away and proceeded to light the kindling around the pyre.

I don't want to see this, Felindra sent.

We don't have to stay for long; just until the fire is going. It would be discourteous to leave before the prince, Tirzah Lin replied.

Once Prince Kazim was sure the fire was burning, he took Lemaya's arm and returned to the temple. Most of the other attendees followed him, leaving only the anti-witchcraft contingent behind.

"I wonder why they want to stay," Felindra murmured.

"It could be that they are the only ones mourning his loss," Tirzah Lin replied. "They probably profited greatly during his reign."

"That must be why they hate the prince," Rasamé commented. "Kazim won't allow them to continue their activities."

***

The days passed slowly for them, waiting for the investiture. Sastin was fully recovered from his illness, but Felindra recovered slowly. The head injury was taking time to heal, leaving her often tired and headachy, but she made the best of her time when she had the energy. She had been granted permission to do the one thing she'd been longing for, to visit the stables and spend time with the horses. She also discovered that there was an extensive farm attached to the rear wall of the palace compound, part of which was devoted to raising livestock.

That was another place she liked to visit. Visiting the pigs and fowl was a nostalgic reminder of time she'd spent in the islands of Moto Ataahua.

She was accompanied by guards everywhere she went, outside of their suites. The next time she had a chance to talk to the prince, she asked him why.

"You never know where they'll strike," Prince Kazim replied. "They could be all around us and we wouldn't know it until they struck. It's like trying to separate good rats from bad ones. They all look alike and have the same habits." He sighed and rubbed his forehead. "Two days ago, we found the mutilated body of a kitchen maid in an unused stairwell."

He stood up to leave but thought of something else. "I am impressed with your ability to commune with animals. May I ask something?" Felindra nodded. "What do you talk about with them?"

Felindra smiled. "Oh, I ask them how they are feeling … mostly I put images in their minds. I can often tell if they are unhappy or in pain and sometimes I can help them get better."

"Do you mean healing?"

"Not exactly. For example, if a cow or a horse had stomach pain, I could feel what sort of pain it has, or ask what it had been eating, and then warn it not to eat that particular plant again; if it's something more serious, I could help an animal healer examine it and tell him where it hurts and how."

"I'm even more impressed now," the prince said. "I have to go. It's been a pleasure talking with you, Sister Felindra."

The Albasinians spent a lot of time walking in the palace gardens, talking about home and the forthcoming journey.

"Let's hope we don't have any more trouble," Felindra said on one occasion.

One time, Farah managed to arrange a three-way conversation between Felindra and Varan. Ashavan linked Varan with Farah who completed the circle by linking them with Felindra. At first, she had been unable to think of anything to say, although Varan had showered her with questions. She'd become more animated, as consciousness of other listeners faded, especially when she started talking about their travels, playing down the various disasters they'd encountered.

Vertan and Barengush had been working with the palace, using their gifts to flush out any remaining witch hunters. They'd managed to uncover three, one of them a woman who worked in the staff kitchen. All three had been relegated to the dungeons to await trials. Prince Kazim said there would be no more arbitrary executions without trials and witnesses. He'd also delegated senior guards and his legal advisors to survey the prisoners in the dungeons from his father's time and release any who hadn't committed serious crimes. About half the prisoners questioned had been jailed because they'd upset the Shah in some trivial way: a page who'd accidentally spilt some wine near the Shah's booted foot, a cook who had given him roasted goose for his dinner instead of duck, a seamstress who'd forgotten to remove a pin from one of his tunics when she mended it. And there were also several girls from the harem that had either failed to please him, or with whom he'd become bored.

The palace was abuzz with activity as preparations were made for the investiture of the new Shah. Kazim had become Shah the moment the former Shah's body had been cremated and the ashes examined by the council of advisors to witness he was truly gone; the investiture was merely a ceremony formalizing this fact.

So many guests had been invited, mostly nobles and clerics from outside the city, that rooms had to be cleaned and made ready for their arrival. There was a complicated process for assigning rooms as enmities between various nobles, and their ranking, had to be considered when assigning them. The kitchens were busy night and day preparing the massive amounts of food that would be needed to feed the guests.

Felindra and her group were invited to select new clothes from the palace wardrobes for the occasion. She was mortified when they couldn't find anything small enough to fit her and she'd had to choose something from the older children's wardrobe. There was nothing plain available in any of these wardrobes; everything was ceremonial in brilliant colors and highly ornamented with bead work, gold thread trim, embroidery and lace. The favorite color in Goa Sun seemed to be turquoise.

"I'm going to look like Ashavan in this outfit," Barengush complained. His outfit consisted of black knee-length britches with matching stockings and boots, and a turquoise satin tunic embroidered in gold thread, with a black and orange cape.

"You could do worse," Felindra replied with a grin. "Ashavan is one of the best-dressed men I know, and the nicest."

"I'm glad my friends won't be there to see me dressed up like this," he replied

"Everyone will be wearing similar clothes," Farah added. "No one will even notice what you're wearing; it's your fair hair that will make you stand out."

"How would you like to be me?" Felindra said. "I have to wear children's clothes." She would be wearing long, cream satin culottes with a knee-length filmy tunic in lace-trimmed turquoise silk and a long cream mantle also made of a filmy material with gold trim.

"You really must gain some weight now that you're feeling better," Sastin said.

When the day finally arrived, everyone was woken at dawn. After breaking their fasts, a couple of women helped them dress in their ceremonial garments, then another woman came in and explained the protocol.

"The men in your party will be travelling separately, as all non-familial guests do; the child will ride with the women. You will be taken to your carriage and seated. The procession to the High Temple will take you through the main thoroughfares of the city. You must keep your veils in place at all times and do not draw attention to yourselves. Now that you are dressed, I'll send someone to take you to the north exit, where you wait for your carriage to arrive."

"What fun," Rasamé said when the woman was gone. "Let's go and see what's happening." She went out on the balcony and looked at the crowd of nobles and their families milling around in the garden below. "They must have different arrangements for the upper class," she commented. "This is the south side of the building."

"Let me see." Zanda held his arms out for her to pick him up.

They all stood along the balcony wall, watching the nobles enter their carriages and join the lineup leading to the gate. Once all the carriages were filled, they saw the Shah and Princess Lemaya climb into a large open, elaborately-decorated carriage, and drive past the others, waving to the nobles as they passed.

A knock on the door alerted them and they trooped back inside. "Hurry, it's time to go," a young man in palace uniform said.

Rasamé picked up Zanda, and they all rushed to the stairs. As Rasamé had suspected, they were being treated differently. This staircase was narrower and less decorative than the others. When they reached the yard, they saw their menfolk were on horseback. "Why couldn't we go on horses?" Felindra grumbled as she mounted the steps into the carriage, noting it was almost the same as the one in which they'd arrived. This time, Rasamé and Zanda had the front seat.

"We're here to protect you, so that any hostiles in the crowd cannot molest you." Tirzah informed the women.

Their carriage, drawn by two black horses, exited the palace grounds and hastened to catch up with the rest of the parade. The people in the crowd were joyous, shouting and singing, waving pennants and ringing little bells as the royal coach passed. The sun was barely at midpoint between dawn and midday and the air was starting to warm up after a chilly night.

"We must remember it's not summer anymore," Farah said. "I wish there were some lap-robes we could use."

"You look cold," Tirzah Lin said. He was riding his horse close to her side of the carriage.

Farah nodded. "Could you ask the driver if there is anything to keep us warm?"

Tirzah Lin asked and turned back with the information. "He said there are some wraps in the boxes under the seats."

Rasamé pulled out a wrap. "Good, they're clean," she said. She shook it out and put it round her shoulders.

Barengush was riding on Felindra's side of the carriage. "What took you so long to come down to the yard?"

"They told us to wait in our suite for someone to show us the way," she replied. "No one came until that man realized we hadn't arrived and came to get us."

"Yes, we had to ask where you were. I wonder why no one came. Maybe someone doesn't like us."

The route to the High Temple took them down through the city on a wide avenue lined with cheering crowds. The people lining the road scattered red and gold autumn leaves on the ground in front of the royal carriage. They turned east around a small circular park and proceeded up another avenue where the temple dominated the summit.

The prince and princess and the other guests had already entered the temple by the time Felindra and her group arrived. They had given the carriage and horses to attendants and went inside to see where they were supposed to sit or stand. One of the temple officials led them to a row of seats at the very back of the temple. The seats were separated in the middle by a low barrier, the women were to sit on the left and the men on the right. Felindra and Vertan exchanged smiles and shrugs when they were directed to the separated benches.

Felindra could see nothing of what was happening at the front of the temple, and could understand little of what was said, so she spent her time exploring the temple's interior décor. A huge dome covered the middle of the ceiling with colored glass panes to let in light and ornate borders of red and gold. The rest of the ceiling had flat panels painted with scenes which she assumed illustrated the history of their religion. Rows of white marble pillars ran down either side supporting the roof. These were ornamented with stripes of azure and gold, real gold by the way it glowed. Even the floors were decorated with panels of abstract mosaic patterns in multi-colored tesserae. It was very beautiful, but not as restful as she would have expected for a house of the Light.

Her attention was suddenly caught by the surrounding guests rising to their feet and starting to chant something, after which, all the men shouted in unison and clapped their hands three times. After that, the congregation sang something joyful with military overtones. She looked down the row towards Tirzah and saw he was smiling. He was probably the only one who understood what was happening. Rather than sitting down again, the congregation turned to face the center aisle.

When some music played on flute-like instruments accompanied by slow drumming started, all heads turned towards the front. After several heartbeats, the new Shah appeared with a military officer on one side and a high cleric on the other. Princess Lemaya, accompanied by two lady attendants, followed a few steps behind them. Felindra noticed that Kazim was now wearing a red tunic with gold ornamentation, whereas before he left the palace, he'd been wearing blue. His headcover was now white, held in place by a gold coronet studded with gemstones.

Vertan, who was sitting closest to the barrier, caught her attention as the people began to file out. "Tirzah said we'd best wait until everyone else has left."

It took a while for all the guests to leave, after which, a parade of richly dressed clerics followed. One of them leaned towards Tirzah Lin and said something, which led him to beckon the others. They followed the clerics from the building and looked around for their horses and carriage, but the was no sign of them. Tirzah went over to talk to one of the temple guards who pointed him to the side of the building.

"I wonder if everyone else was treated like this," Barengush complained,

"It's not deliberate, I'm sure," Tirzah said. "I think they don't know what to do with us or whether we are here as servants or guests."

The sun was high in the sky by the time they left the temple, making the air warm enough to leave off the covers. They trailed the procession back to the palace as the celebrants were dispersing, leaving behind a clutter of trampled leaves and paper food wrapping.

As they approached the palace, they saw that the outer walls had been repaired and painted sky blue, a tremendous improvement over the way it had looked the last time they'd come this way. This time, the drivers stopped at the main entrance of the palace where two footmen gave them directions to their own suites.

"Someone will come for us when it is time to go to the banqueting hall. You will have time to freshen up if necessary," Tirzah told them.

"I hope they don't forget us this time," Rasamé said once they were out of hearing.

"If they don't come, does anyone know the way?" Felindra asked.

"I can find it," Tirzah said. "But let's not panic too soon. I'm sure someone will come."

Felindra and the other women went into their suite, washed their hands and faces, and made sure their costumes were in good shape. Zanda had fallen asleep in his mother's arms on the way back to the palace, so she laid him down in his cot and covered him with a blanket.

When the attendant came to take them to the banqueting hall, Rasamé showed him to her and asked as best she could to have someone watch over him. She knew he would be cranky if she woke him now and she didn't want him to make a scene in front of all the distinguished guests.

The woman smiled and nodded, pointing to herself. "I will take care of him. I will bring him some food."

The Shah and Princess Lemaya were seated on a dais at one end of the room, Lemaya's sister, Donya and her daughter were sitting on the left of the royal couple along with two older women with grey hair peeking out of their veils.

On the Shah's right sat a senior cleric and two other men, one much older than the other.

They must be the families, Felindra thought. The old man with the scowling face is probably Lemaya's father.

All the tables in the body of the hall faced the dais with the guests sitting on the facing side only. After bowing to the royal hosts, Felindra and her group took their seats about halfway from the back on the left side.

Felindra saw the grumpy-looking man lean across and ask the Shah something, watching them as he did so. The man appeared not to like the answer he got.

The four men in her group were seated at one end of the table and the women at the other. With Farah and Tirzah in the middle, like elder relatives, keeping the children apart.

The food was magnificent and Fclindra managed to consume more in one sitting than she had in months. "Sastin said I should gain some weight," she said to her neighbor, Rasamé. "So I'm going to make the best of this feast."

21 – Celebration and Departure
Felindra

Felindra and Rasamé were walking in one of the palace gardens with Sastin, discussing healing, their gifts, and the future, when they were intercepted by a page with a message for them. Fortunately, it was a written message in Trade language, or they might not have been able to read it; the symbols used in Goa Sun were quite different from those of Albasiny.

They sat down on a shaded bench while Felindra opened it. "What is it?" Rasamé asked.

"It is an invitation for all of us to join the Shah and Princes Lemaya for a private supper this evening."

"I'm surprised he has time with all these guests to entertain," Sastin said.

"Maybe he wants to talk about our departure," Felindra said. "We'll find out this evening, I suppose."

When they reached the Shah's private dining room, Felindra saw several other people there. She recognized Lady Donya and her daughter Azita. The others were the people who had sat on the dais at the investiture feast, all but the cleric.

They bowed to Shah Kazim and then to the other guests. "Please be seated," Kazim said. "Then I will introduce you to everyone."

Noticing that the women were all sitting on the same side of the table on the left of Kazim, Rasamé led the two women to that side and seated herself next to the elderly woman. The woman turned and smiled at them as they sat down. The men took seats opposite them, Tirzah sitting next to the younger man.

Kazim said something to Lemaya, who was sitting next to him and she stood up. Nobody else stood so they all remained seated. "Welcome, friends," she said in Trade. "Everyone at this table tonight, apart from our visitors, is a member of my family. The first gentleman is my lord father, Duke Nurghaly of Tindel."

The duke gave a cursory nod of his head but, by the compression of his lips, they could see he didn't look upon them favorably. She continued to introduce the other members of her family, her sister's husband, her mother and her brother. None of them looked as unimpressed as the Duke; the other two men looked puzzled, but the women smiled.

After introductions were complete, Shah Kazim tried to start a conversation. "One of the reasons I wanted to introduce you to our foreign guests is because of the trade interests of your family. Albasiny is well known in the trading community as honest and reliable trading partners and I thought you might like to meet some of them."

"Humph," was the duke's response, illustrated by his sour expression.

"What sort of goods does your nation export?" the son-in-law asked.

The six Albasinians looked at one another. *What do we export?* Felindra sent.

"Mostly manufactured goods," Sastin said. "Things like high quality pottery, medicines, leather goods, glassware, cloth, paper, and wine."

"Hmm," the son-in-law responded. "That's interesting. I've heard from other traders that your goods are excellent quality, and the trading is fair."

He hesitated and looked at his father-in-law who was scowling.

"Witches," the duke muttered.

As the supper continued, the Shah attempted to lead conversation into less controversial subjects, but it didn't seem to matter to the duke. He managed to have an objection to everything brought up, escaped slaves, women travelling with non-familial men, women being independent and having careers. As soon as everyone had finished eating, the Shah stood, looking quite crestfallen, although trying to put on a good face, as he indicated it was over and wished everyone a good night.

As they were returning to their suites, Lemaya caught up with them, indicating that they should continue walking "I'm afraid that didn't go off as well as I'd hoped it would. Poor Kazim is very embarrassed by my father's attitude. I'm so sorry to put you through that. He's been like that ever since my elder brother was killed. He blames it all on magic and that's why he is so against what he calls witchcraft."

"What happened to your brother?" Rasamé asked, once they were inside the suite. When she noticed her brother frowning, Rasame added, "Forgive me, my lady. I didn't mean to pry into something personal."

"It's all right; it was I who brought it up. Before I continue, I should tell you that everyone in my family is gifted in some way. We all inherited it from our mother. Rahim's gift was ... I don't know the proper name for it, but he could do things with rocks and heavy things," she hesitated and looked at them.

"I have a gift like that," Barengush said. "It's related to the manipulation of elements like air, power, and water. We don't have a special name for it except to call it elemental powers."

"Thank you, Barengush" the princess said. "Rahim was trying to move some rocks—he was very young and wanted to impress his friends—he smashed one of the rocks, but that made all the others come loose and one fell on him. It broke father's heart. He was the son and heir. From that day, he won't allow any magic to be used on our lands, and he forbade all of us from using it, even mother."

"Did you have training in the use of magic?" Tirzah asked.

"We did at first until Rahim's accident. We had a very nice teacher from Eleria, but he disappeared after that and we never saw him again. Our father forbade us to use magic ever again, but it's something you cannot just put down and walk away from. You know. It's a part of who you are."

"Yes, we do know that," Barengush said. "My father was an evil man who practiced dark magic. He took away my gifts because I wouldn't do the things he wanted me to do. I felt as if I'd lost a part of me. It was so devastating that I withdrew completely from life. Thanks to that young lady," he nodded in Felindra's direction, "I recovered and found out that he couldn't have taken away my gifts. He had just made me believe he had."

"How did you go on from there?" Farah asked the princess.

"My mother took pity on me and my sister. She sent us to live with my grandmother here in Hil Goa. That's how I met Prince Kazim and Donya met her husband." Lemaya muffled a yawn. "I should let you get your rest. Tomorrow, we are going to plan our marriage. My father gave his consent this morning. We'll probably have it here at the palace. We've had enough of pomp and ritual and want to make it as simple as possible. We'll send you a message in plenty of time."

***

The marriage ceremony took place in the Shah's garden of the palace. It was a short, simple ceremony in which the family of each partner presented him or her to the other spouse-to-be. Because Kazim had no immediate family, the brother of his late mother officiated on his behalf. They were both wearing light blue, with white lace and pearl trim on their tunics, and Lemaya's white headdress was also trimmed with pearls. They made vows of fidelity and loyalty to each other and exchanged gold armbands set with pearls and sapphires. After the vows had been made, the witnesses—everyone who was there, even servants and guards—were invited to add their signatures or marks to the couple's Life Book. The book, which started at the wedding, would also record the births of their children and other significant events in their lives, thereby becoming a history of their lives together. Her title now changed from Princess to *Shahbanu*, meaning Queen.

Refreshments had been set up in the sunroom that opened off the garden for the guests, the sort of food that could be eaten while walking around. Kazim and Lemaya strolled among the guests, hand in hand.

"I like the ceremony," Felindra said. "It's so straightforward and simple. It must be nerve-wracking for a couple to have to go through a long elaborate ceremony." She was thinking about her own forthcoming marriage to Lord Varan, looking forward to it, but also dreading it. She always felt uncomfortable when attention was focused on her.

"Are you going to suggest something like that to Lord Varan?" Farah asked.

"I wish I could, but I'm sure everything will be arranged by the palace. I'll tell him about it, though. I remember how stressful it was to receive that award from Queen Zenobia with everyone watching." When she had fourteen years, Felindra had been awarded a special commendation for her part in the victory of Albasiny against the Dark Brotherhood.

***

The three women were up at sunrise the next day, making their preparations to leave. *Shahbanu* Lemaya arrived just as they finished breaking their fast, followed by a team of servants with armloads of goods.

"I've brought you some things that might be useful on your journey," she announced. "I know you won't be able to carry all this, so just pick out what you may need."

"Rasamé went to the things laid out on the carpet and picked up something that looked like a small harness. "Is this what I think it is?" she asked, eyeing her son.

"For your little boy? Yes; it would make it easier to hold him and keep him from running away. My mother used one when she went out with my little brother." She glanced out the window. "I really must go; I have work to do. We will be there to see you off when you leave. Oh, by the way, my husband is going to send some soldiers to escort you as far as the border." She turned to leave, but then turned back at the door. "I almost forgot, we sent some stable-hands to bring your horses from the Caravanserai." She smiled. "I understand one of them was a bit spirited; it took two of them to control him."

"That's Lex," Felindra said, grinning. "Very few people can handle him. Thank you for bringing them, your highness."

"She looks so happy," Rasamé said after she left. "I know it's a cliché, but those two were really made for each other."

"I know. She's just glowing." Farah added.

"They have much in common, including fathers who hated magic," Felindra said.

They rummaged through the pile of goods and picked out what they thought would be the most useful, relying on their previous experiences. They found metal cups, piles of clean cotton sheets in many sizes." I think these are the most useful thing we could have," Rasamé said. "They come in so many sizes and can be used for everything, from dressings and towels to wrapping food....

I'm going to take plenty." There were also soft leather water bottles, simple clothes, soap and liniments, medicinal herbs, and more bags to carry things in. By the time they had finished, all the bags were bulging.

Tirzah came to their door a while later. "How is your packing coming along?" he asked, from the doorway. "I see you got some gifts too," he added after peering into the room.

When Zanda heard Tirzah's voice, he rushed out to greet him, jumping up into his open arms. "Uncle Lin! Look at me!" he shouted, pulling on the straps of his harness.

"A harness? What, has a nasty wizard turned you into a horse? Well it wasn't me."

"No, silly. It's a boy harness." He struggled out of Lin's arms and ran to his mother. "Uncle Lin silly."

"We're almost ready," Farah said.

"I see there are some warm garments among the things," he said. "Did you pack some. You're going to need them when we reach the mountains."

The three women rushed around picking fleece-lined coats, boots, and long woolen culottes, each one wrapping her bundle in a thick wool blanket.

Tirzah smile and nodded when they had finished. "Remember where we met the carriage to the crowning? Meet us out there. Someone will come and help with your bags."

Still the only one, apart from Rasamé, who could handle him, Felindra was once again riding Lex. She climbed into the saddle and, while they waited to depart she walked him around the stable yard. He was so pleased to have her on his back that he didn't even complain when they secured her bags on the back of the saddle. This time, everyone had a horse; the shortfall was made up by animals from the Shah's stable along with a small cart pulled by two donkeys for their extra baggage.

"Farewell, my friends," Shah Kazim said as they waited for the gate to open and let them out into the city. "I trust you will have a safe journey from now on. I think you have had enough adventures for a lifetime. My men will escort you to the border of Eleria and see you safely across." He indicated two uniformed men on horseback, who were standing to the side. They both bowed from their saddles. "I know you have ample defenses of your own but, with the witch hunters still loose, the more swords to fight them, the better."

Kazim gave the signal for the gates to open, and they rode through onto the avenue that led to the gates of the city.

"I'll miss them," Farah said to Tirzah who was riding beside her.

"We've all had a good rest and enough food to restore our strength, so the next part of the journey should be easy."

"How long do you think it will take to reach Eleria?"

"If the weather cooperates, it shouldn't take longer than five days."

Felindra was elated when they finally left the gates of the city and started on the road north. She would have allowed Lex to gallop if the highway hadn't been so crowded.

22 – The Journey Continues

The road passed through farmland at first, although they could see mountains ahead of them in the distance. Fruit was being harvested in the orchards where they ripened, the last of the root crops were being dug up and prepared for winter storage, and some of the empty fields were being ploughed. Russet, red, and gold leaves flew from the trees and scattered over the landscape. Several huge flocks of migrating birds flew overhead, going south for the winter, their quacking and gabble filling the air.

"Doesn't it smell glorious?" Felindra said to Rasamé who was riding beside her. "It reminds me so much of home. My anniversary is coming up soon, and I'll miss celebrating it with my family again."

"What day is it?"

"It's the last day of the Harvest Moon," she replied. "When is yours?"

"In the spring. I was born on the seventh day of the Seeding Moon."

"Do you remember Eleria?" Felindra asked.

"I remember it quite well really. I had seven years when they abducted my mother, Lin, and me. We'd been collecting herbs and medicinal plants in the woods and were resting by a spring before returning home. We had really gone too far and were tired. But, yes, I remember it. It is a beautiful country even though much of it is mountainous. I remember the green fields, the waterfalls and rivers, the wild flowers." Rasamé looked away and cleared her throat. "Sorry. The thought of being back there after all this time is very … emotional."

As the sun drew close to the horizon, one of the Goan soldiers came and spoke to Tirzah, pointing at their surroundings. Tirzah responded with a nod of his head. "The captain thinks we should stop here for the night," he explained to the others. "It is a good place, defensible, with fresh water and shelter."

They dismounted and led the horses and donkeys to the nearby stream, a little downstream of their campsite, and removed their tack. Vertan and the two soldiers unloaded some of the camping equipment they would need while Barengush walked around the perimeter, looking for potential attack points. The rest of the team started to put up the tents, one for the women, one for the men, but left the soldiers to assemble their own after seeing disapproving looks from them. *They probably think we should be preparing food,* Felindra thought.

"I'm going to look around to see if I can find some edibles," Rasamé said. "Want to come along?"

Sastin joined her, but before they could disappear into the woods, Barengush added himself. "We don't need a chaperone," Rasamé said with a grin. "Sastin will be quite safe with us."

"You do need a guard, though," he replied. "There are probably all sorts of wild animals in these woods, maybe some of the two-legged kind as well."

With the roots and berries and mushrooms they brought back to add to their food supplies, the evening meal was enjoyable. By the time they finished eating, the sun had set, so everyone made ready for sleep. Before she could retire, Felindra insisted in checking the animals once more.

She had noticed a subtle change in Lex since they'd been in Goa Sun; he seemed less aggressive than before and even allowed others to touch him now, providing they showed him respect. He would still strike out if anyone threatened him or was rough with him. He also seemed to get along better with other horses too, at least the mares.

Over the next few days, the land rose steadily until they were in the mountains. The temperature dropped as well so that they needed to add warmer coverings: wool blankets at night, and fur-lined leather cloaks while riding, unless the sun was shining. Occasionally, the atmosphere was filled with a cold fog in the mornings that did not burn off until mid-day if it burned off at all.

Farah was spending more time with Tirzah lately, leading Felindra to wonder if something was brewing between them. She thought they would be a good match; both had the same calm, unflappable temperament, although she thought that might be because of their maturity.

On the fourth day of the journey, about a day's travel from the border, Farah sensed that something didn't feel right. She told Tirzah about it and he scanned the area. "There are people nearby," he said. "And they don't feel friendly to me."

The travelers stopped and gathered in a group. "Does anyone else feel anything?" Tirzah asked. He explained to the guards, and to his surprise, the captain nodded.

"I feel it too," he said in Trade language.

Barengush and Vertan walked around the group, looking outward, and then they turned to the captain. "There seem to be about fifteen men circling that way."

"What do you recommend?" Vertan asked the captain.

The captain scanned the area. "We should continue down the slope to that rock formation and make a stand there ..." He was careful to avoid making any gestures that might alert watchers to the direction "... it's the most defensible position I can see."

They formed a double line with Barengush and Vertan behind and the two Goans leading, and then moved slowly down the slope. They had barely gone twenty paces when two men attacked. One dropped a small boulder on them from above, but Barengush was fast enough to divert it with a small power blast while Vertan dealt with the attacker, persuading him with his gift of conviction to go away. Three more attacked from the sides. First arrows started to rain down on them from behind and then they moved in with short swords.

Everyone responded according to his or her abilities. Tirzah was able to freeze some of the attackers in place, the captain fought with his sword and used his ability to relocate rapidly, which allowed him to overcome one attacker and move instantly to another. Barengush used limited power blasts, while the other Goan soldier protected the women as they sidled down the slope towards the shelter.

Crouching down behind the rocks with their horses and donkey cart, they could hear the screams of wounded men and horses, Farah peered around the rocks to see what was happening and screamed, then fell face down on the ground. Felindra and Rasame rushed to her. They saw an arrow embedded in the meaty part of her upper arm and blood seeping from the hole in her coat.

"Don't move," Rasame said. "You have an arrow in your arm."

Tirzah Lin came running to their hiding place, fear and anxiety straining his face.

"Farah! Are you all right, my love?"

"It hurts," Farah moaned.

"Let's get her into the shelter," Tirzah said. "But be careful. I'll take her shoulders, you hold her legs."

"What's happening? Who's hurt?" Sastin crawled into the shelter. When he saw Farah lying on the ground, he went to the cart for his satchel. "Let me see."

"I'm all right," she replied. "Do you want me to roll onto my side?"

"Just a little so I can get to the arrow. I'll put something behind you to prop you up." He looked around and saw a backpack. While Tirzah and Rasamé gently rolled her, he tucked it under her back.

"It doesn't look too serious. I think your thick coat prevented the arrow penetrating too deeply." Sastin reassured her. "First I'm going to put you to sleep while I get the arrow out." He put his hand on her forehead and held it there until her eyes closed and she relaxed.

"We'll have to get this coat off her," he said.

"We could lift her and pull it to that side." Tirzah suggested. "I can cut a hole in it large enough for the sleeve to go over the arrow. But first we should cut the shaft off to make it easier. I'll do it." Tirzah's hands, holding the arrow shaft, were shaking when he'd finished.

Once the coat was out of the way, the sleeves of Farah's tunic and undershirt had to be cut up to the shoulder. Rasame did that.

Sastin used all his healing skills and experience to cut the arrowhead out of Farah's arm. He then knelt over her and started the healing process on the damaged tissue. After he'd done as much as he could with his gift, he added some sutures to hold the edges together. When he was finished, Rasame had a bandage and some padding ready to cover the wound.

Now that Farah was taken care of, Felindra became aware of the activity outside their shelter. She heard a horse scream and ran without thinking about the danger she was putting herself in, especially after what happened to Farah. The Goan soldier who was guarding them called her, but she wasn't listening, she was too focused on the injured horse. She found Vertan on the ground, one leg trapped under his horse, which had an arrow sticking out if its haunch.

"You'll have to get it to stand up," Vertan said. "Get me out of here so I can go on repelling them."

Felindra went to the horse and stroked its forehead. *Come on, big boy, stand up. We'll help you and make you better.* It wasn't easy to convey this in images, so she concentrated on one image, the horse standing up, while she sent waves of comfort. The Goan soldier saw what she was trying to do. He went to the horse's side and took up the reigns. With Felindra's urging, the soldier's pulling on the reins, and Vertan's conviction, they managed to help it stand, but it was breathing heavily, snorting and groaning from the pain in its hip.

Tirzah Lin, who had followed the guard, took the horse's reins, leaving Vertan and the guard free to continue with their defense.

Vertan stood up and brushed the dirt off his tunic and then looked around for his sword. Before he could reach it, one of the attackers jumped on him from above, landing on his shoulders and driving him face down on the ground. He had a nasty-looking knife in his hand and started to pull Vertan's head up by his hair to get at his throat, all the time mumbling, "die, witch, die, witch," as if in a trance, but the Goan soldier was too fast for him and slashed the hand holding the knife, almost severing it.

The man screamed and grabbed his wrist, rolling off Vertan into the road.

The fighting seemed to be slowing down. Felindra was able to lead the limping horse back to the rocks, which seemed to be free of attackers. The shouts and screams carried on for a while longer, then another horse screamed, and she heard Barengush curse loudly. It was almost silent now, apart from a few groans and whimpers from the injured. A small explosion startled her, and another yelp of pain told her that Barengush had used his power again.

Tirzah Lin

Tirzah went back to the shelter behind the rocks, dusty and out of breath. He wiped his face with the back of his hand and sat down on a small boulder. "How's Farah?"

"She's fine, still sleeping," Sastin replied.

"Is it over?" his sister asked, handing him a water bag. She was trying to sooth Zanda, who had been woken up by all the noise and screaming of men and horses and was now clinging to her with one hand and sucking the thumb of the other.

Tirzah stroked his nephew's head. "The ones who could still walk have retreated," he said. "Now we have to take care of the wounded. That's what I came for, the healers. Are you ready?" He looked at Sastin and Rasamé.

"Were any of our people hurt?" Sastin asked as he reached for the bag he always kept handy.

"The captain is limping; he may have dislocated his knee, and Vertan has a nasty cut on his arm. Other than that, everyone seems to be healthy."

Felindra was already on her feet, eager to do something about the injured horses. "Can you spare someone to help those horses?" she asked Tirzah.

"I'll go with you," he offered. "Leave the more practiced healers to help the wounded men, but first, I have to talk to the wounded".

"Why should we give our best to the enemy?" Barengush grumbled.

"To teach them a lesson," Tirzah Lin replied.

"What sort of a lesson?"

"To show them that we aren't what they think we are. We are not evil and will help even those who want to harm us."

"So we're going to let them go?"

"Of course," Tirzah said. "We are not equipped to keep prisoners."

There were five wounded witch hunters, one with a broken wrist, two with stab wounds, and two more seriously injured, one with a deep gash in his throat, and the one who'd attacked Vertan and had a partially severed hand.

They were all terrified of their captors and lay pale and trembling on the ground amidst their spilled blood.

Tirzah knew he had to ease their fear, otherwise it would be hard to heal them. Healers needed some cooperation from the patient if they were to succeed. He spoke to them in their own language and did his best to put them at ease and reassure them that no action would be taken against them. Then he went with Felindra to help the horses.

Barengush was standing by his wounded horse, trying to keep him from moving too much. The animal had been slashed across its haunch with a sword. Tirzah examined the cut while Felindra put her arm over his neck and soothed him.

"I'm going to have to put some stitches in this cut," Tirzah said. "Is there any way you can put him to sleep?"

"I don't think so, but I can try" she replied.

"Never mind," Tirzah said. "I can freeze it while I do the repairs. Barengush can help hold him still."

It didn't take long for Tirzah to finish and cover it with an antiseptic salve. From Felindra's point of view, monitoring the horse's feelings, he had felt little more than a slight sting as the needle pierced his skin.

"He'll be free of the freezing in a few moments and should be able to walk," Tirzah said to Barengush. "Now for the more difficult one."

The horse with the arrow in her hip was in obvious pain, holding the injured leg away from the ground and swishing her tail. Her ears were flattened, and she tossed her head, her breath coming in wheezing gasps. Felindra approached her cautiously, all the time sending out soothing thoughts. "Can you freeze her?" she called to Tirzah, who had been waiting for her to still the mare.

"I'm going to need help," Tirzah replied. He saw the Goan soldier hovering nearby, and after a short exchange with him, the Goan came to his side. Felindra continued to sooth the poor creature while Tirzah froze the horse's rear and removed the arrow. After that, he used the same procedure Sastin had used with Farah, and then he gave the soldier some instructions and packed up his equipment.

"She's in good hands now." he said to Felindra. "Let's go and see how our healers are doing."

Vertan and the captain had been taken care of. Vertan with sutures and bandages, the captain with a splint to immobilize his knee joint after the tip of the bone had been restored to its socket. Rasamé had given him a walking staff, telling him not to put too much weight on the leg. They were now working on the enemy casualties, who seemed to have calmed down considerably, although they still fired resentful glares at the healers.

"I don't want no she-witch touching me," one of the less seriously wounded casualties snarled.

"I see you are being well taken care of," Tirzah said, receiving more glares.

"We didn't ask for it," a stringy man with receding hair and a dull countenance said.

"No, but we are giving it. Even though you may not appreciate our help, we give it for our own sakes."

"What are you going to do with us?" another asked. This one looked a little more alert than the first one.

"We'll leave you here. What you do after that is your own business. I'm sure, after your experience this day, that you will not try to attack us again."

"We could take them back to the city for punishment," the captain said.

"That is up to you," Tirzah replied. "But I think our way might be more effective."

"Damned witches," someone mumbled.

"Are any of you hungry?" Tirzah asked after the healers had finished.

"We don't need your magic-cursed food," one of the more belligerent men said. He was also one of the less seriously injured. He stood up and looked around the area until he found a backpack and picked it up. "We've got our own rations."

"Well, since you are all comfortable, we'll leave you to it."

As they walked back to the group's haven among the rocks, Tirzah said, "We ought to at least take them some fresh water. Do we have a clean bucket?"

23 – Crossing the mountains

Felindra

Felindra sat down near the Goan captain to eat her evening meal. "I saw you using the relocation gift, while you were fighting" she said to him.

He looked puzzled for a moment and then nodded. "Is that what you call it where you come from?"

"Yes, we do in Albasiny. It's a rare and amazing gift. The only other person I know who has it is my father."

"Are there many people with magic in your country?"

"Oh, yes. More than half the people are gifted in some way. We have monasteries where we are trained. We look upon our magic as gifts from the Light, the Great Spirit."

"You are very fortunate," the captain said. "It is more difficult for us, but that may change with the new Shah."

"Were you in the Goan military during the old Shah's reign?"

"No. Once the *Shahbanu* died, the witch-hunts started, and I decided to retire. It is hard not to react with one's gift in a tight situation, and I knew if I did, I would be in trouble. I returned to my family's estate in the south."

"So how were you chosen to accompany us?"

"I've known the prince for many years and often took assignments from him, undercover of course. Mostly it was rescuing people he'd discovered were in danger. When the old Shah passed, Prince Kazim contacted me and invited me to return to my old position in the army, with a promotion." The captain made as if to rub his wounded knee, but quickly thought better of it. "Tell me about your father; is he in the military?"

"He was," she replied. "We call soldiers 'defenders' in Albasiny. He was the Commander of the Trethawynd Defenders of the Light in the last two conflicts with the Dark Brotherhood, but he's retired and makes swords now."

They were interrupted by Barengush. "Excuse me," he said. "Do you want us to join the watch again tonight? Vertan would have to be a passive watcher, but he could still use his gifts," The two defenders had been part of the watch throughout the journey, but with Vertan's injured sword arm, Barengush wanted to be sure.

"That would be acceptable," the captain said. "You and Vertan take the first watch and we'll take over from you at midnight." The captain started to stand up but thought better of it and stretched his arms instead. He called his subordinate. "This damn leg," he said. "Please go and check on the raiders; see what they're up to."

"Do you need help getting up, sir?"

"No. I'll rest here until you return, and then you can help me to my pallet."

"Should I go with him?" Barengush asked.

"Yes. Your presence may intimidate them more than one of us if they become hostile."

***

A misty drizzle greeted them when they awoke the next day. "Thank the Light for the warm coats Kazim gave us, although mine is messed quite badly." Farah said as she tried to stand up.

195

"Let us help you," Rasame said, rushing to her side. Once Farah was on her feet, Rasame put a blanket round her shoulders. "Would you like me to take you to the latrine?"

Farah looked at the ground, her face scrunched up, then she looked up. "I can manage," she said quietly.

"With only one hand?" Rasame replied.

"I hate needing to have someone help me, like a child, but yes, I may need help. Thank you for offering."

Felindra quickly rolled up her bedding and tied it into a bundle ready to stow in the wagon. Once she had her coat on, they took down the tent and put everything in the wagon, remembering to find a new coat for Farah to replace the damaged one. Felindra went to check the horses while her companions went to the cooking fire to help with their morning meal.

She found the two wounded animals together under some trees. Their ears pricked up when they heard her approach and the female whinnied softly. Out of the corner of her eye, she could see Lex secured to a sapling nearby. He looked restless, tossing his head and pawing the ground with his front hoof. She veered away from the wounded horses towards him. Stroking his forehead, she reassured him. "You don't have to be jealous. You're still my number one, but your poor friends are hurt, and I must check on them. I'll come back soon and take you for a nice ride."

"Do you think he understands all that?" Sastin asked.

"Oh, Sastin! Good morrow. I didn't see you," she answered, flustered. "No, he doesn't understand a word, but the images I send him might calm him for a while. He's certainly the most demanding horse I've ever encountered, but he's worth it. Dom Ash must be heart-broken to lose him."

Sastin smiled and shook his head. "Would you like to help me examine these two?"

Together, they gave care to the horses that had been hurt, Felindra by telling Sastin what they were feeling, and giving them comforting thoughts, while Sastin checked their wounds, He removed the old dressing from the leg of the stallion and did some more tissue repair on both, then added more medicated salve.

"I'll leave the dressings off now. They seem to be mending nicely. They should be well enough to ride in a couple of days."

"I wish I had your healing skills," Felindra said. "I could be much more use to the sick animals if I could heal them, not just feel their pain."

"What you do for them is just as important," Sastin added. "I'm sure your soothing touch does wonders for them."

They returned to the campfire and helped themselves to some porridge and honey, and then sat down in a dry spot under some overhanging trees.

"How are the witch hunters?" Felindra asked.

"They've gone," Barengush replied.

"All of them, even the badly wounded?"

"Yes. There's no sign of them. They probably rounded up some of their horses that were still wandering around in the forest."

"The healing Rasamé and Sastin did on them must have helped them become more mobile," Farah said. "As it did for me."

24 – Entering Eleria

Felindra

The next two days were spent travelling a road that rose and fell around the contours of the mountain, always ending up at a higher altitude at the end of the day. The drizzle turned to a steady rain the second day, and the air was very cold. Everyone was now wearing woolen undergarments and hose under their fur-lined waterproof coats and woolen culottes.

"I don't know how we would have survived without the garments Kazim gave us," Felindra said. "Although I don't like the idea of wearing animal pelts, I appreciate the warmth."

"I wish we were able to see some of the scenery," Farah said. "There must be magnificent views from up here."

"Indeed, there are," Tirzah Lin said. "But once we're in Eleria, we won't want for views."

That night as they were preparing for sleep, Felindra noticed Farah wasn't there. "I wonder where Farah is," she commented. "It's cold out there."

"Well, there are two possibilities: She's either using the latrine, or she's with Lin," Rasamé replied.

"But what...?" Felindra immediately felt stupid and naïve about the question she had been about to ask. "You mean they're...?" *Why do I keep asking stupid questions?*

"Surely you've noticed how they're always together. And please don't ask why!" Rasamé punched her gently on the arm.

"I guess I've been too distracted by other things, but now you mention it..." she was rescued from further embarrassment by the arrival of Farah.

Even in the weak lamplight, they could see the white specs glittering on her coat. Her cheeks and her nose had taken on a dusky red color. Rasamé helped her take off the coat and shook it towards the door. "Would you believe it's snowing out there?"

***

They were greeted the next day by sunlight from a purplish pink sky. As soon as they were dressed, they all trooped outside to look around.

"There's our view," Farah said joyously. "It's even more glorious than I imagined."

Looking towards the east, they could see the yellow disc of the sun peering over the jagged horizon, the mountain peaks adorned with caps of rosy pink. Directly below there was nothing but treetops, mostly evergreens, but there were a few splashes of orange and ochre among them from deciduous trees. Farther out, they could see patches of cleared land with clusters of tiny houses, all releasing puffs of smoke. At one of the closer villages, they saw a tiny man herding little puff-ball animals towards their pasture.

"It's so peaceful," Vertan said. "It's hard to imagine the atrocities men are capable of happening here."

"And yet it does." Tirzah approached Sarah and rested put his arm around her waist. "I told you there'd be views."

She looked over her shoulder at him, a smile on her lips and sparkle in her eyes. "It's unimaginably beautiful. I'm so glad we decided to come this way, despite everything that's happened to us on the way. It's like being on top of the world. Which way is Eleria?"

"You can't see it from here," Tirzah replied. "It's over those mountains." He nodded towards the mountains behind them to the left.

"How long before we reach it?" Felindra asked.

"The evening of the morrow," he replied. "That is if we don't have more snow."

There was more climbing this day, a steep mountain road where the bare rock formed the surface, and moisture of the previous day had turned to ice during the night.

"I don't understand why it's so cold with the sun shining," Felindra said.

"It's a phenomenon of northern highlands in wintertime," Tirzah Lin replied. "The air temperature is actually warmer when it's cloudy, the clouds act as a blanket to keep the heat in. The nights get longer, too."

"It's like that in the extreme north of ValkonenMaa sometimes," Vertan said."

"Don't worry," Tirzah said. "When you're in direct sunlight, it's not so bad, and where it hits the ground, it will gradually melt the ice.

"It's the horses I'm worried about," Felindra continued. "If one of them slipped on the ice ... and it's very hard for them to climb carrying riders."

"Let's stop for a while," Tirzah said. "Give them a rest. Would you like to read them and see how they feel about it?"

Felindra slid down from Lex's back and left him to nibble some vegetation while she went to assess the other animals. Most of the ridden horses were tired and their legs ached from the constant climbing, but the donkeys seemed to be taking it in their stride.

When she'd finished, she went back to her companions, who were leaning against tree trunks or rocks. "I think we should lead them," she said. "All of us can walk except the captain and Farah. Lex is the strongest and so far, he's all right. How would you like to ride him?" she asked the Captain.

He looked at her, surprised at the offer. "Are you sure he would allow me to?"

"He'll do what I tell him," she replied. "He's changed a lot since we left Kum. He's starting to realize that he depends on us just as much as we depend on him. He's growing up, I suppose, just like a little boy. I'll talk to him before you mount."

"Do you really think we should walk?" Tirzah Lin asked.

"I recommend it, while the road is so steep and slippery. We should lead them for a while."

"What about Zanda?" Rasamé asked. "He can't walk on his little legs, and he's too heavy to carry."

"Let him ride your horse and you lead them in case she slips on the ice."

By midday, everyone was tired and hungry, but not as cold as they had been earlier now that the sun had come around their side of the mountain. Even so, they lit a fire to warm up some food and make tea.

"We're nearly at the top," Tirzah informed them. "We should reach the summit by sunset."

By the mid-afternoon Felindra was so tired, she had to ride one of the horses, although she was reluctant to put the strain on it. "You're still recovering from two serious injuries. Not only that, you are slowing the rest of us, so do it for us," Tirzah said. He smiled to show he was teasing, so she reluctantly agreed.

Felindra chose one of the stronger mares for herself, feeling that Lex might be jealous of another stallion. He was very possessive that way.

Later, as they settled down for the night, they heard wolves calling from far away in the forest. This set Felindra thinking of her own wolf Ashala, who had died just before she left Albasiny, and she felt a strong yearning to find them and make friends with them. Her eyes filled with tears. She stifled a sob and wiped her cheeks with her sleeve.

It reminds you of her, doesn't it? Farah sent. *I feel your sorrow, Felindra.* Farah reached out her hand and stroked Felindra's forearm.

"Will they attack us?" Rasamé asked.

"No," Felindra replied. "They prefer to stay away from people. We are dangerous to them. They're just talking to one another."

As if wolf calls weren't spooky enough, the wind started to moan through the trees, but everyone was tired enough to sleep despite the sounds.

Tirzah Lin

The clouds of fog had returned when they awoke the next day but, although they couldn't see much, the air was not as icy as it had been the previous day. They hadn't quite reached the summit and still had some climbing ahead of them, but by midday, the ground had flattened out enough for them to ride and gain some speed. The ride down the other side was more nerve-wracking than the climb had been. Now that the clouds had dispersed, the heat from the sun melted most of the ice, but the meltwater turned patches of earth to mud and slush.

"This will freeze again when the sun goes down," Barengush said.

"We should be down in the valley by then," Tirzah answered. "It's not as far down as it was coming up the other side."

As the fog lifted, more details of the valley emerged. Most of the valley floor appeared to be devoted to agriculture, although several mid-sized towns could be seen at various points, and small villages and hamlets dotted the landscape.

At the base of the hill they were descending was a small community of five or six wood and stone buildings. Several people could be seen going back and forth on the single paved street, although from a distance, it was hard to see what occupied them. A wide road meandered from the mountain across the valley to the other side, and many smaller roads and tracks ran all through the valley, linking the different towns and villages.

"What's that over there?" Felindra asked, pointing to an assembly of domes and spires on the hillside across the valley, with sunlight reflected from the buildings.

"That is Camakäsara, the capital of Eleria, our destination." Tirzah replied.

"It looks as if it's glowing," Farah said.

Tirzah nodded. "The name means *City of Light.*"

You must be happy to be home again after all these years.

That's putting it mildly. He wiped his eyes with the back of his free hand.

"What's that place down there?" Vertan asked. "It doesn't look much like a village."

203

"That's the frontier station," Tirzah said. He cleared his throat and continued, "Actually, we've been inside the border of Eleria since we crossed the summit, but it wouldn't be convenient to have a frontier post up there, although the area is patrolled at intervals." He reached out his left hand and took Farah's right, looking at her with glistening eyes and said softly, "Welcome to the home of my heart."

"The frontier station has facilities for travelers, an inn, stables, and a small market where we can stock up on supplies" he said to the others. "We're almost there,"

It took all their willpower to resist urging their horses to gallop down the serpentine road to the frontier post

The frontier guard wanted to keep them talking about their journey, but when he saw how droopy some of them were, he said "I see you and your honorable friends are tired, so I won't delay you longer. I presume you will rest at the inn before continuing your journey?"

"We will," Tirzah Lin replied. "Is there anything else you need to know before we continue?"

"We can deal with that on the morrow," the captain replied, although he looked mildly puzzled by the presence of the two Goan soldiers. "I'm sure none of your companions would be a threat to Eleria."

Felindra

After leaving their horses and donkeys at the nearby stables, they went through the gate of the inn. Although surrounded by a stone wall, the rest of the structure was natural wood. The inn consisted of three buildings set at right angles to one another. The remainder of the grounds were landscaped with a restful array of sanded paths through small trees and flower beds, although there weren't many flowers blooming at this season, enough color was provided by the changing leaves of the trees and bushes. The small, beautifully arranged pools that dotted the grounds had gold and red fish swimming among the lily pads. This they saw as they walked from the gate to a raised verandah in the center of the buildings where a woman in an elaborate costume awaited them.

"This place is beautiful," Felindra said. "It's so peaceful."

"That's the purpose of this type of landscaping and layout," Tirzah Lin said. "Serenity and peaceful surroundings are very important to my people. Beauty and tranquility are balms to the soul."

"It's strange," Rasamé said. "I feel at home here."

Tirzah Lin patted her shoulder. "That's good."

They followed him up the steps where he spoke to the woman. After he'd told her what they needed, she led them inside the center building and she continued to explain things. She beckoned to a boy who looked around twelve.

"First, we need to change our footwear," Tirzah translated. "We leave our boots here and use the slippers." He indicated a row of straw slippers in assorted sizes lined up on a mat just inside the door. "This building contains the public rooms," Tirzah continued. "The pavilion on the north side is the men's and the one on the south is the women's."

"What about couples and families?" Rasamé asked.

"There are suites at the back of this building," he replied. "Now Sister Kelsang is going to show you your accommodation, and her son will take us to ours. After we bathe, we can meet here and have a meal."

Sister Kelsang bowed to the three women and led them towards a side door that led to a short, covered wooden walkway. They entered the other pavilion through a matching door into a wood-paneled room with a large, multicolored rug on the floor. The walls were decorated with paintings of flowers, and exotic animals and birds on sheets of bark. The roof overhead was, like the one in the public pavilion, gabled and had glass panes to provide light for the plants that sat around the floor in pots.

"This is beautiful," Farah said.

Kelsang said something to Rasamé, gesturing with her hands towards various parts of the room.

"The bathing room is through that door at the end. Now, she will show us to our sleeping rooms."

There were small, head-high panels made of horizontal bamboo poles interspersed along the walls. She led them to one of them and pushed it gently, causing it to swing inwards, then she held it open, so they could see inside. The room had a window overlooking the garden, with a roll-up blind made of woven bamboo, and on the floor two thick sleeping pads with pillows and folded blankets. The only other furnishings were several wicker trunks and four lanterns.

"She said you can have a room each or share in pairs. I'm going to share one with Zanda." She thanked Kelsang and turned towards the next room.

The first thing Felindra wanted to do was bathe. "I wonder if there are towels in the bathroom; I don't see any here.

"Let's check the trunks first," Farah suggested.

There weren't any, so they picked up clean clothes and went to the bathing room. Rasamé was already there with Zanda, who was splashing in the pool. It was a large pool edged with polished wood and lined with smooth stones the size of duck eggs. There were not only towels on a bench near the pool, but also ceramic bottles of various liquids. "What are these?" Felindra asked Rasamé.

"The green one is soap, the yellow is for washing your hair, and the blue one is to put on your skin after you dry it."

"How do you know all that?" Felindra asked.

"My mother taught me. These are the standard symbolic colors for the contents." Rasamé replied. "You have to wash first, using the green soap, then wash your hair with the yellow and rinse everything off with clear water from the barrel.

The two women went ahead with their washes. "I think I'll get dressed and go back to the room to fix my hair," Felindra said when she'd finished drying herself.

"I'll come with you," Farah responded.

Rasamé joined Zanda, who was still splashing joyfully in the pool.

"This would be a good time to call home," Felindra said as she massaged oil into her scalp. "I'd like to know when they will arrive at the port. What did Lin call it? I've forgotten."

"Zimnyaya-gavan," Farah replied. "I agree it's time to get in touch, now that we have good news for a change. I'll have to figure out what time it is there first; Ashavan will not be pleased to be woken in the middle of the night. I expect Lin will know."

When they returned to the central pavilion, the six men were sitting on cushions—the captain with his leg straight out in front of him—drinking something steamy from ceramic mugs. The men stood up when the women arrived. "What took you so long," Vertan asked.

207

"The usual," Felindra replied. "I was trying to make my hair behave."

"It looks fine to me," he said barely glancing at it. "We can have a meal now. This way."

They followed him through an opening in the wall opposite the entrance. On the right was a large area with small tables arranged in a row, each one with a padded stool and a small lantern. "We can move the tables into a rectangle if you like," Tirzah said.

The opposite side of the room was enclosed with wood paneling through which tantalizing aromas filtered. A face appeared in a round aperture in the wall and, a few heartbeats later, Sister Kelsang came out. She nodded her head when she saw the men moving the tables and asked Tirzah Lin a question. After he responded, she went back behind the screen and they heard dishes being moved.

"She just wanted to know if we are ready to eat," Tirzah said. "She said everything is ready to serve. She will also bring more tea." He held up his mug.

The new table arrangement was two rows of five facing each other. The moment they sat down, Kelsang, her son, and a young girl came out with dishes and trays.

The girl filled everyone's bowl from the steaming kettle she carried, and then poured the rest of the liquid into the pot on the table. She smiled shyly at them and left through the opening to the kitchen.

"Is this the tea? Felindra asked.

"It is. We call it *chatan.*" Noticing her looking at the bowl, perplexed, he added, "Just lift the bowl with the palms of both hands, like this."

The main ingredient of the solid food was rice, but there were bowls of sauces and small pieces of meat and fish with which to make a flavorsome dish. In addition to the savory dishes, there were sweets made from coconut, and a selection of fruits and nuts, both dried and fresh.

"What are our plans for the next few days?" Barengush asked.

"First, we need to go to the capital and announce ourselves to the Prime Master of the School of Wizardry. All gifted persons who enter the country must do this. I might also visit the castle and seek an audience with the king. His father was a friend of my father who served on the Royal Council." Tirzah Lin said."

"Does your father still live?" Farah asked.

"Sadly, no. He is at rest now."

"How did he die?" Rasamé asked her brother.

"I thought you knew," Tirzah relied. "Didn't mother tell you? He was killed in an avalanche twenty cycles past."

"Will we be able to do some sight-seeing?" Vertan asked.

"It depends on when you have to leave," Tirzah replied. "We can sight-see on the way to the capital, though, if you don't mind staying at inns."

"I'm going to contact our people tonight," Farah said. "We need to know when the ship will arrive at Zimnyaya-gavan."

"I suppose you'll be returning to Goa Sun on the morrow." Felindra said to the two Goan soldiers.

"We shall," the captain replied. "I would like to say it has been a pleasure travelling with you and I wish you peace and contentment."

"Are you going to take the spare horses back with you?" she asked.

"We can do that," he replied. "Just show us the ones to take."

"They probably have the Shah's mark on them."

"I'd also like you to take a message to the Shah and Shahbanu," Tirzah Lin added. "I'll have it ready before you leave."

25 – The Home of Tirzah's heart.

Tirzah Lin

After breaking their fast the following day, they prepared for the next leg of the journey. They stopped at the market on the way to the road and stocked up on food, mostly dried fruits and vegetables, and some tea and cheese.

The market also had more winter clothing, but they still had the ones they'd received from Shah Kazim, but everyone bought sheepskin-lined mittens.

"As you may have noticed, Vertan, our people are somewhat smaller than Albasinians, but you may be able to get boots your size in Camakäsara. They are essential in the winter here, although the boots the shah gave us are adequate."

The sky was misty when they left the inn, although Tirzah reassured them it would burn off before long. From the inn, they descended into the valley and eventually arrived at the wide paved road that led to Camakäsara. The distant mountains and scenery were obscured by the mist, but they could still see local features. Animals grazed in fields along the roadside, some of them, like sheep were familiar, but there was one incredible animal Felindra had never seen before. They had curved horns like cows, but ten times as long. Their bodies were covered with dark and light brown hair, which almost reached the ground, and they had humps on their shoulders. The herd was grazing on long grass in a pasture that was so vast, it faded into the distant mist.

"What are those?" Barengush asked.

'Those are yaks," Tirzah replied. "They are only found at high altitudes like this. Normal cattle wouldn't survive the winters here, but the yaks are equipped for this climate. They are our dairy herds."

"What about the sheep," Felindra asked. "How can they survive?"

"These are special sheep that have lived in this region for many hundreds of cycles," he replied. "They are growing their winter coats now. You will see them becoming thicker and bushier."

Once the mist wore off, the air became a little warmer. They could see as far as the distant snow-topped mountains that formed a wall around the valley. Men and women were working in the fields, bringing in the last crops, and tending their livestock. Almost all the houses had poultry pecking around in their yards. The houses themselves were built of wood with stone around the lower parts and were surrounded by stone fences. The windows were small, and the doors were set deeply in the thick walls. Smoke rose straight up in the air from chimneys that poked out from the stone walls. The people wore the same costumes, men in baggy woolen trousers tucked into knee-high boots with wool coats and fur-lined hats; the women in woolen skirts instead of trousers. They would have looked drab were it not for the decorations, either embroidered or painted on the garments in bright blues, reds, and greens. The people they passed stopped work and waved to them as they rode by.

Tirzah looked up at the sky which was clouding over. "It looks as if we'll have snow before long. It's time to get some yaks. They are much more sure-footed in the snow on mountain trails.

"Where from?" Rasame asked.

"Every town of any size has places where you can buy them. There's one not far from here. When we arrive, I'll get you settled at the inn and then go and make the arrangements."

"Don't you need help with them?" Barengush asked.

"We won't be picking them up until we leave on the morrow. I'm just going to make sure they have enough and pay the herder to reserve them for us."

"What are we going to do with the horses?" Felindra asked.

"Maybe we can sell them later, but we'll keep them until we leave for the coast."

Felindra

Felindra, who was riding Lex, thought about what Tirzah had said. *Don't worry, big man. I won't sell you. Even though you would fetch a good price,* she thought to herself.

"Does that mean you will be travelling with us until we reach the port?" Farah asked.

"You'll need someone to translate for you and get the information you'd need."

Felindra felt Farah's excitement when she received this information and smiled at her.

After passing several places where they saw men and women hacking chunks off large cube-shaped piles of brown stuff, Barengush asked, "What are they doing?"

"They're preparing for winter," Tirzah replied. "There aren't enough trees to supply firewood, so they use yak dung. They're cutting it into bricks, so they can be dried ready for winter fires."

"You mean that's excrement!" Barengush exclaimed. "I don't smell anything."

"Ah, that's the secret. Yaks don't have any smell. Their bodies, their wool, and their wastes don't have any particular aroma."

"How strange," Felindra said. "I wonder why."

"Their diet may have something to do with it," Tirzah replied. "They eat nothing but vegetation and drink only pure water. You may not have noticed, but the same is true of humans. Those who refrain from eating the flesh of animals don't produce the unpleasant odors that meat-eaters do, neither in their body wastes nor their sweat."

"That is interesting," Farah said. "Maybe we need to change our diets."

Felindra remained silent. She had abstained from animal flesh for many sun cycles, except when she had no choice.

The sun set early in these mountains, slipping down behind the peaks to the west. Tirzah had led them off the highway onto a narrower road towards a distant cluster of lights. As they came closer, it revealed itself as a good-sized settlement, a small town with lanterns hanging from every building.

"There's a good inn here, or there was when I was a child," Tirzah said.

213

The small town had one main street with several narrower ones branching off it. The streets were covered with packed earth, topped with gravel. The place they wanted was halfway down the main street. They waited outside while Tirzah went inside to talk to the owner.

"Everything is well," he said when he came out. "There is a stable behind the inn. Let's take the animals there."

They dismounted and led their horses and donkey cart around the back of the inn to a stable yard. When they arrived, they saw three large yaks staked out in the yard wearing elaborate saddles. The horses were a bit skittish at first, but maybe the yak's lack of a scent made them calm down, although Lex objected to their presence with a loud snort. Two young men came out of the small barn and met them. Once Tirzah had explained their needs, they led their mounts into the barn. There were no stalls for the horses, only posts to which they could be secured. In the middle of the floor were troughs with water and fodder. Tirzah showed them where they could stow the harnesses and saddles.

"They should be all right," Felindra said. "Would you tell them that if they have any problems to call me please, Lin?"

That taken care of, Tirzah departed to find some yaks and the rest of them went inside the inn. The public room of the inn was lit with oil lamps. Warmth was provided by two small stoves at opposite sides of the room.

Three men, a little girl, and a young woman sat on pads around a low table, eating a meal. They looked curiously at the newcomers and offered head-bows with palms folded together. The travelers returned the greetings and the diners returned to their meal.

A man and woman, who were the owners of the establishment, came forward from an alcove at one side and greeted them. Rasamé spoke to them and after they'd finished, she gestured to the women to follow her. She led them through an archway at the back of the room into a long narrow room arranged like the one they'd stayed at the previous night. As before, the hostess took them to doors on the left-hand side, but this time they all had to share one room.

During the night, they heard the child crying and the woman trying to comfort her. *I wonder what that's about,* Felindra thought.

I can't get any details, Farah sent in response, but she obviously doesn't want to go where they're taking her.

The following day, Felindra told Tirzah about the girl crying in the night.

"There's nothing we can do," he replied. "Her father has sold her to a wealthy man in the capital. It is a tradition of wealthy people to pledge their children at an early age to the offspring of another family with whom they want an alliance. It cements the relationship of the two families."

"But she's only a little girl," Felindra protested. "Doesn't she have any say in the matter?"

"None," Tirzah replied. "In this case, the future husband is an older man who already has children. That's probably why she is upset. His wife died in childbirth when the last child was born."

"How awful! I think I'd kill myself ... no, but I would do something, maybe run away or make myself look ugly."

"Dear Felindra, you have a tender heart." He patted her shoulder. "Really, there's nothing anyone can do now that the pledge has been made. And legally, anyone who tried to interfere would be liable for penalties."

"What sort of penalties? And how do you know all this?" Felindra asked in her usual pile-up of questions."

"I talked to the men last might. One man is her father, one her uncle, and the other represents the family to which she is pledged. As for penalties, deliberate obstruction could be punished with prison time, loss of personal assets, and in cases where someone's life is lost, execution."

They saw the young girl being lifted in to a palanquin resting on the back of one of the yaks, her female companion sat in front on the same animal. The three men arranged their yaks around the girl and woman as they left the yard. She heard the little girl's voice as they left and one of the men, probably her father, scolding her.

"Did you find out who the woman is?" Felindra asked.

"She's the wife of the girl's brother," Tirzah replied.

They passed the little caravan taking the girl to the city on their way to the paddocks to pick up their yaks. The side flaps of the girl's cage were rolled down, concealing her.

Riding the yaks was a strange experience for the Albasinians. The saddles were more like armchairs on the wide hairy backs of the creatures, but it didn't take long for them to become accustomed to the smooth plodding ride. Yaks didn't gallop or trot like horses, they just kept up the same calm, steady pace.

"You have to remember these are not equine animals, they're bovine, like cows." Tirzah said when Barengush complained about their lack of speed. "The only time they will go faster is when they sense danger, a fire or an avalanche."

Felindra was the only one still riding a horse. She was afraid Lex would make a fuss if she deserted him for one of these strange beasts, but she vowed to change over when they came to the icy mountain roads.

In all Felindra's distraction with the young girl and the new animals, the subject of Farah's contact with Albasiny, had escaped her mind. Now it came to the fore. "Did you contact the ship?" she asked Farah.

"Yes. I got through to Ashavan. He said they estimate they will reach Zimnyaya in half a moon cycle, weather permitting. Apparently, the weather can be quite stormy at this time of year."

"Is it the ship that tried to rescue us when we were captured by the slavers, the Blue Ranger?"

"I believe so, but I didn't ask. He did mention Captain Morelli, so it could be. I also got the latest news from home." Farah said with a self-satisfied grin on her face.

"Well, are you going to tell me?"

"Your family is well and send their love."

"And?"

"Guess who is also on the ship?"

"Dadi?"

"Yes, and someone else."

"Light, Farah, tell me."

"Lord Varan. He managed to convince his father to allow him to come."

Felindra was speechless. Her heart did a flip-flop and her mind blanked out. Varan! That was the last person she'd expected. "Is it true?" she asked hesitantly, half expecting Farah to start laughing.

"Of course it's true. I wouldn't make a jest of something like that."

"Sorry, Farah. It's just ... I'm so surprised." Felindra's eyes filled with tears, which she swatted away with her mitten. "Anything else?"

"The queen sends her good wishes and says you had better make it home this time. I think she is concerned about all the misadventures we've been having."

"Varan! I'm flabbergasted. I never thought he'd be able to persuade his father."

Once they'd crossed the valley, the road started to climb into the mountain, zigzagging back and forth along the contours of the slope. Walls of stone protected the down-slope edges of the road to prevent people and animals sliding over the side.

The terrain was very much like the mountain range that divided the duchies of Trethawynd and ValkonenMaa. The same steep mountain slopes, similar coniferous trees and ground plants. It smelled the same too, the strong piney and cedar aromas. It brought so many memories back to Felindra, both good and bad. The memories of the times she had spent with Ashala, her beloved wolf companion, but also her abduction and subsequent imprisonment in the Valkonen monastery dungeons. She turned her head and looked at Barengush who had been her abductor, and Vertan who was a fellow prisoner. She sighed and wiped a tear from her cheek, once again pining for her beloved wolf, realizing that more than a full cycle of seasons had passed since she'd passed on.

"It smells wonderful," Vertan exclaimed, as if reading her mind. "It's so much like home."

They were about halfway to the capital, Camakäsara, when a snowflake landed on Lex's head. She looked up at the sky, which had clouded over since they started the climb, and saw flakes like grey feathers fluttering down towards them. At first only a few, but after a while they started to come down more heavily, as if to show they were serious this time. Before long, Lex's mane and her coat were covered in a layer of white.

"Let's hope it doesn't last too long," Barengush replied. "We don't want to get stranded out here. What do you think, Lin?"

"Like you, I'm hoping it's just a shower, but it's hard to tell."

Felindra exchanged Lex for a yak at their next stop, but before mounting the yak, she had to mollify him. All the horses were now tethered together in a single file and the only place suitable for him was the front of the pack. It not only made him the leader—a position he obviously felt entitled to—he wouldn't be able to attack any of the others because his tether was long enough for him to get ahead, making him less likely to kick the one behind him.

***

Felindra moved her mount closer to the wall on the edge of the road and looked out over the valley. The sun was shining towards the southwest, but it looked as if clouds were building up over the mountains to the north. She soon got used to riding the yak and appreciated its calm docility. Unlike horses, it didn't complain or shy at shadows and sudden noises.

Despite their docility and robustness, the yaks needed to rest periodically and to drink and graze on the roadside vegetation. During one of these stops, the Albasinians got together to take some refreshment and exchange observations.

"I hear Lord Varan will be on the ship from Albasiny," Vertan said. "You must be excited."

"I am, of course, but it hasn't quite sunk in yet. It seems too good to be true."

"How about you, Farah? What are you going to do?" Sastin asked.

"I think Lin wants me to stay here. I'd like to; it's a beautiful place, but I still have a yearning for home. I can understand how he must have felt so far from home for all those years. We've been talking about it but haven't really decided on anything. I'd feel guilty dragging him half way around the world when he's only just got here."

"Are the two of you going to marry?" Sastin asked. He seemed to be taking an inordinate amount of interest in the topic and Felindra wondered if he'd had hopes for her himself.

"We've talked about it, but we haven't made any definite plans. We are very fond of each other and would like to spend our lives together, but there are so many factors involved. I know he is hoping to become an instructor at the Academy."

"Would you be willing to stay here?" Felindra asked.

"I might. We'll have to wait and see."

The snow continued to fall in large flakes and soon the trees were covered in white mantles and the ground with a mushy layer of cold slush.

"Let's hope we can get there before sundown," Tirzah Lin said. "If this slush freezes, it will make walking much harder."

It was mid-afternoon by the time the road began to level off and they could see more of the capital city; not everything though, because it was protected by a three-span high stone wall. The snow had turned to sleet and didn't settle the way snow did, so they were hopeful they would reach the gates before it got too cold. Lantern light began to appear on the buildings that showed above the wall. Many of them had high slanting roofs, some which were like tall towers that narrowed towards the top and were ornamented with colored pennants.

The pair of massive carved timber city gates was still open, although there was no traffic either entering or leaving, when they reached it. A cluster of guards stood under a large wooden canopy that stretched over the opening, watching their approach. It wasn't until the caravan stopped that they moved towards them in a line blocking the way. The one in the center, whose garb was more decorative than the others, stood with the butt of his long spear resting on the ground and called out to them.

Tirzah Linn dismounted from his Yak and exchanged a ceremonial bow after which they talked for a while, with the officer casting glances their way from time to time.

Tirzah returned. "It's all right, we can enter. We're lucky; they were just going to close the gates for the night." He climbed back onto his yak and led them into his city.

26 – Disappointment and Change of Plans

Felindra

They found an inn close to the wall where there was a grazing field for their yaks and a small stable for the remaining horses. The inn was a different structure from the ones on the road and looked much older. The lower exterior was built of stone with an upper level of wood, possibly added later. Inside it was spacious and lively with patrons, most of whom looked like workers. Lanterns suspended on chains from the ceiling and two stone fireplaces, added to the body heat of so many people, provided enough heat to warm the whole room.

The travelers stood inside the entrance for a moment while Tirzah looked around for a proprietor, giving the other patrons a chance to look them over. Felindra noticed that there were no women among the patrons kneeling at the low tables drinking steaming liquid from earthenware bowls or picking morsels of food from dishes laid out on the tables.

After a few moments, they saw a portly man coming towards them. Tirzah held a short conversation with the man and then turned to his companions. "We have to enter by another door. He's going to show us the way."

The man led them out the door and turned right, after another right turn, they came to a smaller door on the opposite side of the inn. The proprietor lifted a chain of keys on his belt and chose one to unlock the door, and then he stood back and allowed them to enter. The room inside was only dimly lighted by two flickering lanterns, so all they could distinguish in the dim light was that it was a smaller room than the one at the front and was furnished with a few tables.

Another conversation took place between Tirzah and the proprietor, after which the man lighted two more lanterns and left by the inner door.

"He's going to get us some service," Tirzah said. "Apparently, this room is for the use of parties that include women."

"Don't tell me they discriminate against women here too," Rasamé said. "I thought we'd finally left all that behind."

"No, it's not discrimination. It's more to protect you from the behavior of the patrons in the public room. He said they can become quite rowdy and may try to give female patrons unwanted attention." He looked around the room. "Why don't we sit down? He's going to have someone light a fire in the fireplace. I see the bricks are already laid, all it needs is a flame to start it."

"I can do that," Barengush said, crossing to the fireplace. Just as he knelt in the hearth, the door opened to admit a man and a woman carrying utensils and a tray of mugs. Before they could do anything with them, Barengush created a small flame in his hand and applied it to the kindling. When it caught fire, he stood up and brushed the dust off his trousers. The pair who had just arrived stood looking at him wide-eyed.

After Tirzah spoke to them reassuringly, they put the trays and utensils on a table, then pushed the five remaining tables together and left the room.

By the time everyone was settled and eating a meal, they were yawning or trying to suppress yawns. When two women came in to clear the tables, Tirzah asked them about sleeping arrangements. One of them went out with a loaded tray and returned moments later with another woman, in more elaborate clothes, who was probably the female counterpart of the proprietor. She led them through the inner door and up a polished wood staircase to the next level.

The three women and Zanda shared one room and the four men another. The proprietress left after lighting some candles.

"This whole place seems to be gloomy," Rasamé said. "It even smells old."

"It is old," Farah said. "At least we have a fireplace. I imagine it gets very cold at night."

The whole room was lined with wood, the floors, ceiling, and window shutters, which were now closed. An iron stove with a pipe leading up through the roof stood on a brick-tiled square in the center of the room.

***

"What are we going to do now?" Rasamé asked her brother as they broke their fast the following day. "Are there any kin we could visit?"

"I'm sure there must be some; as to whether they'll want to see us, I can't say."

"Can we look around?" Felindra asked.

"What we need to do first is find a place where we can settle down for a while. I want to call at the Academy and make my presence known. It's possible we might be able to find accommodation there since you are all mages."

"Can we all go with you?" Rasamé asked. "Mother used to talk about it all the time, and I'm longing to see it."

"That would be best," Tirzah replied. "It is a steep climb, so we should take the horses. You'll be able to see much of the city on the way, and the view from the top is breathtaking."

"How are you going to find out about the family?" Rasamé asked.

"The Academy is the best place to start," he replied. "If they are registered there or have been students, they are bound to have records."

When they left the inn, the sky was misty, but it looked as if the sun was trying to break through. The roads were cobbled with drainage channels between the footpath and the road. It seemed to be a very clean city without a lot of litter, although there was a rotting vegetable smell from a market they passed. The buildings were fascinating, almost all were built with stone and had sloping slate roofs and tiny windows with wooden shutters. Although there were few flowers—probably because of the season—many of the houses were decorated with streamers of tiny colored flags.

"Do the little flags have any significance?" Farah asked.

"They identify the people who live in the house," he replied. "If you went closer, you'd see writing on them. That relates to relationships and lineage. On some of the larger structures, like that one," he indicated one with a woman and child coming out the door, "are places of business—I believe you call them shops—and the pennants give information about the merchandise and the owner. That one sells textiles. She advertises that they also make garments."

"That's marvelous," Farah said. "They are so much more decorative than plain old script."

"The people here are very fond of decoration and color, probably because of the long winters, which are completely colorless."

"That's right! I've noticed how all their clothing is decorated with embroidery and painted designs. I think we should buy some of those scarves; they're so rich and vibrant." They had just passed another shop that sold knitted goods."

"Many of the country women spend their winters knitting. The rest of the year, they take care of the sheep, card and spin the wool, and in their spare time, they create dyes from plants and other sources."

Every so often, they turned onto another street where the incline was less steep, but they continued ever upwards.

Felindra was impressed by Lex's good behaviour. He hadn't once tried to kick another animal or human; he seemed to be satisfactorily tamed now but hadn't lost his old spirit and showed it by tossing his head and snorting occasionally. Since they reached the mountains, all the animals had warm blankets over their backs to protect them from the icy winds. *I'm so proud of you,* she sent, stroking his neck. *You are being so good. Is it because you missed me?*

He tossed his head in response.

"Barengush...." she said to her neighbor. "Do you think horses are as intelligent as wolves?"

"They might be smarter," he replied.

"I'll have to check that when we get home. There must be something in the library about it."

"Ooh, look at that," Rasamé exclaimed. "What is it, Lin?"

It was a structure at least forty paces wide, built of polished white stone. It was decorated with horizontal strips of mosaic, hundreds of brilliantly colored tesserae forming patterns, outlined in gold. From the corners of the roof, cone-shaped towers rose into the sky. The spires were covered in gold, decorated with three mosaic bands near the bottom.

"That's the Grand Temple," Tirzah said. "It replenishes my soul to see it again. Let's stop here and rest the horses for a while," he said, dismounting.

Almost as if welcoming him, the sun broke through the clouds and illuminated the ground before them. Tirzah sighed and reached for Farah's hand. "Come with me," he said, leading them up the broad steps towards the massive door.

"How are we going to get in?" Rasamé asked. "That's a heavy door."

"Don't concern yourself, little sister. I know the way."

The door was made up of several panels, all butted smoothly together with no sign of an opening. Each panel was decorated with carvings of men and women wearing a variety of costumes and headdresses. The only things missing were door latches or knobs. Instead of stopping in front of the door, Tirzah went to an alcove almost concealed by a pillar to one side of the door. When they got closer, they saw a small door set in the back. Tirzah spun a wheel in the stone beside it and the door slid smoothly aside.

"These doors are useful when one doesn't want to bother with the big one," Tirzah said.

"Does the big door open at all?" Rasamé asked.

"Oh yes, mainly for ceremonial occasions. It can only be opened from the inside and it needs a special key. We have time for a quick look around, and then we must be on our way."

The interior of the temple was as spectacular as the exterior. The walls were polished white stone on which hung large paintings interspaced with gold candelabras. The central section had large statues standing between the pillars that supported the roof. Lanterns hung from beams about halfway from the ceiling. The central portion of the floor was spread with colorful rugs with piles of seating cushions stacked nearby.

"We won't go any farther," Tirzah said. "We would have to remove our footwear before treading on the rugs. I just wanted you to see it. You can come back another time for a more thorough viewing. There's a lot more to see."

"It is magnificent," Farah said. "Thank you for showing us, Lin."

They left the temple, remounted, and continued to the Academy.

Tirzah Lin

Tirzah felt almost giddy with anticipation as they drew near the Academy. It was almost thirty sun cycles since the last time he'd been here. He'd been a student then, about to finish his final year before being granted his primary classification of Wizard Preliminary. He would have remained at the Academy to continue his studies for advanced levels had it not been for the fatal expedition to the nearby forest to gather medicinal plants.

Tirzah's mother had been a Master of Wizardry and Healer First Class and she had continued to instruct him and encourage him to practice and develop his skills. Under her tuition, he'd reached the same level as she held, a Master of Wizardry. It had not been easy for her to continue teaching him after they had been sold to different owners and it was only his good fortune—being purchased by the father of Dom Ash—that had made it possible at all. The dom had not objected to their keeping in touch and had persuaded their owner, a friend of the dom, to allow them to meet periodically.

As they approached the familiar gate, his heart started thudding. If he could be granted a teaching post here, he would be content for life. This was the moment he'd dreamed about for many cycles. The others slowed down as they got close to the gates, allowing Tirzah to go ahead of them. The wrought iron gates were wide open, guarded by two men wearing the garb and insignia of guardians. He dismounted and led his horse forward, feeling as if his heart was expanding in his chest. Everything looked just the same as the last time he'd see it so long ago.

One of the guardians came to meet him. "Blessed meeting, brother," he said, "What is your business here this day?"

Tirzah cleared his throat. "I was a student here many cycles ago and I would like to reacquaint myself with my old school. I have been traveling with these worthy friends for many moon cycles and would like to show them the Academy. They are also gifted and have come from a distant land. But I believe the first thing I should do is report my return to the First Master."

"May we know your name?" the guardian said.

"I am Tirzah Lin, son of Tirzah Kusho and Nyama Maya."

"Ah, your family is well respected at the Academy. I'm sure the First Master will be delighted that you have returned. Please be welcome."

"Is the Master's office still in the Jade Hall?"

"It is, brother."

Tirzah beckoned his companions forward and remounted his horse.

He led them via a meandering path through some vegetable gardens and an orchard to an empty field behind a wood fence. A couple of yaks were nibbling some bushes on the far side of the field. "We can leave the horses in here. There is enough grass to keep them happy for a while, and a pond at the other end in case they were thirsty. You can hang the saddles and harnesses on the fence." He dismounted, opened the gate, and led them into the field. They quickly removed the tack and hung it where Tirzah indicated.

"What about the yaks?" Felindra asked him. "Won't the horses bother them?"

"No, they're placid animals, although you might warn your friend there to leave them alone." He said, referring to Lex. "If he attacks one of them, it would defend itself, and as you can see, it has the equipment to do serious damage."

"I'll tell him that," she replied, patting the stallion on his shoulder.

They went out, closed the gate and stood in a cluster for a moment looking at the horses.

"I have to go to the Master now, so why don't you look around? If it gets too cold out here, you can go into one of the libraries, or the public refectory. You understand enough Elerian to manage, don't you, Rasamé?"

"I can't read the writing symbols very well," she replied.

"Well, you can ask someone if you get lost. I'll meet you at the public refectory in about five degrees."

Tirzah started towards Jade hall, taking a deep breath to help him relax. He was so excited about being home, he felt like breaking into a sprint, but he managed to restrain himself. Jade hall was a medium-sized building, among some of the more massive structures. It was so named because of the decorative jade patterns around the doors and windows, setting them off against the grey stone of which it was constructed. He pushed open the double front door and stepped into the terrazzo-tiled entrance hall. A young woman, probably a student, sat on a low bench inside the door, sorting texts on a higher bench in front of her.

"I am at your service, brother," the woman said, standing up to give him the traditional greeting, palms together and bow.

"I'm honored, sister," he said returning the bow. "I wish to see the First Master. Is he, or she, available?"

"I will find out brother. I know he's here, but ...." she stopped, looking a bit flustered.

"You don't know if he's busy," he finished for her.

She nodded with a weak smile. "Please allow me to send a page to tell him you're here," she replied. She picked up a small brass hammer and struck the gong that stood on the end of her table. "May I inform him who wishes to see him?"

"I am Tirzah Lin," Tirzah replied.

Her eyes widened in surprise when she heard this, but a boy came running down the stairs before she could respond.

"Tibo, would you go and inform the Master that Brother Tirzah Lin is here to see him?"

Tibo nodded and bowed to them, and then repeated the name. "Tirzah Lin?" with a surprised look on his face. He turned and ran back up the stairs.

"You are Tirzah Lin! Everyone at the Academy has heard of you. The instructors say you were one of the most promising students in many decades before you disappeared. You are a legend. Your disappearance was a great mystery. Would it be proper for me to ask where you were all these years?"

"Suffice it to say that I did not go willingly and have been in Basrind for the last twenty-nine cycles."

Vicki Wootton

The young woman's lips formed a circle, but Tirzah was saved from further questions by the return of the page.

"Master Rigzin will see you now," he said, gasping for breath. "Please follow me."

As Tirzah turned to follow him his mind was distracted by the name of the Master. *Surely it couldn't be him. Should I ask the boy? No. If it is him, let me have a few heartbeats of peace before I meet him.* But of course, trying not to think of something was futile. It only locked his attention on it more firmly.

This time the boy walked up the stairs. Whether it was for Tirzah's sake, or because he'd already used up all his energy, he didn't know, but he was thankful for it.

They reached the familiar second floor landing with its white marble paving and aged wood paneled walls, and continued ahead, passing alternating lamps and old paintings hanging on the walls. Two lamps marked the Master's suite, halfway along. The boy paused and pulled down on a heavy braided silk rope next to the door, ringing a bell inside the room.

Tirzah's apprehension increased when door opened, and he saw who it was. The man was older now and his body had thickened around the torso, but there was no mistaking the smug face of his old nemesis.

"So, Tirzah, you've decided to return at last." He held the door open wider. "Come in. Tell me what you've been up to all these years. You can go, boy," he added to the page.

Tirzah walked into the large, ornate room, filled with rare woods and much gilded ornamentation. The carpets on the floor looked new, but little else had changed. "You've done well for yourself, Rigzin," he said blandly.

232

Rigzin scowled. *Oh, excuse me; did I forget your esteemed title?* "Sit down and tell me what you've been up to since you disappeared. Everyone thought you'd been killed." He offered Tirzah a small padded stool near his own ornate padded chair with a back and arms.

"What happened to you?" the First Master asked. His chin rested on his folded hands, his elbows on the desk, as he peered down at Tirzah.

"I can't believe you don't already know," Tirzah replied.

"Surely you don't think I had anything to do with it," Rigzin replied, indignantly.

Tirzah was not surprised to find that Rigzin was fully warded. "I would have thought everyone would have known when it happened. My mother—you remember my mother, don't you? Second Master Nyama Maya, whom everyone thought would be the next First Master. She sent many messages back to the Academy trying to get help for us."

"I never heard of any messages," Rigzin said. "Everyone I knew thought you'd all been killed."

Tirzah shook his head and sighed. It was useless following this line of discussion. Whatever happened long ago, no one was going to claim responsibility for it. "To be honest, Rigzin, I didn't come here to discuss the past. Now that I've returned, I'm looking for a post at the Academy."

"You mean teaching?" Tirzah Lin nodded. "Oh, that's quite out of the question, brother. You don't have the qualifications. Unless you want to start at the bottom as a novice."

I will not grovel, Tirzah thought. "Oh, I'm eminently qualified," he said. "Don't forget my mother was a leading master of wizardry and she taught me all she knew. I could pass any test you would care to challenge me with."

"Much as I respected your mother; she was a great teacher, but you have to be qualified here at the Academy to win a teaching post here."

Tirzah stood up. *I knew the moment I heard that name that I was wasting my time.* "Is that a new rule, or did you just make it up spontaneously?"

Rigzin stood up. "We're wasting our time here, Lin. I'm afraid you don't belong here anymore."

"Yes, I can see that," he said. "You haven't changed in all these years, Choti."

"I wish you good fortune," the First Master said insincerely as he led Tirzah to the door.

"I already have that in abundance," Tirzah Lin replied. "Despite our history, I want to assure you that, even though I am disappointed by your decision. I hold no resentment towards you. It is your nature and who am I to expect that to change?"

The last image he had of Rigzin was the contempt on his face as he closed the door.

Head held high, Tirzah walked down the hallway and descended the stairs. In a way, he felt lightness of heart, as if a decision had been made for him, not an outcome he desired, but the opening of a new path in his life. There were so many choices open to him, but the most important one centered around Lady Farah.

His friends were waiting for him when he arrived at the public refectory. Like everything in his homeland, little had changed there, maybe some new furniture and wall decoration, but the arrangement was still the same: waist-high tables around the stone walls with dishes of food resting on charcoal warmers, the same tea urns, and lanterns hanging from the rafters. He took it all in as he picked up a bowl and loaded it with food, then filled a large beaker with tea and took it to the cluster of tables they'd arranged for themselves.

Farah scooted her padded seat over to make a space for him next to her and looked at him curiously. When he was settled, he took her hand and kissed it.

"You're looking pleased with yourself," Rasamé said. "Have you been offered the First Master's position?"

"Not that, but I'm quite content with the way things are turning out." He poured some sauce over the chicken, rice, and vegetables in his bowl and tasted it. "Mmm, this is delicious."

"What are you going to do?" Farah asked Tirzah.

"There are many options available to me, for example, I could go back to Basrind as a free man…" he was interrupted by several groans. "Or, I could go to Albasiny and do research at their Monastery, what else…?"

This last comment was met with astonished silence. Farah put her hand on his wrist and squeezed it. "What happened?" she said.

Tirzah sighed and took a mouthful of tea. He put the beaker down and looked at each person in turn. They all seemed to be waiting anxiously for his response, especially Farah.

"I met an old rival," he said. "We began our education at the same time, but he was one of those people who need to be on top of everybody else and resented it when I came out ahead of him. He could be quite vindictive at times. Let's just say we didn't get along." It was hard for Tirzah to talk about this; it brought back so many memories. He took another mouthful of food and chewed for a moment. "He is now the First Master, and he hasn't changed a bit. Apparently, there is no place here for me, unless I want to start over as a novice. He obviously blamed me for suddenly disappearing, without actually putting it into words."

"Did you...?" Rasamé started to ask at the same time as Farah said, "But that wasn't..." the two women looked at each other. "Go ahead," Farah said.

"I was going to ask you if you told him we were abducted?"

"No. For a moment there, I had a feeling he'd been responsible for that, but ... I don't know. I couldn't accuse him without proof anyway, and that was a long time ago. He had a powerful ward, so I couldn't read him." He turned to Farah. "What were you going to say my dear?"

"Just that it wasn't your fault you were abducted." She squeezed his hand. "Would you really come to Albasiny?"

"I'm giving it serious consideration," he replied. "Do you think they'd have me at your Monastery?"

"I think they'd welcome you," she said.

"Farah's right," Felindra added. "You'd be able to teach us so much."

"I'm sure I'd learn much, too," Tirzah said.

27 – Preparing to Leave Eleria

Tirzah Lin

They stayed in Camakäsara for a quarter of a moon cycle. During this time, not only did they see most of the sights and buy as much as they had coin for, but Tirzah had tracked down his uncle's family and the joy of seeing them almost changed his mind about leaving but love for a woman often surpasses family relationships.

Tirzah also visited the royal palace and discovered that his childhood friend was now the King of Eleria.

Tirzah had told him briefly about his rejection at the Academy.

"I could hire you here to be the Court Wizard," the king offered.

"What about the incumbent?"

"He was my father's wizard and he's getting old. I know he would welcome a chance to retire to the country while he is still active."

"It's very tempting, your grace. I'll have to think about it."

"Do you have any plans?" the king asked.

"There is a woman I wish to form a bond with. She's from Albasiny and has invited me to go with her. She also thinks I would be welcome at their Monastery. That's where all their gifted people are trained."

"You're a lucky man! Will this be your first bond?"

"Yes," Tirzah replied. "It's not easy for a slave to form a permanent bond."

"Well, think about my offer, and if you get homesick, we'll still be here."

Rasamé and Zanda went to stay with their uncle, this left Tirzah and the Albasinians waiting to depart for the coast.

The weather improved for two days and they used the opportunity to see more of the remarkable sights in the city. The most memorable place they visited was the ancient catacombs. It was not an easy approach. To get to it, they had to cross a shelf of rock jutting out from the almost vertical rock-face. Luckily, a stone wall had been cemented together along the drop-off side. The wind was fierce the day they went, sometimes laced with fine ice pellets that abraded any exposed skin.

"It's a good thing we brought face masks," Sastin said. "Even though the wind keeps trying to tear them off." They had face masks that covered their faces all but for narrow slits over their eyes.

"How did they bring the bodies up here?" Barengush asked. "This shelf is so narrow."

"It was a lot wider at one time," Tirzah replied. "The cliff fell away gradually with the fierce pounding it got from the weather. Rock will crack when ice forms in crevices."

The entrance had two doors which now hung lopsided from their rusted hinges. Barengush and Vertan had to use all their strength to open a space wide enough for them to go through. At first, Barengush had wanted to use a power blast to get them out of the way, but Tirzah told him that would be tantamount to desecrating a sacred site. Everyone carried a small closed lantern which they lit once they were out of the wind.

The leading tunnel appeared to be a natural cave. Its walls, which had been smoothed and engraved with text, were lined with carved wooden statues. The statues were so smoothed by weathering and being touched by visitors that their surfaces were hardly recognizable as the persons or creatures they represented.

"What do these statues represent?" Farah asked Tirzah.

"Some of them are ancient gods, and some saints. It's hard to tell now."

The actual internment chambers were in tunnels that had been excavated from the mountain rock. In the first tunnel they entered, which was probably the oldest, the bodies were sealed in rock tombs resting on ledges carved in the walls, but farther in, the bodies were laid on three rows of shelves, one above the other. The individual apertures had enough space for objects to be laid to rest with their former owners. Each body had been wrapped in garments, most of which had now disintegrated into shreds, just as the flesh of their owners had worn away, leaving only bones, although the occasional sparkle as the light of their lamps were reflected indicated that some of the coverings had included gems and gold threads.

Felindra was amazed at the variety of objects that were left with the corpses, weapons, armor, covered urns, even jewelry and body ornaments, tools and household items. "Some of them must have been women, judging by the items they were buried with."

"Who were these people?" Vertan said. "Judging by their possessions, they don't look like ordinary people."

"No, these are the aristocrats, the wealthiest people. I don't know if you've noticed, but each section of shelves belongs to a specific family. That's why you see women and men together. The carvings below each section tell the family name and dynasty."

They walked on and turned a corner into a newer tunnel. As they progressed, the bodies and objects were less decayed, and details of their burial finery were more recognizable. The colors and patterns were still visible.

"Oh, look here," Farah said. "Isn't this sad?"

She was standing by the body of a young woman holding a new-born baby in her arms. Their skin had turned dark and leathery, but it was still mostly intact.

Even more poignant was the tiny cradle lying next to them.

The end of this tunnel widened into a large semi-circular chamber, elaborately ornamented with carvings and paintings, their paint faded and flaking. There were at least sixty persons interred here including children of all ages, men and women, and at the end, a headless man with his head lying on his torso. His body was not caparisoned as richly as the others, in fact, all he had covering him was a strip of soiled cloth. An inscription in blood-red paint was attached to the top of his aperture.

"What happened here?" Barengush asked. "I can see there's a story in it."

"You're right," Tirzah replied. "This is the family of the last sovereign of the Gampo Dynasty. The king is the headless one. Our land was overrun by invaders from the north, who executed him and his whole family."

"But these other bodies haven't been desecrated," Farah said.

"Many of them predeceased him, and some of them were killed with poison, however, there may be wounds on the bodies that are hidden by clothing. The best indication is their facial expressions. You can see that some of them suffered much pain."

"And look there!" Vertan exclaimed. He was looking at something on the top shelf, which was a little too high for the shorter people to see.

"What is it?" Felindra asked.

"That, my dear was the queen. She was carrying an unborn child. They cut the child out of her body—that's probably what killed her—and interred it with her."

On their way out of the catacombs, Farah asked Tirzah, "Was there a reason for bringing us to see this?" She already suspected there was.

"Oh, I just thought you might be interested in some of our history, and the knowledge you gained here gives you some background on someone we are going to visit later this day."

"Who?"

"King Nyima, of the Tsarong Dynasty, has invited us to dine at the palace this evening."

"And why would our visit to the catacombs be relevant?"

"It was the Tsarongs who overthrew the Gampos."

The wind had died down while they were inside, and now big feathery snowflakes fell steadily. It didn't seem to be piling up on the path they followed; most of it was melting as soon as it hit the ground, nevertheless, they had to tread carefully. After leaving the path along the rock face, they descended through a small wood that led to a gate in the city wall.

"Unless you have anything better to do, we can return to the inn and have a meal," Tirzah Lin said.

Felindra

They were relieved to go back to the inn. The excursion to the catacombs had been tiring and they felt chilled to the bone. They took off their heavy outer garments in their dormitories and washed their hands before going to the inn's communal dining room.

"What are we going to wear for the King's dinner?" Farah asked while they were eating.

"What would you wear to visit your queen?"

"Oh, it's very elaborate and there are protocols that have to be followed," Felindra replied. "Even down to the kind of headdress and the right footwear."

"Well, we are not such sticklers about ceremony," Tirzah replied. "We just dress like everyone else. If what you are wearing is clean and in good repair, no one really minds."

"But don't we have to wear Elerian costume?"

"No, it's not necessary. My advice is to wear the best you have." He smiled. "I know you've been shopping, so you must have something. Oh, and make sure you don't have mud on your boots."

"You didn't finish telling us about the overthrow of the Gampo Dynasty," Farah said, changing the subject. "How did that come about?"

"It's quite interesting really," Tirzah replied. "Merchants and travelers passed through the Kingdom of Eleria on their way to the northern ports and had noticed how happy the people there seemed to be, and there wasn't as much poverty as there was here. They talked to local traders and merchants and discovered that taxes there were not so high as to leave them destitute.

"Here, the royal family and aristocrats lived lives of pleasure and debauchery, while everyone else was struggling to survive. Any small disaster, like a fire, could ruin a shopkeeper or tradesman and leave them destitute, so there was a great deal of discontent, though to express their anger and dissatisfaction was to invite severe penalties. It was a cruel, ruthless regime. There was no justice for the people, only for the aristocracy. Things were ripe for change."

"Did they rebel?" Barengush asked.

"Not exactly," Tirzah replied. "I think word got around in Eleria that the people here were dissatisfied with their royal family and might not resist too hard if they were invaded."

"Did the people help the invaders?" Felindra asked.

"In some ways, but not by taking up arms. Anyone seen carrying a weapon would have been executed on the spot. They did things like leaving gates unlocked, and some of the more courageous acted as guides."

"I noticed you said the invaders were from Eleria," Vertan said. "That must mean that they annexed this country. What was it called before?"

"You're right, brother. This part of Eleria was called Shan-Gāo"

"You imply that the invaders were good people, so why would they do that to the queen?" Felindra asked.

"These things happen in war," Tirzah replied. "But legend has it that that it was a palace employee who did that, in payment for their killing his sons. The invaders did execute the sovereign, but, once they knew they wouldn't be punished, many men went on a rampage against the aristocrats. Not many aristocratic families survived those times."

"How long ago was that?" Sastin asked.

"Close to two hundred sun cycles," Tirzah replied.

"How did you become friends?" Farah asked.

"We met at the Academy when we were boys. We were all about the same age, Nyima, Rigzin, and I. I think Rigzin's animosity towards me began there. Nyima and I became friends, but Nyima didn't take to Rigzin, so he felt left out. It would have been a boost to his vanity to have been able to claim the crown prince as his friend."

"If he was at the Academy, does that mean he's gifted?" Felindra asked.

"He has two gifts, he's a Truth Seer, and also has a gift for making people feel comfortable."

"Excellent gifts for a leader," Farah said. "I wonder if they were bred into his ancestral line."

"It's possible, I suppose." Tirzah let out a long breath. "I don't know about you, but I'm ready for siesta."

"I thought it was only in hot countries that people took siestas," Vertan said.

Tirzah shrugged. "We can adapt it to fit the circumstances, and I'm tired."

The dinner with King Nyima was most enjoyable, mainly because the King was so informal and treated them all as equals. He was a roly-poly man who stood only half a head taller than Felindra. The food was plain, but obviously prepared by skilled chefs. After eating, he insisted they stay and talk to him. He led them into another room that had a semi-circle of cushions on the floor around a low table in front of a fireplace. After the servants served them tea and sweet pastries, they left and King Nyima spent the rest of the evening questioning them about Albasiny. He had a keen interest in the far-off land.

When they were about to leave, he said to Tirzah, "I should make you my ambassador to Albasiny. Would that suit you?"

Tirzah looked at Farah, who gave a tiny nod. "Indeed, it would, your excellency. Do you have an ambassador there now?"

Nyima shook his head. "It's so far away, I never considered it until now. Talking to your friends has shown me what an excellent nation it must be, and I think we would be missing out if we didn't form a friendly relationship with them." He beamed at the Albasinians.

"What would it entail?" Tirzah asked.

"We would prepare a document from me, which you would present to the queen of Albasiny along with your credentials. If she accepts my request for a diplomatic relationship, you would receive a residence and other trappings that would assume the status of Elerian property. Once inside the property, it would be synonymous with being in Eleria. What do you think?"

"I like the idea, but I have a question: I was planning to form some sort of relationship with the Monastery in the duchy of Trethawynd, maybe as a consultant or teacher. Would that interfere with my ambassadorial roll?"

"I think you would have to talk to the queen of Albasiny about that, but I'm not averse to the idea." Nyima replied. "When do you leave?"

"At dawn, two days from now," Tirzah replied.

"I should be able to get everything ready by then. I have enough advisers and clerks; it's about time they had something to do." He winked at them to show he was joking.

28 – Departure

Tirzah Lin

"Today, we must prepare everything we are going to take with us," Tirzah Lin announced while they broke their fast the following day.

"Will we have time to visit the market?" Felindra asked. "I'd like to get some gifts for my family."

"You could do that," Tirzah replied. "Do you need me to show you around.?"

"Not if you have other things you must do," she replied.

"We'll be fine," Farah said. "I know you want to say goodbye to your family. I'm sure that between us, we can find the way."

"Before you go, we have to decide what to do with the animals. I'm sure you don't want to take them on the ship."

"I wish there was a way we could send Lex back to Dom Ash," Felindra said.

"Why would you want to do that?" Barengush asked.

"I don't know. Maybe it's because of how much he loves him. And he was good to us; he treated us well, on the whole." Felindra thought for a moment. "It's the thought of someone having him that doesn't understand him and might abuse him."

"I have two suggestions," Tirzah said. "Take your pick. You could sell him to King Nyima; I know he likes a good horse, or send him in a caravan to Basrind and hope he actually reaches the dom."

"You mean ... why would he not reach Dom Ash?"

"Many things could happen on the way: accidents, bandit attacks, even mistreatment by the drivers. The traders might not be honest and sell the horse to someone else."

"What if we said the dom would give them a big reward for bringing Lex back?"

"That might do it, but we'd have to make sure Dom Ash would agree."

"Do you think the king would buy him and treat him well?"

"I'm sure he would. I know he deplores abuse of animals. Would you like me to approach him about it?"

"Could we contact Dom Ash and tell him what we are doing with Lex, to reassure him that he's safe?"

"I think I could do that. I'm curious to know how things are going in Basrind and I know of at least two wizards I could contact. Who knows, the dom might even decide to come and reimburse the king for taking care of Lex. His trading ships, what's left of them, sail all over the world; there's nothing to stop them coming this way once the war is settled."

"All right," Felindra replied. "I'll leave that to you, but maybe I should go with him, if the king agrees, to introduce him to the stable hands."

"Now, about the other animals. We'll need transportation to the coast. I suggest we try to sell the whole herd at a low price if the buyers will agree to let us use them to reach the ship. That way we will have yaks for the mountains and horses for the lowlands, with both to carry baggage."

***

"Did you contact Dom Ash?" Felindra asked when they returned to the inn

"I did. One of my former apprentices was able to go to the plantation and connect us."

"How's he doing?" Farah asked.

"He's having a hard time still, but his health has improved. He can't get over the disappointment he felt when we left. They're surviving with what they can produce on the plantation, but there is very little food being imported from other countries."

"What about the war?" Barengush asked.

"It's over. Once Pangast got what they wanted out of it—mostly food for their people and release of the slaves—they called a truce and eventually the two countries signed a peace treaty. One of the conditions was that Basrind would not continue to recruit slaves in neighboring countries, or transport slaves through their territory."

"How does Dom Ash feel about that?" Felindra asked.

"He said he would be quite happy if slavery were abolished in Basrind, but he'd have some opposition if he spread those feelings abroad. He says that, with the slaughter of so many slave owners, things might change gradually, with fewer left to perpetuate the practice. Their families, what is left of them, will certainly think twice before bringing in more slaves."

"What did he say about Lex?"

"He's happy that you found him and took such good care of him. He thinks we've done the best we could for the horse and one day he might see him, but right now, he has other problems. Several of his ships were lost, in addition to his warehouses, and now he must hire Basrindians to work on the plantation and laborers are in short supply, and those who will work, are lazy. That's what he says."

By the time night fell, they barely had enough energy left to eat a meal before retiring for the night, but most of their problems had been solved. One drawback came with the sale of the animals. The new owner agreed to their terms but insisted that they only take one animal per person. Without draft animals, there would be a problem with carrying baggage. "I told him we would keep the donkeys and cart in that case." Tirzah told them.

Farah had been in touch with Ashavan on the Blue Ranger and discovered that they hoped to reach the port in three days, if they had smooth sailing, but he reported that clouds were building up and they might run into a storm.

29 – Descending into the Plain

Everyone was delighted the next day when the sun rose in a cloudless sky.

"I'm glad you persuaded that trader to let us use the donkey cart," Felindra said as they were preparing the animals for the journey. "I was afraid I would have to leave my gifts behind."

"What did you buy that was so heavy?" Barengush asked.

"I wanted to get something really spectacular for the duke and Varan, for the palace really, so I got two ebony carvings … little statues."

The King had sent two guards to accompany them, and the trader sent two more men to accompany the livestock. The four of them would take the 'borrowed' animals back to the capital. The four men in the Albasinian party started out riding the horses while Felindra and Farah took the yaks, because they were lighter, leaving them room for baggage. The cart carried the heavier load, camping equipment and food supplies.

Now that they had more coin, they would be able to buy fodder when it was needed.

The first leg of the journey took them down the mountain, not retracing the way they'd come, but using a road that zigzagged largely towards the northwest. The sunshine held out until midday, but after that it was gradually overcome by mists that developed into full-blown clouds. By sunset, a light rain set in. They could still see the plain below, but without much detail apart from the lights of some of the communities scattered over the lowland.

"I think we should set up camp now while we can still use trees for shelter," Tirzah said as darkness approached.

***

They reached the plain around midday the next day, and, with better roads, began to make more progress.

"You must be getting excited," Farah said to Felindra as they prepared for bed at an inn on the second night.

"I can barely breathe sometimes, thinking about being home and seeing my family again."

"And Varan?"

"Of course." Felindra rolled over and raised herself on her elbow. "Do you think I've changed much?"

"You've changed in many ways, Felindra," Farah replied. "But you are still the loving, innocent girl who left Trethawynd eighteen moon cycles gone. You are still you."

"Thank you, Farah. But do you think Varan will recognize me when he sees me? Will he think I'm a different person? He probably has an image of me in his mind that may not correspond with the way I look now."

"If you're worried about the way you look, I promise you that a little weight loss and a few minor scars are not going to affect the way he loves you."

Felindra sighed. "I guess I'm being silly about it. It must be because I'm tired."

"When I get anxious, I think to myself, *everything will work out as it should, so why waste energy worrying about it*, and it always does, eventually," Farah said. "Sleep well!"

30 – Leaving Eleria

Once they crossed the border between Eleria and its northern neighbor, Mesalar, they felt the need to be more cautious and stay alert to possible threats. Along the border, the people of Mesalar were not very different from the borderland people of Eleria, but as they moved farther into the country they gradually changed into a stockier people with narrow eyes and dark reddish-brown hair. They were not as outgoing as the people farther south, slow to speak and abrupt when spoken to. They seemed to be a gentle race overall, although there was no telling how they would react if displeased.

At first, the terrain was a grassy plain that seemed to go on forever. The settlements, usually spaced far apart, were just clusters of large tents with an occasional stone building. Large herds of livestock littered the plain, sheep, ponies, and yaks, although yaks were less common.

"Why do they live so far apart?" Vertan asked.

"These people are herders," Tirzah replied. "Each settlement belongs to a single family. They need a lot of space for their animals to graze. If they were any closer, they would completely deplete the grassland."

After travelling half a day, they came to a small town with a marketplace. Most of the buildings were of mud bricks or stone, and the road earth with gravel trodden into it.

"Now maybe we can get some real food at last." Barengush exclaimed. "I'm tired of meat and hard cheese.

"We'll be able to get some fruit and vegetables as well," Felindra said, winking at him. When she'd first met Barengush, he didn't eat any vegetables.

Buying meat entailed choosing an animal and watching it being slaughtered and seeing it being cut into pieces. "No, we can't do that," Felindra said, knowing she couldn't tolerate feeling its pain and fear. "Please don't let them...." she begged.

"I agree with sister Felindra," Tirzah said unexpectedly. "We have no way of preserving the meat, and we don't have time to cook it before we go on."

The others agreed more for Felindra's sake than the inconvenience it would cause.

"There are plenty of other things we can eat, some fruit already preserved by drying."

Tirzah tried to start conversations with some of the vendors, but they had no common language, so most of their buying was done with signs and gestures.

As the weather became colder, they were glad of the sheepskin coats and lined boots they'd acquired in the Elerian capital, Camakäsara. They also had thick wool blankets to sleep in.

About half a day after leaving the plain, the road entered a forest. At first, it was thinly populated by deciduous trees that had almost finished shedding their leaves, spindly types like poplar, birch, and ash. These were gradually replaced by pine and fir as they progressed north. The terrain rose through the forest, not steeply, but enough to tire the horses and require more frequent rest stops.

On the third day, a drizzly rain started to fall, a dreary shower that seemed as if it would go on forever. Despite the fragility of the raindrops, they soon managed to penetrate their clothing, and by nighttime, the only way they could dry themselves was by lighting a fire in the shelter of some forest giant. It abated by dawn the next day, but still hung in the air as a light fog around the treetops.

"How are things on the Blue Ranger?" Vertan asked as they ate some spit-roasted fish to break their fast.

"I'm afraid they've run into a storm," Farah informed them. "Ashavan says they had to anchor in a cove, but Captain Morelli thinks it will blow over in a few hours."

"Is this going to make them late?" Felindra asked anxiously.

"I imagine it won't be by much, maybe arriving in port at night instead of early in the day."

"Is the weather like this in Valkonen at this time of year? Sastin asked.

"Not this bad but, although it can get cold in the north; it's not as far north as we are here," Vertan replied.

That night, they heard wolves howling from one direction, answered by another pack from another location.

Sastin shuddered and hugged his arms around his body. "Are they going to attack us?" he asked.

"No," Felindra replied. "For one thing, wolves seldom attack humans; we're much too dangerous for them to risk getting into a fight with us, and secondly, there is plenty of game for them in these woods."

"So why are they making all that noise?"

"Oh, don't worry about that; it's a social thing with them. They like to get together and howl. Or they might be warning other wolf pack about some danger." She sniffed and then continued. "I could try to listen to them, if you like and see what they're excited about," she added.

"Can you do that?" Tirzah asked.

"Maybe," she replied. "Now I'm getting curious".

As she saddled the yak, she started sending out mental feelers over the surrounding area. She encountered a herd of deer drinking at a pond, some rabbits, a flock of rowdy crows. The crows were the easiest to contact. She entered the mind of the bossiest one, assuming he was the leader. *Greetings, winged friend.* She sent, with an image of herself and her companions. The crow reacted with curiosity, without fear. *We are travelling through your territory on our way to the great ocean and we mean you no harm.* She imagined him perking up and looking around, then she sensed he was preparing to take off and fly. *I'm curious about the wolves. Have they sensed a problem?* This message was sent with an image of wolves howling and a sense of curiosity.

Suddenly a large crow flew over the road and landed in a tree ahead of them. He cawed a few times, and more crows joined him, spreading among the branches. Felindra slowed down and waited. The crows spent a few moments sharing information with one another, and then quieted down and waited. She realized they were waiting for her.

Do you know what the wolves were excited about? she sent.

Bad humans, she received from the one she assumed was the alpha crow. He visualized it for her by showing five or six men dressed in furs, carrying bows and spears. They appeared to be hiding in the trees beside the road not far ahead of Felindra and her companions.

Lin, stop. There are bandits ahead. She sent hurriedly and urged her horse to go a little faster.

She saw Tirzah coming towards her, warning everyone.

"How did you find out about it?" he asked her. "I just sensed it too."

"I was talking to the crows. They told me that was why the wolves were howling." By now they had coalesced into a group, surrounded by crows circling around them cawing.

"They sure make a lot of noise," Sastin said.

"It's because they're excited. I understand by what I sense from them, that they aren't often able to communicate with humans. They're also keeping watch on the 'bad humans', as they call them."

"If there are bandits ahead, we should prepare," Barengush said. "Wait here, everyone, while I go and scout ahead." He dismounted from his horse and gave the reins to Vertan.

"I'll come with you," Vertan said, dismounting.

"No, you stay here to protect the others."

Vertan nodded. "Why don't we all get off the road," he said to the others and led the two horses into the trees.

"It must have been exciting, talking to the crows," Farah said. "I heard they are very intelligent."

"They are," Felindra replied. "If being able to understand other species defines intelligence."

They were interrupted by a man's cry up ahead and then a howl of pain, followed by the sound of people crashing through the bush. Barengush returned moments later, barely out of breath. "They're gone," he said casually.

"What happened?" Felindra said.

"They were all hunkered down near the road as if waiting for someone to pass. They looked pathetic with their ragged furs and crude weapons. I just went up behind one of them and gave him a little shock. Then they all ran."

"You didn't kill him, did you?" Felindra asked.

"No, it was just enough for them to get the message. They must have understood from it that they were playing with some dangerous people and ran away."

They stood around for a while longer, eating some of their rations and taking a few sips of water. "We'll have to look out for a stream soon," Tirzah said, holding up his water skin.

As if the clouds had understood what he said, they released some rain.

It was hard for them to tell when the sun set because of the heavy cloud cover, but once it started to get too dark to see far, they decided to look for a place to camp.

31 - The Northern Forest

They continued to trek through the forest, enduring the torment of the drizzling rain and the insects it brought. It seemed that the damp northern forest was the habitat of every biting and stinging insect in the world. Because of the cold, their bodies and hands were already covered with clothing, but the nasty little bugs could still reach their faces and necks.

"We'll have to make masks from some of the cloth. We can cut slits for our eyes," Tirzah advised. "And we must have something we can use to repel them." He took his satchel from his shoulder and put it on his lap to search through his healing supplies. "There's not much here. Have you got anything?" he asked Sastin.

"Not for that specific purpose," Sastin replied after rummaging through his own satchel. "But I've got this. It might help." He held up a small bottle of clear liquid. "We could dilute some of it with boiled water and dip our face masks in it. It's very pungent, so you don't need a lot of it."

The next time they stopped, Sastin put a small pot filled with water over the fire and added a few drops of the oil.

Barengush leaned over the pot to test the steam. After one sniff, he stepped away, "You weren't fooling; that stuff is powerful. How are we going to tolerate it so close to our noses?"

"It will evaporate," Sastin replied. "You could wet your mask with water to dilute it more before dipping it."

"What is it?" Tirzah asked.

"It's eucalyptus oil from the leaves of a tree that grows in the tropics. I discovered it when we were in Motu Ataahua. It's good as an antiseptic as well."

"How much longer are we going to be in this dismal place?" Vertan asked. "It feels as if we've been here half a lifetime."

One of the Elerian guards laughed and said something to Tirzah. "He said you must come from a very comfortable place," Tirzah translated. "And we should be out of here after sunrise on the morrow."

They packed up their things, donned their face masks, and remounted. The next leg of the journey took them through a swamp. There was a road going through it, but the constant rain had turned most of it into sludge that ran down between the cobbles, leaving them slick and the surface uneven. The trees were becoming smaller and spread farther apart, providing less shelter. The swamp was the breeding ground for a multitude of mosquitos— some of which were almost as long as a finger joint— constantly buzzed and hummed around the travelers, although very few alighted on them.

Just before the sun went down, a sunset that they could see because the rain had finally stopped, Felindra heard an animal whining somewhere nearby. "Stop! It's lost, poor little thing. It's only a baby, out there all alone." She slid down from the back of the yak. "I'm going to see if I can help it."

"Oh no, not another!" Vertan said, recalling all the other creatures she'd helped in the past. He dismounted. "I'll come with you."

Felindra was already on her way towards the little creature. She turned her head. "Stay back," she said softly. "Don't make a sound."

She had to push her way through some wet bushes to find where the whining came from. She could sense the little creature lying terrified on the ground and realized it was next to a larger animal that had no life signs. *Don't be afraid, little one*, she sent out as soothing, calming waves. *I want to help you.*

She pushed aside a rain-soaked branch and looked down upon the most pitiful sight she'd ever seen. A baby wolf, lying against the body of its mother who had three arrows piercing her body, one in the neck, one in the shoulder and one in the chest. The little wolf didn't look more than a moon-cycle born. When it sensed her close by, it snarled at her and tried to burrow under its mother's body. Felindra knelt on the wet ground and crawled towards it, all the time sending feelings of tenderness and love. "I'll take care of you, little one. Don't be frightened." The creature barked and snarled at her, its hackles rising.

When she was close enough to touch it, she sent calming thoughts, trying to make it relax. Felindra couldn't bear to see any creature suffering and this one, being a wolf, touched her heart. She slowly reached out her hand and started to stroke it. At first, it tried to back away, struggling vigorously when she held it back, but she kept her touch firm and it gradually relaxed and sniffed her hand. "I'm going to pick you up now," she murmured, sending an image of herself lifting it and holding it close against her heart.

As she grasped it with both hands, its struggles to escape became more frantic, but Felindra didn't relent. She held it tightly and responded by holding it against her and stroking gently. It soon calmed down and snuggled in. As she looked back at the dead wolf and saw the trail of blood leading to the hideout in the bushes, tears filled Felindra's eyes.

Another thought came to her. It needed something familiar for reassurance. Holding it with one arm, she pulled out some of the mother's hair and tucked it inside her coat. The baby wolf sniffed it and yelped, then rested its head against her chest and licked her coat.

The first obstacle she had to pass with her newest rescue was Vertan, who was standing on the other side of the bush, waiting for her.

When he saw her, he stood up and brushed the wet leaves off his pants. "Uh, oh! You're doing it again. What have you got this time?" he said shaking his head.

Felindra wrapped her arms protectively around the little wolf. "It's all alone. Its mother has been killed."

"What is it this time?"

They started to walk back to where their companions were setting up camp and preparing their evening meal.

"A wolf," she replied.

"I might have known. Surely it belongs to a pack," Vertan said. "They would take care of it."

"If they haven't all been killed or driven away by hunters. Its mother had three arrows in her body. If I knew the pack was close by, I would leave it with them, but I don't sense any wolves in the area."

Felindra sat down a short distance from the fire, knowing how afraid wild animals are of fire. Tirzah Lin came and sat down beside her. "I see you've found a new friend. What do you plan to do with it?"

"If I could find its pack, I'd release it to them. They'd take care of it. But I can't just abandon it. It would die all alone in the forest." She looked down at the cub and tried to stroke its head, but it snapped at her hand, threatening to bite her. This reminded her of Pico, Ashala's son, who had been raised at the Monastery. He'd been a little terror as a cub, biting everyone that came close enough, and chasing them if they ran away, biting their ankles. *I wonder what he's doing these days; I hope he went back to join the pack. He'll be full grown now,* she thought sadly.

"I'm going to have to find some way to restrain him until he gets used to being with us," she said.

She noticed the Elerians were watching her now with amused expressions. "Could you ask them if they have something I can use as a lead, Lin? Something soft and not too easy for it to bite through."

Tirzah stood up and held a short conversation with the two men who were going to take the horses and yaks back to Camakäsara. One of them produced a long strip of leather, the kind used to make reins.

Felindra emptied her water bag into a metal bowl and put it on the ground. While the wolf was drinking, she made a collar from a piece of soft cotton and tied it around its neck, tying it loosely, but tight enough to keep it from slipping over its head. "That'll do for now," she said, stroking its head and scratching under its chin. The little creature didn't agree with her and began to scratch furiously in a vain effort to free itself. *Maybe some food would distract it,* she thought. She visualized a slab of raw meat. The cub looked up at her and whined.

"What sort of meat do we have?" she called out. "Preferably raw."

"We trapped a few rabbits," Barengush replied. "I suppose you want to feed it now?"

"I can't let it starve," she replied.

"My brothers also have some fresh meat," Tirzah Lin said, indicating the four Elerians." He went to where they were preparing two small foxes for the pot and returned with some liver and kidneys. "Do you think he'll be able to eat these," he asked, holding out the offering.

261

"Him! It's a boy baby?" she said. "I never thought to check. I think he could manage. He's old enough to eat meat. Put a piece down and see how he does. He must be starving."

Tirzah put a piece of liver on the ground near the baby wolf and stood back. It disappeared in a flash with barely a chew and then he looked up for more. Felindra beamed. "He must be very hungry," she said. "Give him the rest. The cub gobbled up the rest in a moment."

Barengush came over with a few more pieces of raw meat. "Do you need more?" he asked, grinning at her."

"Could we save it for later?" she asked. "Right now, he needs to answer a call of nature."

Barengush nodded and went to find something to wrap the meat in. Felindra looped the leather strap through the neck collar and allowed the little fellow to pull her into the woods. *I wonder if he would come back if I let him go free. I'd better wait a day or two before I test him.*

When he'd finished, he stood, looking up at her and made little murmurs in his throat. He shook his head and scratched his neck, trying to rid himself of the bothersome restraint. *Come on, let's go back to the pack.* She sent him an image of himself and her walking together without restraints, hoping to plant the idea firmly in his head. She then recalled how Ashala had hated the collar and leash but had accepted them eventually when they were necessary. But Ashala had been a mature wolf when Felindra had bonded with her; this one was a baby. She sighed. *I'll have a lot of work to do training this one.*

She ate her own meal, which contained no meat, when they got back, leaving the cub restrained at her feet.

One of the Elerian drovers had been milking a female yak every day and keeping the milk in leather bags attached to his saddle. This provided them with more protein in the form of curds and soft cheese. There wasn't much food to be found in the forest; the berry season had passed, so all they could harvest were some mushrooms, and a few nuts from the trees.

Felindra asked if she could have some for the cub, and received a small cup of fresh milk, which he consumed in a few laps.

"Do you think I should set him free?" she asked Farah when she went to her tent,

"I don't know." She stopped and thought for a moment. "How about this? Let him stay here for the night and set him free on the morrow. See what he does? You haven't named him yet, have you?"

Felindra laughed. "Not yet. I want to see if he'll stay with us first. I've already lost two animals on this trip," she said, recalling the baby monkey and the little panther she'd rescued in Motu Ataahua. "I like your idea, but he'll have to sleep with us in the tent. If he starts making noises, I'll take the restraint off."

She tied the lead to the tent frame and persuaded him to lie down, then she went outside and got another bowl of water for him.

You must be a good boy and sleep, she sent when she returned with the water. She stroked his neck and scratched behind his ears, and then sent an image of him sleeping and her sleeping to give him the idea.

They were awakened in the middle of the night by the tent collapsing on them, and the wolf gone, leaving some chewed leather and cotton on the ground near the tent frame.

"He must have spent half the night chewing and finally given up and pulled the frame from the ground," she said as she scrambled around under the tent canvas, searching for her outdoor clothes. "I should have left him untied. I hope he'll be safe out there all alone."

"He may find his pack," Farah said. "And he may come back. This is the test."

"I know, but the hunters might kill him," Felindra replied. "He's so young, I don't think he can hunt alone. Ashala had to show her cubs how to hunt."

The two women spread the tent canvas on the ground after donning their outdoor clothes. They wrapped their blankets around them and tried to sleep once more.

"Where's the cub?" Vertan asked when they came to the fire to break their fast.

"It collapsed the tent and got away while we were sleeping," she answered. "It's probably gone looking for its pack." She took a bite of the hard bread dipped in curds.

"I thought you'd want to keep it," Barengush said.

"I wouldn't mind," she replied, "but I'm leaving it up to him."

Felindra looked at the surrounding trees, and then stood up to stow her dishes in her saddlebag. *We'll see.* The animals were already harnessed, ready to leave, all she had to do was put on the saddle. As she was climbing onto the back of the yak, she heard a wolf howl close by, but there was no response from other wolves. The howl was repeated, still no answer.

Suddenly, she had an idea. "Vertan, Barengush, come to me!"

They brought their horses closer and looked at her curiously.

"Can you imitate a wolf howl?" she asked her two friends.

The two men looked at each other and shrugged.

"It's important," she said. "Please!"

"All right, I'll try," Vertan acceded, but I can't promise it will sound like a wolf. The wolf howled again, just in time for him to imitate the sound. It seemed to be getting closer now.

He put his head back and did a passable imitation.

"You too," she said to Barengush. "Everybody!" she waved her hands at the travelers, who now surrounded them.

The lone wolf howled again. "Now!" she said. She put her head back and howled with Vertan and Barengush, and then again with several others joining in. She stuck her thumb in the air and nodded. "We can go now," she said. "If there are any around, they're probably ignoring us because they think it's a trick to lure them into a trap." *They're not stupid.*

As they continued down the road, Felindra asked Tirzah Lin, "Have they told you how far it is to the edge of the forest?"

"They expect we will be on clear land before the end of the day," he replied. "That means occupied land, farms and villages, and so on."

Felindra's attention was drawn to the surrounding bush by a soft bark. She sent out sense feelers and found the cub a few steps away, standing expectantly, ears up, alert to possible danger and ready to retreat immediately.

"Go on," she said to the others. "I'll catch up with you." At the same time, she sent reassurance to the wolf cub, urging him to stay where he was until everyone was gone. The Albasinians smile knowingly at her as they passed, but the Elerians, all except Tirzah, looked curious.

As soon as they were a few paces away, Felindra slid down from her saddle on the yak and knelt on the ground. *Come to me,* she sent. *I am your pack now.*

She heard a soft whine and rustling of vegetation and then a small canine head emerged from the bushes.

It occurred to her then that the yak might be afraid when it caught the scent of a wolf, so she stood up and put her arm over its shoulder. She sensed its nervousness and sent calming and reassuring feelings to it, trying to assure it that the little cub wouldn't hurt it. The yak blew a cloud of air from its nostrils and shook its head, pawing the ground with its front hoof. *You'll be all right, I won't let it hurt you,* she sent in images and it seemed to calm down a little.

Now all I need to do is find a way to do all those things. I daren't try carrying him on the Yak's back. She sighed. She rummaged in her satchel and came out with a small piece of cooked meat. She took it over to where the cub was waiting at the edge of the road and gave it to him as a token of her promise. *You must follow us.* She sent an image of herself riding on the yak, and the cub walking behind.

She climbed onto the yak and shook the reins to start it moving. He's so small, she thought, he'll never be able to keep up, but I can't hold up the whole caravan. It's the best I can do. If only his pack would come back and find him.

They rode on through the forest, stopping near a wide stream at midday to have a meal and attend to other necessities.

"We've almost run out of meat," Tirzah said. "We'll have to rely on hard bread and cheese until reach somewhere with a market."

"We could hunt for something," Barengush said.

"We don't have time to stop," Farah replied. "The Ranger arrives in the port in two days, and we still have about three more days on the road. As Lin said, we will reach civilization on the morrow and maybe there'll be a village where we can buy something."

"At least we can set some traps when we stop for the night," Vertan said. We may be able to catch something to tide us over."

He realized that Felindra was standing behind him. "What happened to the wolf?" he asked her.

"I told him to follow us, but he's too small to keep up. And now we can't even leave some food for him." Tears filled her eyes. "I'm sorry, I should never have...." She turned away and wiped her eyes.

Farah stood up from the fallen tree-trunk where she'd been sitting and joined Felindra. She put her arm around Felindra's shoulder. "Let's take a walk," she said,

"I feel so stupid," Felindra said, wiping her nose with the back of her mitten. "I just get carried away when an animal needs help. I wasn't thinking of all the complications involved."

They arrived at the place where the animals were grazing, having taken their fill of water from the stream.

"This is a beautiful place," Farah said, taking a deep breath of the fresh air. "I'm glad the rain has stopped. It reminds me of the forest in ValkonenMaa."

"It does," Felindra replied, trying to hold back a sob. Unfortunately, it also reminded her of Ashala

Farah hugged her. "I wish I could help you," she said. "I know you have many conflicting feelings right now, and if you wanted my advice, I'd counsel you to concentrate on all the good things you have to look forward to. Seeing Varan and your father again, returning to Albasiny..."

"I know you're right," Felindra replied. "But I still feel...."

"Felindra, you have a loving heart, as we keep reminding you. That is not something to apologize about, it's a great gift, but you can't help every creature in need that crosses your path. I think you need a child of your own to smother with love." She squeezed Felindra's shoulder.

As they rode away from the stream, they heard a high-pitched wolf howl close by. Another wolf farther away answered, and soon several more joined in.

32 – At sea

The final stage of the journey to the port of Zimnyaya-gavan was not without incident, but the travelers felt more secure being out of the forest and on the northern plain.

One evening, on a lonely stretch of road, some bandits attempted to hold them up, but they hadn't expected to be driven off so easily. All it took was a demonstration by Barengush of his blasting gift and Vertan's conviction that they wanted to leave. Barengush blew up a tree stump and the bandits turned and ran.

Another time, a horse was lamed when its foot was caught in a pothole. Both Sastin and Tirzah went to work trying to heal it while Felindra stood by to keep it calm.

"I don't have many medicines," Sastin said as they assessed the injury.

"Neither do I," Tirzah said. "But it doesn't look too bad. At least it's not fractured. It's more torn ligaments, I think."

The horse was standing on three feet, favoring the injured one by keeping it off the ground. Sastin ran his hand over the leg about a finger's width away. "I agree," he said. "What do you recommend?"

"I've got something for the pain," Tirzah replied. "Let's give him some and then heal as much of the damage as we can. After that, we can wrap the leg to hold it steady."

"Do you think we should talk to the men who represent the new owner first?" Sastin said.

Tirzah nodded and went to consult the two men from Camakäsara who were standing with the others, watching the two healers.

"They tell us to go ahead. It's better than killing the poor creature; they didn't want to arrive back in the capital short one horse."

It took Sastin and Tirzah about ten degrees of time to finish making the horse reasonably comfortable. It wasn't totally free of pain, but they had reduced it to a minimum by mending the tendons and muscles that had been torn.

After they'd left the forest, the road widened and sloped downward onto a plane interspersed with small coppices of trees and low hills. However most of the land was devoted to agriculture, both pastures and growing fields, which were now bare from harvesting. From the summit of the hill they were now descending, they could see farms and villages as well as several major towns, plus two rivers and several streams meandering towards the north coast. Some of the ploughed fields were whitened with frost, another indication that winter was almost upon them.

When it reached the first river—a raging torrent flecked with foam—the road turned to meander along its bank. It was twilight by the time they reached the first small town. The lantern light shining from the windows created a warm, welcoming atmosphere.

"We'll take the animals to the paddocks first, and then we can look around and find an inn," Tirzah said after a few words with the two drovers from Eleria.

"They seem to have a lot of space for horses and Yaks," Vertan said as he dismounted. "It looks almost like a caravanserai."

"It is in a way. That's because this is a trade route," Tirzah replied. "You'll also find good inns and places to buy supplies."

They walked through the town, taking in all the different structures: homes and shops built of wood, and more grandiose stone buildings whose purpose was undefined unless you could read the symbols and signs above their doors. The inn was obvious, though, from the sounds of laughter and the clink of pottery drifting through its door and windows.

One of the Elerian drovers took care of making their arrangements. He'd obviously been this way before, and Tirzah didn't know the language.

The days that followed were much the same, except that the closer they came to the port, the more traffic there was on the road and the more crowded the inns. On the third day after leaving the forest, they arrived at

Zimnyaya-gavan, where they were sure they would find the Blue Ranger resting at the dock, but it wasn't there. They'd already unloaded their belongings from the yaks and cart and said farewell to the guards and drovers. Their baggage was stacked up in front of them, on the dock.

"What could have happened to them?" Felindra cried. "They said they would be here today." She saw that Farah was communicating and waited for her to finish.

"They wouldn't allow them to enter the port," Farah reported.

"Why not?" Vertan asked.

"Because they're a warship," Farah replied. "They had to wait over there." She pointed out a small fleet of ships anchored away from the shore.

"So how do we reach them?" Felindra asked. This final obstacle, after all they'd been through to get here, brought her to the edge of despair.

Tirzah Lin put his arm around her shoulders and hugged her. "We're almost there," he said. "They'll pick us up, won't they, Farah?"

"They are on the way," Farah confirmed. "Look! See the boat being lowered?"

"I'm sorry," Felindra said, wiping her eye. Now her heart began to pound with anticipation. In less than ten degrees, she would be in Varan's arms and with her father.

The boat being rowed towards them looked awfully small. She wondered how the six of them would all fit in, but as it came closer, she knew there was ample room. A stocky man sitting in the bow waved to them. Even though they couldn't tell who it was, they all waved back.

Suddenly, Felindra let out a scream. "Dadi. It's dadi!" She began to wave frantically, having a hard time keeping her feet on the ground. She suddenly wondered if he would recognize her in her current costume, sheepskin-lined hooded coat and boots. She pushed the hood back and shook out her hair. *Now he'll know it's me.* She glanced at her companions, wondering if they thought she'd gone crazy. *I can't help it ... after all this time ...* She calculated they'd been away from home for six seasons and had undergone enough experiences to last a lifetime.

The boat drew close to the dock and Felindra held her breath, not taking her eyes off her father until his image was blurred by a film of tears. When the boat finally bumped against the edge of the dock and the mariners had secured it to a bollard, Daryan left his seat and hurtled up the ramp.

"Dadi!" she called and rushed to meet him.

He enfolded her in his arms and kissed her on the forehead and both cheeks. "I was afraid I'd never see you again," he murmured into her hair. "Thank the Light you are safe. Come on, let's go home." He wiped the tears from her eyes with his thumbs, gave her another squeeze, and then turned to greet the other Albasinians.

They didn't talk much on the boat back to the Blue Ranger; everyone was so overwhelmed with emotions. Felindra kept her eyes on the ship, hoping to catch a glimpse of Varan. Once, the flash of a telescope caught her eye and she was sure he was the one wielding it, but she didn't see him properly until they were a few spans away. The reason she hadn't recognized him sooner was the hood of the heavy dark blue wool coat he was wearing almost hid his face. All the mariners on the ship wore identical cold weather gear.

A wooden ramp had been lowered from the side of the ship. It had slats nailed across it to prevent them slipping as they climbed the steep slope. A section of the rail had been opened to allow them to step onto the deck.

Strong hands reached out to help Felindra climb onto the ship. When she looked up, she found Varan looking down at her. He pulled her into a hug and whispered in her ear, "Welcome back, my love." He kissed her cheek. "I thought I'd lost you. You can't imagine my turmoil when I heard what had happened to you."

He led her away from the rail where the others were landing. Holding her at arm's length, he looked her up and down. "You look well. You might even have gained some weight."

She smiled at that. "It's the clothes, Varan. It gets so cold where we've been, they line everything with fur. This coat is sheepskin with the wool on the inside."

He linked her arm and led her towards an open hatch in the deck. "Speaking of cold, let's go somewhere warm." They turned to the right at the bottom of the stairs and went towards an opening from which came the enticing aromas of food. "First, we should take off these warm coats." They stopped at a row of hooks on the walls which were already burdened with cold weather gear. "We can leave them here for now and take them to our cabins later." They unfastened their coats and removed their gloves and then placed them on the hooks. Felindra noticed that most of the garments were decorated with crests marking rank. "Are they all officers?" she asked.

"Yes. This is their mess. The mariners have their own mess down that way; the one where all the noise comes from."

Felindra heard the rest of her friends descending the stairs, and saw her father was leading them. They all trooped into the room furnished with long tables and benches. When they saw Lord Varan, everyone stood up and bowed. Varan smiled at them. "Please sit down. I thought I said we should not stand on ceremony here. We're all shipmates together now." After they sat down, he put his hand on Felindra's back to guide her to a table. "I would beg your attention for a moment, though. I want to introduce you to my betrothed, Lady Felindra Peshanar, the daughter of Sir Daryan Peshanar." The officers started to rise again, but Varan waved them down, so they bowed and clapped their hands instead.

Remember me? Felindra jumped and turned around to see who was sending.

"Ashavan! Of course, I remember you. You are the most unforgettable person I know. How are you? You're looking good." He was wearing one of his trademark outfits, a butter-yellow tunic trimmed with magenta braid, and black leather culottes. "Come and join us," she said with a glance at Varan.

He bowed to Varan, "My Lord!" and sat across from Daryan who was sitting next to Felindra. The rest of her friends filled the remaining seats and were soon feasting on grilled fish and rice with an assortment of spicy and tangy dressings.

Introductions were made, and the travelers settled down to the long sea voyage. The one constant of the voyage was the bitterly cold weather. The changeability of the weather was another matter. Sometimes the wind was fierce, raising great mountains of ocean for them to battle and making sick those not accustomed to such powerful motion. In places close to the shorelines, even the sea was frozen.

Felindra and Varan tried to walk on the deck together at least once a day, so warmly wrapped in wool and fur, they looked like chubby bears. It was the only time they could talk to each other in privacy. She gave him a rundown of her adventures since she'd left Trethawynd, carefully culling, or downplaying, some of the worst horrors she'd endured. He told her about the advances made at his father's palace, and Trethawynd in general. They sometimes saw Farah and Tirzah arm-in-arm walking the deck, deep in conversation.

"I think those two are heading for marriage," Varan commented one time. "How long have they been like this?"

"It's hard to say," Felindra replied. "At least since we were still on the plantation. About two seasons."

"I'm happy for them," he added. "She's a nice woman and he seems like a remarkable man."

"He is. It's hard to think he played a role in our enslavement, although he showed his compassionate side even before we landed in Basrind. He didn't stray too far away from his loyalty to the dom though. He was still a slave, although he didn't wear the yellow. He was afraid to go too far because of his sister who was a slave on another plantation."

"What do you mean by 'wear the yellow'?" Varan asked.

"It's the tradition in Basrind for all slaves to be dressed in yellow garments, although some only needed a yellow band or tunic, depending on their occupations. The more trusted a slave was, the less yellow he had to wear."

"What about you? Were you a trusted one?"

"Of course!" she replied with a grin. "But it was a different kind of trust. I was a stable hand and we had to wear grey coveralls while working, so I only had to wear a yellow head cover."

"Why a head cover?"

"All women in Basrind had to cover their heads, and sometime their faces, when they were out. It has something to do with their religion."

He put his mittened hand behind her neck and pulled her towards him to kiss her. "I'm so glad you're here. I missed you terribly. Do you remember the stars?"

It took her a moment to realize that he meant the pledge they made before she left Trethawynd: Every time they looked up at the stars, they would think of each other.

She looked up now and all she saw were clouds. "It's so dreary," she said, "not a patch of color or warmth anywhere. Shall we go inside and warm up?"

They had to walk carefully across the deck because it was covered in a thin layer of ice and frost. The mariners had sprinkled it with sand when it first started to freeze, but they'd soon run out of sand, so now they just had to be careful and try to hold onto something when they went on deck.

About halfway to Albasiny, the ship began to veer southwest and after a couple of days, they faced a much warmer wind.

"Which way is Albasiny?" Felindra asked one of the mariners when she was walking on deck on a day when the sky was blue.

He looked up at the sky for a moment and then at the shadows on the deck. "That way," he answered, pointing narrowly to the right.

"Why don't we sail straight to it?" she asked.

"There are some islands we have to circumnavigate before we reach home."

She stood leaning against the ship's rail with Vertan and Barengush, watching the distant islands and the birds swirling overhead with raucous cries and sudden dives into the water to harvest a fish.

"Do you think this is where your ancestors came from?" she asked Barengush.

"I don't think so," he replied. "I think they are farther north. The impression I got from hearing the history and legends was that it was a very cold, icy land."

"How do you feel about being home?" she asked.

"We'll have a lot to talk about, that's sure," Vertan said. "We've seen so many places and met wonderful people, it almost makes me want to switch to naval duty. I certainly wouldn't mind visiting Motu Ataahua again."

"Yes," Barengush added. "You did take quite a fancy to the women. I wouldn't mind seeing them again, either."

Felindra smiled, remembering how Vertan was awestruck watching their native guide, Nagali, emerge from the sea after her daily bath. "And now Nagali is going to marry the Dom," she said. "I don't know whether or not to feel sorry for her, although I hope she will find happiness with the dom. Basrindian way of life is so different from the easy-going islands. At least she is marrying an honorable man."

"You call a slaver 'honorable?" Vertan said.

"I think the war with Pangast has changed him. I don't think he will return to trading in slaves again. She is a strong woman, and her influence will discourage that."

Sastin joined them at the rail. "What are you discussing so avidly?"

"Oh, just reviving some memories." Felindra said.

"Of home, or our recent experiences?"

"The journey we've been on," Felindra replied. "I just realized, we hardly ever talk about home. Even Varan and I, in our private conversations, rarely mention Trethawynd or our future. It's as if we need to shake off all the things that have happened to us before we can advance into the future. Perhaps it will be different when we land and are reunited with our families.

"That reminds me of when the conflict with the Dark Brotherhood was over. Everything seemed unreal to me for a while," Vertan said.

Felindra saw a sad look come over Sastin's face and turned to see what he was looking at. She saw Farah and Tirzah Lin walking hand in hand on the opposite side of the deck.

She touched his hand and nodded for him to follow her down the deck. "May I ask you a personal question about Farah, Sastin?"

He put his hands in his pockets and leaned back against the rail, looking as if he felt trapped. "It's all right, Sastin. I understand if it's too personal."

"No, it's not that," he said. "Maybe if I talked about it, I might get over it. What do you want to know?"

"Remember when we were on that boat after Tumma and his wizards had captured us? You said something about wanting to marry somebody when you were young, but she married someone else." She looked at his downcast eyes, but he didn't return her look. "Was it Farah?"

Sastin turned around and looked out to sea. "Yes, it was Farah. I never stopped loving her. I was hoping that going on this expedition with her might lead to something, but...." He shrugged.

"And now she's with someone else." Felindra sighed. "I'm so sorry it didn't work out, Sastin. I know you are a good man and you deserve to be happy." She hesitated. "I seem to recall saying those very words once before. I am really sorry."

"Perhaps I'm fated to live without a partner," Sastin said with a sigh.

Felindra felt a heavy hand on her shoulder and turned around to see her father. He had dispensed with his cold-weather gear and was now wearing a plain black leather coat with a fur collar.

"Dadi!" She stood on tiptoe to kiss his cheek. "You remember Sastin, our healer?" she asked.

"How could I ever forget the man who saved my daughter's life, on more than one occasion. You must be glad to be home, out of danger, Sastin."

"It was an adventure, but I wouldn't want to repeat it," Sastin replied. "You have a very remarkable daughter," he added.

"You don't need to tell me that," Daryan replied. "Unfortunately, that's the very thing that gets her into so much trouble." Daryan put his arm around Felindra and squeezed her shoulders. "Her mother and I are hoping she's going to settle down and live a normal life. Give me a grandchild or two."

"Dadi!" Felindra felt her face heating up. She shook off his arm and started to walk away. "I'm going to find Varan."

The next day, the ship changed direction again until they were sailing directly westward, and as the sun began to descend in the west, they saw a distant strip of land, it's mountains enhanced in an aura of gold.

Epilogue – Two Years Later, a Dedication

Varan poked his head into Felindra's dressing room. "Need any help?" he asked. He knew she didn't like having maids fussing around her.

She looked up from the shoes she was tying and smiled. "Maybe you can fasten the back of my tunic. I don't know why I had to choose one that fastens at the back." She stood up and turned her back to him. "You just have to put the loops on the left side over the bobbles on the right."

"Easy," he replied. After he'd finished, he kissed the back of her neck. "Is that all?"

"Just the mantle. I can do that myself; it goes on like a coat. Now, how do I look?"

"As beautiful as a princess," he replied. "And I have a gift to go with your gown."

Felindra looked at him expectantly. She was getting used to all the little trinkets he bought her and assumed it would be another ring or bracelet, but gasped when she saw what he withdrew from the box. "It's beautiful, but a crown? I don't deserve something this regal. When would I ever use it?"

"It's just a diadem. My mother used to wear one for occasions like this." Varan replied. "You can use it to hold your headdress in place; you know nothing is too good for the mother of my daughter."

"Oh, that's what I forgot, my veil." She went over to her dressing table where the maid had laid out accessories and picked up a filmy silk veil which she placed on her head, hoping it would control her hair. She looked in the mirror to make sure it was straight and turned to him. "All right, let's see how it looks."

He came up behind her and placed the circlet—gold filigree set with tiny pearls and turquoise beads—over the veil, pressing it in place. "There. You look beautiful, as always. Is the baby ready? We must hurry now; the Grand Master arrived a while ago. He's talking with father now."

"Yes. We just have to get her from the nursery." She took one last look at herself in the full-length mirror. "This hair of mine," she grumbled. "I can't do anything with it as usual." She pressed the diadem down over her thick bushy curls, but it just bounced back. "Maybe I should get Nana to pin it in place otherwise it will fall off." However, she was satisfied with the outfit she'd chosen, wide-leg culottes of creamy silk with a matching tunic and a turquoise ankle-length mantel.

The grand salon was packed with guests. Since they were all important in one way or another, the duke had suggested allowing them to choose their own seats. In that way, no one should complain about not receiving his due respect.

Felindra's eyes were immediately caught by the regal couple sitting together on two of the larger chairs. She had been delighted when Dom Ash and his wife Nagali accepted her invitation to come to the dedication of their daughter. They had brought with them their young son, born just five seasons earlier, his father's pride and joy. He was a big boy like his parents and looked more like a child at least two cycles older. She smiled at them and gave them a little wave to acknowledge them.

Duke Valdor sat at the far end of the room with the Grand Master of the League of Light seated next to him. Two empty chairs were waiting, one on either side of them, and it was to these seats that Felindra and Varan headed. Felindra bowed to the duke and the Grand Master before sitting down and taking her daughter from the nursemaid. The baby girl, just one season born, was a good-natured child with frequent smiles and few cries. Her skin was slightly paler than Felindra's, but her hair promised to be like her mother's, black and curly. Today she was wearing a long white silk gown and bonnet, and a tiny gold bangle on her wrist, which she was trying to chew, with little success. She finally relented and decided to suck it instead.

The Duke stood up and addressed the guests. "We are gathered here this day to celebrate, not only the birth of a child, but also the safe return of our daughter." He turned and smiled at Felindra. "We also rejoice that our country is at peace, thanks to the Light."

The duke turned and gestured to the Grand Master. "We have invited the Grand Master of the League of Light to officiate this day and are grateful for his acceptance of the invitation. I'll turn the ceremony over to you, Grand Master," he finished with a bow to the grand master.

The Grand Master nodded to the duke and stood up. He walked between the young couple to address the guests. "It is a great honor for me to officiate on this auspicious occasion. I have known his grace the duke and his son for many years and was blessed to have them as guests at the Monastery after the tragic loss of their family and home during the Dark Brotherhood crisis. And

The Whisperer Returns

Lady Felindra was a student at the Monastery since she was a young girl, and after that a mage and teacher. I cannot express how happy I am to see her here today, happily married, a mother, and above all, safe!"

There was some laughter at the last comment from those who knew her and knew about her tendency to get into perilous situations.

"She is a very gifted young woman, amiable and courageous, and I'm sure she is a wonderful wife and mother."

He turned and nodded to the young couple, who stood up and brought their daughter to him. "We are gathered today to witness the dedication of this child." He looked questioningly at Varan and Felindra.

"They looked at each other and said, "Nerina," simultaneously.

"Nerina," the grand master repeated and held out his arms for the baby. He held her cradled in one arm and continued, "Nerina, daughter of Varen and Felindra, we hereby dedicate you this day to the eternal Light. May the Light guide you in all your ways and keep you safely in his care for all time." He lifted her up and kissed her forehead—Laughter broke out when she made a grab for his beard. Holding the child in both hands, he held her up to face the guests. "The Light bless you little Nerina. So be it as it is and ever shall be."

Many of the guests repeated the affirmation. "So be it as it is and ever shall be."

Felindra bowed to the Grand Master and took back her baby, who was beginning to look restless. "I think she's getting tired," she said. She turned to Varan, who was a head taller than she was. "Can you see Mila?" she asked. "I think it's time for feeding and a nap for this little girl."

283

"There she is," Varan pointed out a robust woman standing just inside the door and beckoned her.

The servants were setting up a long table down the center of the room and when it was ready, Felindra and Varan stood at one end to thank the guests formally and accept gifts for their daughter. The gifts were as varied as the people who gave them.

Varan's grandmother gave a painting of her daughter, Varan's mother who had been so ruthlessly slaughtered by the Dark Brotherhood. "She will never see her grandmother," the countess said to Varan, "but this will keep her alive for your daughter," He kissed his grandmother and hugged her close.

Felindra's young sister Lydris brought a little stuffed lamb knitted with blue wool. "My teacher made this," she said. "It's for her to talk to when she is lonely."

Dom Ash's gift was one of the most impressive, a gold statue of a magnificent horse one tenth the size of the living model. "I suspect this is as much for the mother as the baby," Nagali said with a smile as she placed it on the table.

Felindra stretched up and hugged her friend, and said, "I suspect it's a portrait of Lex, his favorite horse, but it is beautiful, and we will treasure it." She accepted a gentle— for him—hug from Dom Ash.

When all the guests had finished giving their gifts, Duke Valdor spoke to the assembly again. "Now there will be a short break for everyone, and then we will return here for a celebratory luncheon. If there is anything you need, feel free to ask a page or a footman."

***

It's wasn't until after the evening meal that Felindra was able to have a private talk with Dom Ash and Nagali. They met in the salon of their suite. Felindra thought meeting and talking with Dom Ash might help Varan understand why she could forgive him so easily for his role in her enslavement. They had also invited Farah and Tirzah Lin, who had married the previous year.

"What happened after we left," Felindra asked.

"I recovered from my wounds," Dom Ash replied with a wink at Nagali. "Thanks to the devoted care given me by this remarkable woman."

"You understand that we had no choice. We had to leave," Felindra said. She needed him to know that she and her friends had no intention of betraying him. "They intended to charge us with treason. We would have been executed."

"I understand that," Ash replied. "They had to blame someone for what went wrong, and unfortunately you and your friends were the most convenient scapegoats. It made things difficult for me though. The War Council, or at least some members, wanted to pin the blame on me for giving you shelter. After I talked to the Monarch, he put an end to that idea."

"How are things on the plantation now?" Tirzah Lin asked.

"We're recovering, but it takes time, especially since we lost most of the slaves. But bit by bit, we're pulling everything together again. We have paid workers now, but they are more difficult to handle."

"It's the adjustment that's difficult," Nagali said. "The workers tend to complain a lot and make unreasonable demands." She stopped and looked at Felindra with a grin. "Did you know that all the former slaves who stayed on are now in charge of the work-force? They're the managers and supervisors. The hired hands are not too happy about being managed by former slaves who have the power to dismiss them if they don't measure up."

"I'm also building up my shipping fleet. We managed to salvage enough ships to start on a small scale, and we've been building up from that. No slavery, I guarantee that. I've been talking to the Monarch's council about banning slavery altogether."

"Of that, I heartily approve," Tirzah Lin said. Everyone else nodded in agreement.

Felindra passed around a tray of snacks and refilled some glasses with Albasiny's Summer Wine.

"How about Moto Ataahua? Is everything back to normal?"

Nagali beamed at her. "Better than ever. Now that the extent and value of the crystal mines has come to the attention of the government, it has become a major source of income. Food is plentiful, the refugees have returned." She took a sip of wine. "All thanks to you and your friends." Felindra tried to break in and deny the importance of their contribution, but Nagali held up her palm. "I just want to tell you something more. I hear that they are thinking of having a national holiday named after you?"

Felindra put her hands over her face. "Oh, no," she said. "We didn't do that much. We failed in the end by deserting them."

"It wasn't your fault," Nagali exclaimed. "You were abducted."

Dom Ash stood up. "It's been a long day," he said, holding out his hand to Nagali. "I just remember the day you arrived at the plantation when you told me about how you might one day marry the son of a duke. I was angry at the time, not because you reminded me that you had another life, but because you made me feel guilty for robbing you of it. I just wanted to say I'm sorry about that and I'm very happy to see that things have turned out so well for you and your lucky husband. I'd like to ask you something, my lord," he said to Varan. "Does she still like to go to the stables and talk to the horses?"

"Need you ask?" Varan replied. "Every day. It's part of her daily routine. I'm still expecting the day when she brings home a wolf for a companion."

"Give me time, I've been too busy with other things and haven't had time to look for one yet," Felindra replied, taking her husband's arm and smiling up at him.

End

About the Author

Vicki Wootton was born and educated in England but has spent most of her adult life in North America. She currently resides in British Columbia.

Among her many occupations, she has been a mother, galley girl on a fishing boat, law office accountant, and a government contractor. She is now a full-time writer and book designer.

She is a vegetarian and a Jesusonian and enjoys balcony gardening. To wind down, she does online jigsaw puzzles.

∽◯◇

Thank you for reading these books. It would mean a great deal to me if you could find the time to leave a review on amazon.